'Romancing the Margins'?
Lesbian Writing in the 1990s

'Romancing the Margins'? Lesbian Writing in the 1990s has been co-published simultaneously as *Journal of Lesbian Studies,* Volume 4, Number 2 2000.

The *Journal of Lesbian Studies* Monographic "Separates"

Below is a list of "separates," which in serials librarianship means a special issue simultaneously published as a special journal issue or double-issue *and* as a "separate" hardbound monograph. (This is a format which we also call a "DocuSerial.")

"Separates" are published because specialized libraries or professionals may wish to purchase a specific thematic issue by itself in a format which can be separately cataloged and shelved, as opposed to purchasing the journal on an on-going basis. Faculty members may also more easily consider a "separate" for classroom adoption.

"Separates" are carefully classified separately with the major book jobbers so that the journal tie-in can be noted on new book order slips to avoid duplicate purchasing.

You may wish to visit Haworth's website at . . .

http://www.haworthpressinc.com

. . . to search our online catalog for complete tables of contents of these separates and related publications.

You may also call 1-800-HAWORTH (outside US/Canada: 607-722-5857), or Fax 1-800-895-0582 (outside US/Canada: 607-771-0012), or e-mail at:

getinfo@haworthpressinc.com

'Romancing the Margins'? Lesbian Writing in the 1990s, edited by Gabriele Griffin, PhD (Vol. 4, No. 2, 2000). *Explores lesbian issues through the mediums of books, movies, and poetry and offers readers critical essays that examine current lesbian writing and discuss how recent movements have tried to remove racist and anti-gay themes from literature and movies.*

From Nowhere to Everywhere: Lesbian Geographies, edited by Gill Valentine, PhD (Vol. 4, No. 1, 2000). *"A significant and worthy contribution to the ever growing literature on sexuality and space. . . . A politically significant volume representing the first major collection on lesbian geographies. . . . I will make extensive use of this book in my courses on social and cultural geography and sexuality and space." (Jon Binnie, PhD, Lecturer in Human Geography, Liverpool, John Moores University, United Kingdom)*

Lesbians, Levis and Lipstick: The Meaning of Beauty in Our Lives, edited by Jeanine C. Cogan, PhD, and Joanie M. Erickson (Vol. 3, No. 4, 1999). *Explores lesbian beauty norms and the effects these norms have on lesbian women.*

Lesbian Sex Scandals: Sexual Practices, Identities, and Politics, edited by Dawn Atkins, MA (Vol. 3, No. 3, 1999). *"Grounded in material practices, this collection explores confrontation and coincidence among identity politics, 'scandalous' sexual practices, and queer theory and feminism. . . . It expands notions of lesbian identification and lesbian community." (Maria Pramaggiore, PhD, Assistant Professor, Film Studies, North Carolina State University, Raleigh)*

The Lesbian Polyamory Reader: Open Relationships, Non-Monogamy, and Casual Sex, edited by Marcia Munson and Judith P. Stelboum, PhD (Vol. 3, No. 1/2, 1999). *"Offers reasonable, logical, and persuasive explanations for a style of life I had not seriously considered before. . . . A terrific read." (Beverly Todd, Acquisitions Librarian, Estes Park Public Library, Estes Park, Colorado)*

Living "Difference": Lesbian Perspectives on Work and Family Life, edited by Gillian A. Dunne, PhD (Vol. 2, No. 4, 1998). *"A fascinating, groundbreaking collection. . . . Students and professionals in psychiatry, psychology, sociology, and anthropology will find this work extremely useful and thought provoking." (Nanette K. Gartrell, MD, Associate Clinical Professor of Psychiatry, University of California at San Francisco Medical School)*

Acts of Passion: Sexuality, Gender, and Performance, edited by Nina Rapi, MA, and Maya Chowdhry, MA (Vol. 2, No. 2/3, 1998). *"This significant and impressive publication draws together a diversity of positions, practices, and polemics in relation to postmodern lesbian performance and puts them firmly on the contemporary cultural map." (Lois Keidan, Director of Live Arts, Institute of Contemporary Arts, London, United Kingdom)*

Gateways to Improving Lesbian Health and Health Care: Opening Doors, edited by Christy M. Ponticelli, PhD (Vol. 2, No. 1, 1997). *"An unprecedented collection that goes to the source for powerful and poignant information on the state of lesbian health care." (Jocelyn C. White, MD, Assistant Professor of Medicine, Oregon Health Sciences University; Faculty, Portland Program in General Internal Medicine, Legacy Portland Hospitals, Portland, Oregon)*

Classics in Lesbian Studies, edited by Esther Rothblum, PhD (Vol. 1, No. 1, 1996). *"Brings together a collection of powerful chapters that cross disciplines and offer a broad vision of lesbian lives across race, age, and community." (Michele J. Eliason, PhD, Associate Professor, College of Nursing, The University of Iowa)*

'Romancing the Margins'?
Lesbian Writing in the 1990s

Gabriele Griffin
Editor

'Romancing the Margins'? Lesbian Writing in the 1990s has been co-published simultaneously as *Journal of Lesbian Studies,* Volume 4, Number 2 2000.

Harrington Park Press
An Imprint of
The Haworth Press, Inc.
New York • London • Oxford

Published by

Harrington Park Press®, 10 Alice Street, Binghamton, NY 13904-1580 USA

Harrington Park Press® is an imprint of The Haworth Press, Inc., 10 Alice Street, Binghamton, NY 13904-1580 USA.

'Romancing the Margins'? Lesbian Writing in the 1990s has been co-published simultaneously as *Journal of Lesbian Studies,* Volume 4, Number 2 2000.

Cover design by Jennifer Gaska.

Library of Congress Cataloging-in-Publication Data

'Romancing the margins'? : lesbian writing in the 1990s / Gabriele Griffin, editor.
    p. cm.
    "Co-published simultaneously as Journal of lesbian studies, volume 4, number 2, 2000."
    Includes bibliographical references and index.
    ISBN 1-56023-133-5 (alk. paper)–ISBN 1-56023-128-9 (alk. paper)
    1. Lesbians' writings, American–History and criticism. 2. Lesbians' writings, English–History and criticism. 3. Women and literature–History–20th century. 4. American literature–20th century–History and criticism. 5. English literature–20th century–History and criticism. 6. Lesbians in literature. 7. Lesbianism in literature. I. Griffin, Gabriele. II. Journal of lesbian studies.
PS153.L46 R66 2000
810.9'9206643–dc21
                                                                     00-025542

INDEXING & ABSTRACTING

Contributions to this publication are selectively indexed or abstracted in print, electronic, online, or CD-ROM version(s) of the reference tools and information services listed below. This list is current as of the copyright date of this publication. See the end of this section for additional notes.

- *Abstracts in Social Gerontology: Current Literature on Aging*

- *BUBL Information Service, an Internet-baed Information Service for the UK higher education community <URL: http//bubl.ac.uk/>*

- *CNPIEC Reference Guide: Chinese National Directory of Foreign Periodicals*

- *Contemporary Women's Issues*

- *Feminist Periodicals: A Current Listing of Contents*

- *FINDEX, free Internet directory of over 150,000 publications from around the world (www.publist.com)*

- *Gay & Lesbian Abstracts*

- *GenderWatch*

- *HOMODOK/"Relevant" Bibliographic database, Documentation Centre for Gay & Lesbian Studies, University of Amsterdam (selective printed abstracts in "Homologie" and bibliographic computer databases covering cultural, historical, social and political aspects of gay & lesbian topics)*

- *Index to Periodical Articles Related to Law*

- *PAIS (Public Affairs Information Service) NYC (www.pais.org)*

(continued)

- *Referativnyi Zhurnal (Abstracts Journal of the All-Russian Institute of Scientific and Technical Information)*

- *Social Services Abstracts (http://www.csa.com)*

- *Sociological Abstracts (SA) (http://www.csa.com)*

- *Studies on Women Abstracts*

- *Women's Studies Index (indexed comprehensively)*

Special Bibliographic Notes related to special journal issues (separates) and indexing/abstracting:

- indexing/abstracting services in this list will also cover material in any "separate" that is co-published simultaneously with Haworth's special thematic journal issue or DocuSerial. Indexing/abstracting usually covers material at the article/chapter level.
- monographic co-editions are intended for either non-subscribers or libraries which intend to purchase a second copy for their circulating collections.
- monographic co-editions are reported to all jobbers/wholesalers/approval plans. The source journal is listed as the "series" to assist the prevention of duplicate purchasing in the same manner utilized for books-in-series.
- to facilitate user/access services all indexing/abstracting services are encouraged to utilize the co-indexing entry note indicated at the bottom of the first page of each article/chapter/contribution.
- this is intended to assist a library user of any reference tool (whether print, electronic, online, or CD-ROM) to locate the monographic version if the library has purchased this version but not a subscription to the source journal.
- individual articles/chapters in any Haworth publication are also available through the Haworth Document Delivery Service (HDDS).

'Romancing the Margins'?
Lesbian Writing in the 1990s

CONTENTS

ABOUT THE EDITOR

Gabriele Griffin, PhD, is Professor of English at Kingston University, Surrey, United Kingdom. Until 1998 she was Professor of Women's Studies and Head of the School of Cultural Studies at Leeds Metropolitan University. She has just completed *Visibility Blue/s: AIDS and Representation* (Manchester University Press, 2000). Her previous works include *Straight Studies Modified: Lesbian Interventions in the Academy* (co-ed. with Sonya Andermahr; Cassell, 1997); *Gender Issues in Elder Abuse* (co-ed. with Lynda Aitken; Sage, 1996); *Feminist Activism in the 1990s* (ed.; Taylor & Francis, 1995); and *Heavenly Love? Lesbian Images in 20th Century Women's Writing* (Manchester University Press, 1993).

'Romancing the Margins'?
Lesbian Writing in the 1990s

Gabriele Griffin

When the call for papers for this volume went out in a great variety of journals, newsletters, and bulletins, most of them specifically mentioning 'lesbian' or 'lesbian and gay' in their title, one of the first papers, symptomatic in some respects of the rest, to appear on my desk was one by a man producing a densely argued piece about Gertrude Stein–with not a mention of her lesbianism. The lesbian-free zone seemed to have finally arrived. The paper put me into a serious quandary, demanding clarification of what this collection on *lesbian* writing was meant to be about. I decided that it had to be about what occupies lesbian critical thinking, or critical thinking in relation to lesbian writing now.[1] As Teresa de Lauretis (1993) puts it: 'representation is related to experience by codes that change historically and, significantly, reach in both directions: the writer struggles to inscribe experience in historically available forms of representation, the reader accedes to representation through her own historical and experiential context; each reading is a rewriting of the text, each writing a rereading of (one's) experience' (145-6).

What seemed to have influenced the writers of the papers produced for this collection most are postmodernism and queer, which, between them, generate simultaneously a sense of liberation and of uncertainty: *liberation* in that the apparent boundaries set by 1970s and early 1980s radical lesbian feminism[2] are being exploded in favour of a play (and I use that word with some trepidation here[3]) with identities and differences which allows space for uncertainty regarding the specificities of lesbian identity, for bisexuality, for engagement with the work of lesbians from diverse backgrounds, be these Jewish, Chicana or Black; *uncertainty* in that the relation of such play to politics and materiality is experienced and represented as increasingly uncertain and problematic.[4] Thus Sonya Andermahr's close reading of Sarah

[Haworth co-indexing entry note]: "'Romancing the Margins'? Lesbian Writing in the 1990s." Griffin, Gabriele. Co-published simultaneously in *Journal of Lesbian Studies* (Harrington Park Press, an imprint of The Haworth Press, Inc.) Vol. 4, No. 2, 2000, pp. 1-6; and: *'Romancing the Margins'? Lesbian Writing in the 1990s* (ed: Gabriele Griffin) Harrington Park Press, an imprint of The Haworth Press, Inc., 2000, pp. 1-6. Single or multiple copies of this article are available for a fee from The Haworth Document Delivery Service [1-800-342-9678, 9:00 a.m. - 5:00 p.m. (EST). E-mail address: getinfo@haworthpressinc.com].

Schulman's novel *Empathy* analyses the ways in which Schulman employs both techniques associated with postmodernist writing and positions familiar from 'high' queer theory such as the work of Judith Butler to construct a complex presentation of a lesbian character whose uncertainty about her identity leads her, finally, to adopt what Andermahr describes as an ethical postmodernism, a demand for 'a political stance in a postmodern world of shifting locations.'

In 'Performing "La Mestiza"': Lesbians of Color Negotiating Identities,' Ellen M. Gil-Gomez, too, employs the language of high queer theory to engage with the ways in which lesbians of color deal with their sense of self, both cross- and intra-culturally. Emphasising the importance of context, Gil-Gomez discusses the notion of a border psychology inherent in the mestiza's position which enables her survival because 'choosing to *perform* pluralism within one's cultural tradition can be a useful strategy for the lesbian of color.' Therein, from Gil-Gomez's viewpoint, lies the liberatory aspect of the idea of performance. Drawing on Gloria Anzaldúa, Gil-Gomez suggests that this performance is aligned to a mestiza consciousness, an awareness–and therefore a certain agency–in making choices about the roles one takes on. (A question needs to be asked here about the possibility of such choices existing in the lives of 'real' as opposed to fictional characters.) Gil-Gomez explores the relationship between wholeness and fragmentation of the subject in the works of Anzaldúa, Cherríe Moraga, Paula Gunn Allen, Beth Brant, Audre Lorde and Ann Allen Shockley which is mediated through the writers' and their characters' engagement with the cultural traditions that constitute part of their heritage. Significantly, it is the taking on of these traditions and their rewriting that is constructed as particularly enabling–through context, diachronic and synchronic, text and self are 'made.' Gil-Gomez celebrates the sense of power which the characters she discusses derive from this process.

Terri Ginsberg's discussion of the film *Entre Nous* which raises questions about the representation of the relationship between female erotic bonding in the context of World War II and the Holocaust does not focus on either postmodern or queer notions of identity but deals, nonetheless, with uncertainty and indeterminacy which, Ginsberg argues, results in the women's relationship becoming a 'primary and overdetermining signifier of . . . holocaustic catastrophe . . . and a particularly dubious mode of liberation therefrom.' Where Gil-Gomez shows how context (historical, cultural, social) may be appropriated and reworked towards lesbian integration into hostile cultures, Ginsberg analyses the ways in which context, here the Holocaust, is displaced and thereby erased through the use of a female erotic bond which does not declare a(ny) lesbian content but serves instead to deflect from the narrative drive of the film towards a 'transnational capitalism' as Ginsberg describes it which feminist and other critics alike have been unable to address. Ginsberg demonstrates that the lesbian dimension of *Entre Nous* amounts to a patriarchally conventional form of appropriation of female to female desire, a kind of homosocial exchange in celebration of entrepreneurialism, simultaneously obliterating the significance of the holocaustic experience.

This appropriation bears some relationship to the querying of lesbian identity which has been promoted by postmodernism and queer, and which, as I argue in my essay, has led to a dispersal of the lesbian in some contemporary (lesbian) women's writing where women's sense of self as 'male,' women's relationships (erotic and otherwise) with men, and women's roles in the lives of men, seem to have become the newly central topics. This re-focusing does not amount to the integration celebrated by Gil-Gomez, or the acknowledgment of plural identities within an ethical postmodernism analysed by Andermahr; it is closer to the displacement described by Ginsberg. It raises questions about the 'romance of the margins' and of 'romancing the margins' borrowed from Jeffner Allen and indicated in the title of this volume, a legacy, possibly, of the mainstreaming of gayness in Anglo-American cultures in the early 1990s.

One might argue that all the essays in this collection are concerned with border figures, with writings that explore the indeterminacy of identity. Ana-Louise Keating's analysis of some of June Jordan's poems, for instance, is intent upon what Keating describes as 'categorical breakdown'–the insistent destabilization of categories of sexually inflected definitions of identity. Keating argues that Jordan's use of non-gender-specific pronouns such as 'I,' 'you,' and 'we' explodes the closure of poetry and invites the reader into an 'intersubjective matrix' which allows for ambiguity and possibilities of transformation. Keating is keen to stress that she does not wish to deny 'lesbian' as a category; she also emphasizes her perception of the importance of a politics of visibility. Simultaneously, she attempts to show how Jordan's poetry enables the reader to acknowledge within herself aspects of the self which seemingly more stable categories of identity than those projected in some of Jordan's work erase.

Keating's essay offers, in a sense, a standpoint[5] critique of Jordan's work in that she explicitly interpolates herself as reader into her engagement with Jordan's poetry. A similar process operates in Wendy Leeks' piece on 'Hysteria, Mastery and the Man/Woman Thing' which interrogates, and seeks to reverse, the relationship between analyst and analysand, master and slave, teacher and student, the person who is supposed to know and the one who supposedly does not, as formulated by Jacques Lacan and Sigmund Freud. Leeks demonstrates how Freud's discourse on hysteria produced woman as other, and suggests that feminist rereadings of Freud and psychoanalysis have sought to recover the hysteric as a feminist heroine, and that at the heart of Freud's difficulties with the Dora case lie Freud's investments in heterosexuality and his repression of homosexuality. Leeks argues that the fixed heteronormative categories ('man/woman') within which Freud works do not hold for the lesbian and that lesbians therefore should have an interest in moving beyond them, revealing these categories as an illusion. It is within this context, and in a manner not dissimilar to Keating's position, that Leeks invokes bisexuality as evocative of the plurality of positions which Freud's categorical illusions mask.

Leeks' essay perhaps most insistently and most radically points to the problem of core categories of identity.[6] Rather than asking 'where are the lesbians?' this collection of essays seems to be asking, once more, 'what is a lesbian?' From one lesbian perspective one might maintain that many of the figures and writings addressed in the essays are not lesbian at all, are peripheral to lesbian identity as understood by writers such as Sheila Jeffreys, for example. One might go even further and suggest that in their attempt to negotiate between margin (= indeterminate identity) and centre (= masculine power) as understood within these texts, these writings and figures hark back to the early stages of second-wave feminism, or even earlier, when (heterosexual) women intent upon asserting their equality with men took men as their point of comparison. Indeed, some decades prior to that, in *A Room of One's Own* (1928), Virginia Woolf spent several chapters comparing women's fate in the world of writing with that of men, ending with the notion that the representation of women's relation to each other might revolutionize writing by women–in some respects it is almost as if we have gone back in time to that point, and the intervening seventy years had never happened.

A wholly different way of looking would be to suggest that we truly live in a world in which difference is no longer encoded in oppositional ways and subjects have to come to terms with indeterminacy as the governing principle. Butler (1993) would argue that it is through the latter that we have the possibility of agency and that it is for this reason that we should embrace the dissolution of naturalized categories of identity. The difficulty for many is that the categories in question dominate daily discourses and as such have material effects in lesbians' lives.[7] This generates uncertainty as to the political viability and efficacy of agreeing with the notion of the indeterminacy of identity. Against this may be set the idea that writing becomes a means of expressing and shaping change, both as discourse and as material reality.[8] This, in a sense, is the position adopted by Heather Love in her discussion of Radclyffe Hall's *The Well of Loneliness*. Arguing against a lesbian-feminist critical tradition of condemning *The Well* as an inappropriate role model for lesbian readers since it portrays the lot of lesbians as doleful and masochistically inflected but also because of its insistent reading of lesbianism as inversion, Love suggests that Stephen's suffering in the novel in particular is reflective of the experiences of many lesbians. Rather than demanding a utopically rendered fantasy of lesbian life, Love advocates the embrace of *The Well* as a text with a basis in love letters to Evguenia Souline. There can be no doubt that lesbian critical interest of the 1990s is focused upon what once was viewed by lesbians as the margins, sometimes indeed the beyond, and that this 'romance' reflects changes in lesbian writing.

NOTES

1. I recognize that the two are not necessarily the same but want to retain the ambiguity as it resonates with the content of the essays.

2. It is worth noting that lesbians like Radicalesbians and Adrienne Rich promoted an inclusivity of all women in the category lesbian in their work which itself, not dissimilar to some critiques of queer, subsequently became the object of vigorous criticism. The question of boundaries and of definitions of identity thus has a history which stretches well back past its most recent manifestations.

3. The notion of 'play,' in its association with the ludic qualities of performance and, indeed, performance itself, a term frequently used in postmodern and queer writing, seems to undercut some of the very serious agendas with which lesbians grapple in our daily lives.

4. In a brief and highly relevant essay (1996) Renée C. Hoogland discusses the relationship between the notion of 'the lesbian's cultural invisibility as a site of epistemic privilege' (157) and 'the gradual dropping from sight of lesbian sexuality . . . as an epistemological and hence a political category' (163) during the 1980s and 1990s.

5. For a discussion of standpoint theory see Sandra Harding (1987).

6. In 'Feminist Historiography and Post-Structuralism' (1989) R. Radhakrishnan attempts to analyse how feminist historiography might utilize and differentiate itself from poststructuralist theory. If one replaces lesbian theory for feminist historiography, Radhakrishnan's argument offers a constructive and radical position, akin to Leeks', for a productive engagement of lesbian theory with postmodernism.

7. One need only consider, as one pertinent example, the ways in which lesbian academics seek to address lesbianism in the classroom to realize that discourse and identity are deeply embroiled with the material reality and circumstances in which lesbians operate daily, and in which agency and choice are not necessarily readily available to all and effects cannot be fully predicted (Garber, 1994).

8. The distinction between discourse and reality is of course a problematic one but I make it here in recognition of the view expressed by many lesbians that phrases such as 'playing with gender' do not express the material reality of their lives and that 'discourse' and 'reality' are not synonymous for them.

BIBLIOGRAPHY

Butler, Judith. 1993. *Bodies that matter.* London: Routledge.
de Lauretis, Teresa. 1993. Sexual indifference and lesbian representation. In Henry Abelove, Michèle Aina Barale, and David M. Halperin, eds. *The lesbian and gay studies reader.* London: Routledge. 141-58.
Garber, Linda, ed. 1994. *Tilting the tower: Lesbians teaching queer subjects.* London: Routledge.
Harding, Sandra, ed. 1987. *Feminism and methodology: Social science issues.* Milton Keynes: Open University.
Hoogland, Renée C. 1996. The gaze of inversion: The lesbian as visionary. In Teresa Brennan and Martin Jay, eds. *Vision in context: Historical and contemporary perspectives on sight.* London: Routledge. 155-67.
Radhakrishnan, R. 1989. Feminist historiography and post-structuralism. In Elizabeth Meese and Alice Parker, eds. *The difference within: Feminism and critical theory.* Amsterdam: John Benjamins Publishing Co. 189-206.
Woolf, Virginia. 1928. *A room of one's own.* London: Hogarth Press.

'A Person Positions Herself on Quicksand': The Postmodern Politics of Identity and Location in Sarah Schulman's *Empathy*

Sonya Andermahr

SUMMARY. This article discusses Sarah Schulman's 1993 novel *Empathy* in the context of contemporary debates about the politics of identity and location. It begins by discussing the impact of challenges from postmodernism and from Black, post-colonial and lesbian feminisms on feminist theories of identity, highlighting the concepts of diversity and intrasexual difference. The article goes on to explore Schulman's novel as an example of contemporary lesbian feminist fiction which engages these debates both in its subject matter, by deconstructing the categories of 'race,' gender and sexuality and, formally, in its use of postmodern stylistic devices. It argues that Schulman's novel represents both a postmodern critique of essentialist theories of gender identity, recognising the multiple locations of subjects, and a feminist critique of postmodern cultural relativism and political irresponsibility, insisting on the re-

Sonya Andermahr is Principal Lecturer in English and Women's Studies at University College, Northampton, UK. In addition to several articles on lesbian and feminist fiction and popular culture, she has written (with Terry Lovell and Carol Wolkowitz) *A Glossary of Feminist Fiction* (Edward Arnold, 1997) and is co-editor (with Gabriele Griffin) of *Straight Studies Modified: Lesbian Interventions in the Academy* (Cassell, 1997).

Address correspondence to: Sonya Andermahr, School of Cultural Studies, University College, Park Campus, Northampton, NN2 7AL, United Kingdom.

[Haworth co-indexing entry note]: "'A Person Positions Herself on Quicksand': The Postmodern Politics of Identity and Location in Sarah Schulman's *Empathy*." Andermahr, Sonya. Co-published simultaneously in *Journal of Lesbian Studies* (Harrington Park Press, an imprint of The Haworth Press, Inc.) Vol. 4, No. 2, 2000, pp. 7-20; and: *'Romancing the Margins'? Lesbian Writing in the 1990s* (ed: Gabriele Griffin) Harrington Park Press, an imprint of The Haworth Press, Inc., 2000, pp. 7-20. Single or multiple copies of this article are available for a fee from The Haworth Document Delivery Service [1-800-342-9678, 9:00 a.m. - 5:00 p.m. (EST). E-mail address: getinfo@haworthpressinc.com].

alities of social injustice. The main part of the article examines Schulman's treatment of four key issues: psychoanalysis and theories of sexual difference which pathologise lesbianism; heterosexism as reproducing women's oppression in patriarchy; the politics of representation whereby lesbian desire is written out; and American cultural imperialism and ethnocentrism. The article concludes by highlighting Schulman's assertion that empathy constitutes a valuable political stance in postmodern times. *[Article copies available for a fee from The Haworth Document Delivery Service: 1-800-342-9678. E-mail address: getinfo@haworthpressinc.com <Website: http:// www.haworthpressinc.com>]*

KEYWORDS. Feminism, postmodernism, lesbian fiction, queer theory, psychoanalysis, Jewish writing

INTRODUCTION

Since the advent of the second wave of feminism in the late 1960s, fiction produced by feminist and lesbian writers has provided a powerful engagement with the politics of gender and sexuality. During this period, however, feminist fiction has registered transformations that have affected the theory and practice of feminism more widely. A major shift, dating from the late 1980s, names the theorisation of location and the radical rethinking of theories of identity and difference as one of its main concerns.[1] It suggests a reconceptualisation of identity, particularly gender identity, from a relatively homogeneous model to a more unstable and heterogeneous conception of what identity means. This requires that feminists take the notion of intrasexual difference–that is difference among women–seriously. All three–theory, politics, fiction–endeavour to offer women ways of simultaneously articulating their differences and challenging inequality. Importantly, they attempt to register both the diversity of women's experience and the multiplicity of identities within each woman. As a result, the subject fragments, frequently (and sometimes painfully) traversing borders and boundaries, moving across and within culture, history, 'race' and, sometimes, even gender. In this article, I want to examine one example of contemporary lesbian feminist fiction–*Empathy* (1993) by the US lesbian writer Sarah Schulman–in the light of contemporary feminist debates about the politics of location.

In common with much recent feminist fiction by American and British writers such as Jeanette Winterson, Alice Walker, Michele Roberts and Angela Carter, *Empathy* employs a number of techniques and devices associated with postmodernist and anti-realist aesthetics in order to explore the politics of gender, sexuality, and identity. These include hybridisation or the mixing of genres; metafiction, which comments on its own fictional status; self-reflexivity; intertextuality, in which the text draws on other texts; fantasy; pastiche; and irony. While postmodern devices are not in my view inherently radical, their use by Schulman facilitates the deconstruction of the narratives of (hetero)sexism and imperialism.[3] Like many contemporary feminist novels, *Empathy* combines postmodern stylistics with a feminist critique of postmodernism, sharing its central theme with contemporary feminism: the possibilities of political solidarity and resistance in the postmodern world.

In the course of the article I'll draw on a range of contemporary feminist, lesbian and post-colonial theories including Monique Wittig's (1992) concept of the straight mind and her controversial view that lesbians are not women; Judith Butler's (1991) concept of gender as performance; the notion of strategic essentialism propounded by Gayatri Spivak (1988) and Diana Fuss (1989); Kimberlé Crenshaw's (1989) model of intersectional identities, and the concept of multiple locations of identity proposed by post-colonial theorists Chandra Mohanty (1987) and Lata Mani (1992). First, I want to discuss briefly two of the challenges currently facing feminism–diversity and postmodernism–before going on to discuss how they are negotiated in Schulman's novel.[4]

THE CHALLENGES OF POSTMODERNISM AND DIVERSITY

The challenge of postmodernism is first of all a challenge to the epoch of western modernity and in particular to its concept of knowledge (Flax, 1990). Postmodernism represents a critique of universalistic grand theories and master narratives which provided the grounding for the Enlightenment discourses of rationalism and scientific objectivism, and ultimately for Western capitalism, imperialism and liberalism. It challenges a-historical concepts of the 'self,' 'truth,' and 'science,' and emphasises the contingent and discursive construction of such concepts. In particular, it destabilises the liberal humanist belief in a unified stable subject organised around a core identity.

Feminism in the West has historically drawn attention to many of the same patriarchal master narratives, highlighting, for example, the construction of citizenship as exclusively white and male. But it too finds itself the object of postmodern deconstruction which works to undermine the feminist metanarrative of shared female oppression, in particular its theory of patriarchy as a unified or even dual system, and any transhistorical concept of the sexual division of labour. More generally, feminism, as an emancipatory politics, is itself a product of the Enlightenment ideals of progress now under attack from postmodernism.

The challenge of diversity has been powerfully articulated by lesbian feminists and by Black and Third World feminists. In the field of sexuality, Monique Wittig, Luce Irigaray and Judith Butler demonstrate the centrality of heterosexism to women's oppression. Wittig (1992), for example, advances a powerful critique of heterosexuality as an oppressive symbolic system which she calls 'the straight mind.' Lesbian feminist theorists like Celia Kitzinger and Sue Wilkinson (1996) call on heterosexual feminists to examine the ways in which gender inequalities are constructed and reinforced in and through heterosexuality.

Black feminists such as bell hooks (1989), Chandra Mohanty (1987) and Trinh T. Minh-Ha (1989) have challenged the ethnocentrism of much feminist theory. From this has come a recognition of the need to go beyond the 'adding women in' approach whereby Black women are added to white feminist frameworks. The nature of the relationship between different vectors of oppression–'race,' class, gender–has become a key focus of analysis. The critic Kimberlé Crenshaw (1989) uses the term 'intersectionality' to describe this interrelationship, and sees the understanding of diversity as central to Black feminism which necessarily rejects any single-axis theory about racism and sexism.

For some feminists, these combined challenges would appear to lend support to the view that feminism is outmoded because it is premised on a supposedly unified subject, 'woman,' who no longer has integrity. But for others, the political challenge posed by postmodernism and diversity is one of mobilising strategies of resistance while deconstructing essentialist and universalising categories of identity. Such feminists are acknowledging the need to theorise locations of power as well as powerlessness; to deconstruct whiteness and heterosexuality; and to theorise the Western subject of imperialism.

Feminists have recognised the need to situate their discourse within multiple and often contradictory fields of power. Chandra Mohanty (1987) calls for an understanding of the multiple locations of subjects and the different temporalities of struggle to which they give rise. Increasingly, feminist theories of knowledge emphasise the process of positioning as itself an epistemological act. Donna Haraway (1988) proposes the concept of 'situated knowledge' to capture the idea of knowledge as always partial and embodied. Summing up these developments, the post-colonial critic Lata Mani states:

> As claims to universality and objectivity have been shown to be the alibis of a largely masculinist, heterosexist and white, western subject, both readers and writers have had to confront their particularity and history. Gender, race, class, sexuality and historical experience specify hitherto unmarked bodies, deeply compromising the fictions of unified subjects and disinterested knowledge. (1992: 307)

Sarah Schulman's *Empathy* gives a fictional treatment to many of these issues. The novel's theme is precisely that of feminism in the 1990s: the possibilities for political resistance across multiple and shifting identities. It asks the question of how we can empathise in a confusing postmodern world in a way that is politically and psychologically enabling. As such, it deals with the so-called big issues, thereby confounding the view that lesbian novels are particularist and lacking in general significance.

The novel operates a double gesture, deconstructing and simultaneously inscribing the political meanings of identities. It does this not in the 'add-on' manner of identity politics, but in a radically intersectional way, recognising the 'multiple locations' of contemporary subjects. In the rest of the article, I want to discuss *Empathy*'s treatment of postmodernism and diversity in terms of four major critiques that it undertakes: a critique of the psychoanalytic theory of sexual difference; of heterosexism as implicated in women's subordination; of the politics of representation; and of ethnocentrism and American imperialism.

PSYCHOANALYSIS AND THE STRAIGHT MIND

The themes of psychoanalysis–sexuality, identity, the unconscious and psychic pain–are central to *Empathy*. The novel represents the psychoanalytic view of 'identity' as a kind of psychic violence which is based on the repression of unconscious desire. The aim of psychoanalysis, the novel reminds us, is to help people who suffer by listening to them through a form of empathy. The concept of transference, the psychoanalytic term for this, is integral to the cure. However, the novel highlights the historical role of psychoanalysis as a regulatory and normalising technique with the aim of reconciling subjects to their 'correct' gender identity. It explores the psychoanalytic account of the acquisition of femininity which constructs female identity as lack, and asks 'how can I be a woman and still be happy?' (6). Moreover, in focusing on lesbian identity, *Empathy* foregrounds the double erasure of the lesbian subject within a heterosexist society.

The novel's central tragi-comic conceit is that its lesbian protagonist Anna has never slept with another lesbian but always falls for ambivalent bisexuals. She can't understand why and so goes to Doc, apparently a pavement psychoanalyst who offers three free counselling sessions. In engaging psychoanalysis the text foregrounds its Jewish identity. It invokes and plays on notions of Jewishness, for example, the stereotype that all New York Jews are in analysis or are themselves analysts or the children of analysts. Both Anna and Doc are the children of Jewish psychoanalysts, and therefore 'born' Freudians. There are obvious echoes of Sigmund Freud's (himself, of course, a Jew) relation to his female patients. Indeed, the novel represents a radical intertextual reworking of Freud's female case studies: Anna's lover in the novel is called Dora. Anna O was Freud's first patient, Bertha Pappenheim, who with Breuer, invented the talking cure. Dora, whose real name was Ida Bauer, a resistant heroine for feminism, refused to name her desire for another woman and famously sacked Freud. There is also a character called Herr K, Dora's seducer in the Freudian case study, whom Schulman rewrites as Doc's mentor and as 'a pioneer in the field of interruption theory' (137).

The novel's epigraph comes from Freud's 1920 essay 'The Psychogenesis of a Case of Homosexuality in a Woman' which defines female homosexuality as a combination of masculinity complex and frustrated desire to have a child by one's father. Freud states: 'She changed into a man and took her mother in place of her father as the object of her love' (1991: 158). This misogynistic and homophobic construction is internalised by the protagonist. As a result, Anna experiences extreme alienation from her body and sexuality and becomes a disembodied, dysphoric subject. Schulman represents her subjectivity through a correspondingly fragmented and discontinuous narrative style, split between the two protagonists, Anna and Doc. However, Doc rejects the sexism and heterosexism that inform psychoanalytic theory and, unlike Freud, he deconstructs the power relations of the analytical scene. He is aware both of the value of listening and of the power it confers on the listener. Paradoxically, he himself has never been in therapy because he sees its potential for exploitation:

> You tell them one real thing and then the doctor thinks he knows you. He starts getting arrogant and overfamiliar, making insulting suggestions left and right. You have to protest constantly just to set the record straight. Finally he makes offensive assumptions and throws them in your face. A stranger in a bar could do the same. (72-3)

The novel undertakes a critique of the psychoanalytic theory of sexual difference, describing it as shoring up heterosexuality as a political institution. It articulates the lesbian feminist view that women's oppression is constructed in and through heterosexuality as well as gender. The text negotiates two main theories of lesbian identity, associated with the work of Monique Wittig and Judith Butler, two of the most influential theorists for lesbian feminism in the 1980s and 1990s.

Monique Wittig (1992) defines the straight mind as the 'ensemble of heterosexual myths,' a semiotic system which oppresses us as lesbians and women. Like Schulman, Wittig singles out psychoanalysis as a prime example of the straight mentality, highlighting its reification of gender binarism. She writes:

> with its ineluctability as knowledge, as an obvious principle, as a given prior to any science, the straight mind develops a totalizing interpretation of history, social reality, culture, [and] language. Thus one speaks of *the* exchange of women, *the* difference between the sexes, *the* symbolic

order, *the* unconscious, Desire, Jouissance, Culture, History, giving abso-
lute meaning to these concepts when they are only categories founded
upon heterosexuality, or thought which produces the difference between
the sexes as a political and philosophical dogma. (1992: 27-8)

The sum total of these discourses amounts to the message 'You will be
straight or you will not be' (1992: 28). Schulman's depiction of Anna's
sexual relationships with women shows the straight mind and compulsory
heterosexuality in operation. In one episode, Anna recalls one of her female
lovers who, after making love, rolls over and pronounces, 'You're narrow
because you're gay but I'm universal because I'm not' (119). Another lover,
the 'woman in white,' constructs Anna as a masculinised lesbian 'other,'
using her to bolster her own feminine identity and 'prove that she is heterosexual' (163). As Anna says: 'that woman in white really made me feel like
one of the guys' (163). The 'woman in white' represents the failure of
empathy and, specifically, homophobic disavowal. Moreover, her association
with whiteness gestures towards a racialised level of meaning. In chapter 25
Doc dramatically shoots her; however, in the following chapter the reader is
told, in postmodern style, that this is a lie: 'That was just Doc projecting his
worst fears onto the page' (161).

LESBIANS AND FEMALE MEN:
THE CRITIQUE OF HETEROSEXISM

It is impossible to discuss *Empathy* without reference to another lesbian
novel–Joanna Russ's brilliant sci-fi satire *The Female Man* (1975). The latter
is itself intertextually related to another feminist and lesbian classic, Virginia
Woolf's comic fantasy *Orlando* (1928). Like Russ and Woolf, Schulman uses
humour and irony to subversive effect. Their texts highlight the interconnections between the construction of gender and sexuality in a heteropatriarchal
society which privileges masculinity and heterosexuality at the expense of
other subject positions. In the ideology of heterosexuality the definition of a
hero is essentially male; a lesbian can't compete. In response Anna, like Russ'
protagonist Joanna, adopts a male persona because men are taken more seriously, carry more authority and of course have easier sexual access to women.
Her transformation becomes a means of keeping her self-respect: if maleness is
the only signifier of humanity, then it makes sense to become a man. In a key
episode Anna and Doc discuss Anna's problem with identification:

'Anna, why are you dressed like a man? . . . Listen Anna, in this entire
event there is only one word that has no meaning and that is the word
he. Why do you use it?'. . .

> 'I use he,' said Doc, 'Because it's easier and I need all the help I can get.' . . .
> 'But Anna, what does all this have to do with you being a lesbian?' . . .
> 'Since I was a child,' he said, 'there have been two epithets that I have truly feared. I feared being told "You want to be a man," and I feared being told "You hate men." . . . The end result was that I, Anna O., could not exist.' (156-8)

The confusing slippage of pronouns and proper nouns generated in this dialogue is owing to the fact that Anna and Doc are really the same person: Doc, it transpires, is a projection; he is Anna's split-off male persona. 'He' has to exist because the person who loves a woman has to be a man. For his part, Doc realises that he is alienated from his femininity, from Anna, both because of its denigration in patriarchy and its construction as heterosexual in relation to men. The conceit therefore points to the repressive regime of heterosexual binarism which limits sexual identification to two categories. Another way of looking at it is to say that Anna and Doc are suffering from empathy; as Doc says: 'transference was just another kind of love' (11). Indeed, they are presented as mirror images of each other: 'They looked so alike. The only difference was that Anna had to wear clothes she hated' (31). Like Woolf's *Orlando* whose sexual persona changes through the centuries according to the clothes he/she wears, Anna and Doc are represented as both the same and different, demonstrating simultaneously the fluidity of subjectivity and its containment within rigid gender categories.

In its depiction of Anna, *Empathy* bears out Wittig's contention that lesbians are not women in a heterosexist system. Wittig argues:

> Lesbian is the only concept I know which is beyond the categories of sex (woman and man), because the designated subject 'lesbian' is *not* a woman, either economically, or politically, or ideologically. For what makes a woman is a specific social relation to a man. (1992: 20)

However, while Wittig sees this as to lesbians' advantage, placing them outside, in opposition to the symbolic order, *Empathy* sees it in terms of oppression, alienating lesbians from their embodiment as women. The novel rejects Wittig's extreme anti-essentialism and it ultimately teaches Anna that she can be both, a woman and a lesbian: 'I forgot I was a woman,' she says to Dora, who responds, 'Don't do it again. You don't have to' (164).

In exploring the relationship between heterosexual women and lesbians, the novel addresses the issue of diversity within the women's movement. Despite the centrality of lesbians to so-called first and second wave feminism, lesbianism is commonly articulated as threat. The preferred feminist narrative of female solidarity is a non-sexual sisters-in-arms affair. Lesbians, as the novel shows, pose a challenging question: what happens when you eroticise relations between women? The sign lesbian works to detach gender from its assumed connection to heterosexuality. Lesbian difference thus complicates the concept of female identity. The novel uses this insight as a source of humour. At one point Anna remarks:

> Maybe that's the problem I've always had with female identification. It's like looking at Picasso's Three Women only to come away thinking, 'My breast is your thigh.' (68)

THE POLITICS OF LESBIAN REPRESENTATION

The issue of representation is central to the novel. It asks 'what are the conditions for the inscription of lesbian existence?' The use of postmodern stylistic hybridity is a means of experimenting with modes of representation productive of lesbian meanings. The fragmented character of the text testifies to the lack of an authorised/authentic script for the articulation of lesbian desire and the necessity of employing intertextuality. For Judith Butler the unrepresentedness of lesbianism is a strength. She sees the sign 'lesbian' as a catachrestic one which can be made to unfix sexual meanings generally:

> I would like to have it permanently unclear precisely what that sign signifies . . . I am permanently troubled by identity categories, consider them to be inevitable stumbling blocks, and understand them, even promote them as sites of necessary trouble. (1991: 14)

The novel's blurring of identity boundaries, its rejection of essentialist conceptions of self and its focus on intra- as well as inter-sexual difference all correspond to Butler's model.

Empathy's representation of identity is insistently anti-realist and highly stylised. The novel incorporates text in the form of plays and film scripts, vignettes and conversations from daily life. It subverts the self-discovery narrative which is a staple of much feminist fiction. As Anna says about 'the coming out' narrative expected of her: 'How many times do I have to come out? And do I always have to do it anecdotally? When it's not a story, but a constant clash of systems. When it's a traveling implosion?' (158-9). Anna presents her autobiography not in the revelatory manner of the traditional Bildungsroman but as a film or play script, thereby accentuating the performative role of the family members and defamiliarizing the heterosexist ideology of family life. In the Sedar Jewish holiday episode all the family members are presented as playing a part which foregrounds the theatricality of identity. Anna's doctor father acts the paternal figure always there for family and friends; Anna herself plays the Black sheep, continually politicising her sexuality. Schulman's emphasis on the performative aspects of identities and roles constructed within the discourses of gender and sexuality recalls Judith Butler's discussion of the being of gayness as a necessary drag:

> If gender is drag, and if it is an imitation that regularly produces the ideal it attempts to approximate, then gender is a performance that *produces* the illusion of an inner sex or essence or psychic gender core. (1991: 28)

This is highly relevant to *Empathy*'s postmodern representation of identity as a set of stylistic repertoires and performances. Schulman fully endorses Butler's contention that 'there are no direct expressive or causal lines between sex, gender, gender presentation, sexual practice, fantasy and sexuality' (25). Indeed the insistence that there is and must be is part of the normalizing discourse of psychoanalysis in particular and heterosexist discourse generally.

However, unlike Butler who resists naming lesbian oppression in language implicated in essentialist categories, Schulman insists on the continuing validity of a vocabulary of oppression:

> I look back on my own life story and see the history of the distortion of our imagery. I'm talking about something that has nothing to do with nostalgia. Within that story there is the total history of my oppression and my refusal to be oppressed. (166)

The passage plays on the distinction between sincerity and irony. 'Distortion,' 'nostalgia,' 'a total history,' 'oppression' and 'resistance': this is the language of political movement, but one which understands the problems of postmodernity, working with and against these to challenge heterosexist norms. In a metafictional move and ironic lament the text meditates on the postmodern condition, saying that analysis has been replaced by catharsis: marxism by postmodernism, psychoanalysis by twelve step programmes, and that we are witnessing the 'end of content' (146). The novel deploys what Spivak (1988) and others have called a strategic essentialism, whereby the critic makes use of particular narratives such as marxism for liberatory purposes while acknowledging their complicity in structures of power.

MULTIPLE LOCATIONS: DECONSTRUCTING ETHNOCENTRISM AND THE AMERICAN DREAM

Finally, the novel includes a critique of the American dream and its relationship to American imperialism. *Empathy* was written during the Gulf War (1990-1) and is marked by an awareness of US military intervention in global politics. It asks how one can act authentically in a postmodern world that is not yet post-imperialist. In a satirical representation of American culture, Schulman humorously highlights the important symbolic role food has played in the hegemony of conservative American values. The text incorporates recipes for classic American dishes such as 'Spam Patio Dip' and 'Three Musketeers Treasure Puffs' which come from what Doc sees as the most dangerous magazine in America–*Family Circle*. As Doc observes:

> This was special food . . . It came from the time when America had dreams. When Americans didn't mind being geeky and weird because soon the whole world would be that way too. It didn't mind eating slop because America would make slop important. Slop would have meaning. Slop would mean power. (82)

The novel attacks US indifference to human suffering on a global scale. At one stage Anna accompanies her girlfriend on a trip to Indonesia and is shocked by her lover's cultural insensitivity to her surroundings. She typifies the First World stance of treating the Third World as her playground, seeing it as nothing more than a picturesque backdrop. It represents what Spivak (1988) calls the worlding of the Third World. Responding to Anna's account of her trip, and her dismay at her friend's refusal to see beyond the ideological construction of the East as tourist paradise, Doc says:

> 'Wow . . . That's very Heart of Darkness of you. I mean, there's no way to be there and be polite because your presence there is rude.' Yes, Anna reflects, 'I mean something different in the World than I mean in my world.' (111)

This comment perfectly captures the post-colonial feminist concept of multiple locations of identity, highlighting the difference within as well as between cultures and subjects. Alongside this critique of imperialism the novel presents an ethnically heterogeneous American culture through its representation of contemporary New York. The text is full of vignettes of New York street life, portraying different ethnic communities and their uneasy co-existence. It exemplifies Bakhtin's (1981) concept of heteroglossia, containing a plurality of social discourses and a cultural intermingling which is both exhilarating and risky. And, understandably in a novel by a Jewish writer about psychoanalysis, the language, humour and cultural references of Jewishness are particularly marked. Moreover, the variety of styles and genres used in the novel–plays, cinema, dreams, recipes–foreground the world of representations in which we live. The novel asks that we recognise and challenge the deep structures bolstering this world of surfaces; the continuing realities of women's subordination, of imperialism, racism and homophobia.

CONCLUSION

It should be clear that *Empathy* articulates a postmodern politics of location, recognising the fact that 'a person positions herself on quicksand' (165). In the course of the novel, Anna acknowledges the need for a new ethics, distinguishable both from the old overarching metanarratives and from politically quiescent models of postmodernity. She recognizes

> that every single individual has to rethink morality for themselves and at the same time come to a newly negotiated social agreement. That's how Anna learned to be many people at once and live in different worlds of perception at the same time each day. (165)

In subscribing to an ethical postmodernism, the novel rejects the politically disengaging mode of postmodernism, refusing the simulacrum, and insisting on the political meanings of identity and desire. It articulates a critique of postmodern relativism, of a world without depth, meaning or value and demonstrates that postmodernism is a heterogeneous phenomenon, containing 'worlds of difference.' Schulman's text represents a symbolic exploration of women's unequal differences as articulated in contemporary feminist theory and in the process exhorts feminists to take seriously the possibilities for empathy as a political stance in a postmodern world of shifting locations.

NOTES

1. The sense of redirection within feminism is widely evidenced in feminist scholarship and publishing in the 1990s. *Doing Things Differently: Women's Studies in the 1990s*, edited by Mary Maynard and June Purvis, examines the impact of recent debates on the discipline of Women's Studies. In their chapter, Mary Maynard and Joanna de Groot identify the crisis around the *identity* of the subject, arising from

> challenges to the idea that there can be a universal feminist approach or a generally valid framework for feminist analyses or politics. The early concerns with the ways in which men exercise power over women have been complicated by the increasing awareness that women comprise a diverse and varied group. It is no longer appropriate to talk about 'women' in the homogeneous way that Women's Studies previously did. (1992: 149)

2. There are of course many continuities as well as discontinuities across feminist fiction of the 1970s, 1980s and 1990s in terms of style, theme, etc. Typologies of second wave Anglo-American feminist fiction which chart its development up to the end of the 1980s (e.g., Palmer, 1989) often identify a dichotomy between, on one hand, texts with a social and political approach to identity and, on the other hand,

texts with a more psychoanalytic focus. Political fictions chart the struggle of individual or groups of women to liberate themselves from patriarchal constraints. While 'political' fiction could be criticised for frequently presenting a simplistic and unified image of the 'female' subject, psychoanalytic fictions could be criticised for failing to make connections between women or offer a wider social relevance. Moreover, both types of text could be criticised for privileging a limited concept of white femininity. While this split is still in evidence, I would suggest that many contemporary 1990s lesbian and feminist texts such as *Empathy* succeed in articulating valuable aspects of the two models, achieving a dual focus on commonality and difference, politics and the psyche. They combine a political critique of the social status quo and represent women's identity and subjectivity in a sophisticated and nuanced manner.

3. In her analysis of second wave feminist fiction, Rita Felski (1992) argues that some forms of feminism have privileged an avant-garde modernist aesthetic at the expense of realism which, she suggests, is the mode most feminist writers have actually utilised. I would extend Felski's argument to postmodernism: while some contemporary lesbian and feminist texts are formally innovative *and* politically radical, I do not think that postmodern aesthetics are inherently more politically radical than realist ones.

4. Maynard and de Groot (1992) identify postmodernism and diversity as two of five challenges facing Women's Studies; the other three are Gender Studies, 'Doing' Theory, and Feminist Scholarship.

WORKS CITED

Bakhtin, Mikhail. *The Dialogic Imagination: Four Essays.* Ed. Michael Holquist, trans. C. Emerson and M. Holquist. Austin TX: University of Texas, 1981.

Butler, Judith. 'Imitation and Gender Insubordination,' in Diana Fuss ed., *Inside/Out: Lesbian Theories, Gay Theories.* London: Routledge, 1991.

Crenshaw, Kimberle. 'Demarginalizing the Intersection of Race and Sex: A Black Feminist Critique of Antidiscrimination Doctrine, Feminist Theory and Antiracist Politics,' *The University of Chicago Legal Forum*, pp 139-67, 1989.

Felski, Rita. *Beyond Feminist Aesthetics: Feminist Literature and Social Change.* London: Hutchinson Radius, 1989.

Flax, Jane. *Thinking Fragments.* California: University of California Press, 1990.

Freud, Sigmund. [1920] 'The Psychogenesis of a Case of Homosexuality in a Woman,' in *The Standard Edition*, Vol. XVIII. London: Hogarth Press, 1991.

Fuss, Diana. *Essentially Speaking: Feminism, Nature and Difference.* New York and London: Routledge, 1989.

Haraway, Donna. 'Situated Knowledges: The Science Question in Feminism and the Privilege of the Partial Perspective,' *Feminist Studies*, Vol. 14, No. 3, pp. 575-99, 1988.

hooks, bell. *Talking Back, Thinking Feminist, Thinking Black.* London: Sheba Feminist Press, 1989.

Kitzinger, Celia and Sue Wilkinson. 'Deconstructing Heterosexuality: A Feminist Social-Constructionist Analysis,' in Nickie Charles and Felicia Hughes-Freeland eds., *Practising Feminism: Identity, Difference, Power.* London: Routledge, 1996.

Mani, Lata. 'Multiple Mediations: Feminist Scholarship in the Age of Multinational Reception,' in Helen Crowley and Susan Himmelweit eds., *Knowing Women: Feminism and Knowledge*. Cambridge: Polity Press and the Open University, 1992.

Maynard, Mary and Joanna de Groot. 'Facing the 1990s: Problems and Possibilities for Women's Studies,' in Mary Maynard and June Purvis eds., *Women's Studies in the 1990s*. London: Taylor and Francis, 1992.

Minh-Ha, Trinh T. *Woman, Native, Other: Writing Postcoloniality and Feminism*. Bloomington: Indiana University Press, 1989.

Mohanty, Chandra T. 'Feminist Encounters: Locating the Politics of Experience,' *Copyright*, Vol. 1, No. 1, 1987.

Palmer, Paulina. *Contemporary Women's Fiction: Narrative Practice and Feminist Theory*. Hemel Hempstead: Harvester Wheatsheaf, 1989.

Russ, Joanna. [1975] *The Female Man*. London: The Women's Press, 1985.

Schulman, Sarah. *Empathy*. London: Sheba Feminist Press, 1993.

Spivak, Gayatri Chakravorty. *In Other Worlds: Essays in Cultural Politics*. New York and London: 1988.

Wittig, Monique. *The Straight Mind and Other Essays*. Hemel Hempstead: Harvester Wheatsheaf, 1992.

Woolf, Virginia. [1928] *Orlando: A Biography*. London: Hogarth Press, 1990.

Performing 'La Mestiza': Lesbians of Color Negotiating Identities

Ellen M. Gil-Gomez

SUMMARY. Even with the major movements in current gender studies that attempt to expand the simple notions of monolithic identity there are still major blind spots that perpetuate what they seek to disrupt. These blind spots are sometimes heterosexist, sometimes racist, or sometimes both. This essay analyzes how the lesbian of color is situated at the interstices of many fields of identity studies–gender, queer, and ethnic–and the specific difficulties she has with this position. By using the theories of Judith Butler and Gloria Anzaldúa, I describe how the lesbian of color can survive numerous sites of hostility by constructing a positive identity within her own ethnic/racial community through creative acts of cultural revision. After considering the power of these acts I call for the empowered performance of the mestiza state–the state of contradiction wherein the lesbian of color finds herself. *[Article copies available for a fee from The Haworth Document Delivery Service: 1-800-342-9678. E-mail address: getinfo@haworthpressinc.com <Website: http:// www.haworthpressinc.com>]*

KEYWORDS. Lesbians of color, la mestiza, performativity

Lesbians of color "lov[e] in the war years"–to borrow a phrase from Cherríe Moraga–and so they must live out their lives in the crossfire. These

Ellen M. Gil-Gomez is Visiting Senior Lecturer of Latino/a Studies at Ohio State University, developing a curriculum on identity studies, cultural studies, and women of color.

[Haworth co-indexing entry note]: "Performing 'La Mestiza': Lesbians of Color Negotiating Identities." Gil-Gomez, Ellen M. Co-published simultaneously in *Journal of Lesbian Studies* (Harrington Park Press, an imprint of The Haworth Press, Inc.) Vol. 4, No. 2, 2000, pp. 21-38; and: *'Romancing the Margins'? Lesbian Writing in the 1990s* (ed: Gabriele Griffin) Harrington Park Press, an imprint of The Haworth Press, Inc., 2000, pp. 21-38. Single or multiple copies of this article are available for a fee from The Haworth Document Delivery Service [1-800-342-9678, 9:00 a.m. - 5:00 p.m. (EST). E-mail address: getinfo@haworthpressinc.com].

women are "outlaws" within multiple communities: their "home" ethnic/racial community, the white feminist community, and the white lesbian community. If the lesbian of color is to align herself with anyone, Moraga concludes, she must somehow choose because "her very presence violates the ranking and abstraction of oppression" (*Loving* 53). As Moraga illustrates, when lesbians of color acknowledge their identities they necessarily challenge the "camps" that are defined by individual facets of identity–and call attention to the abstractions within those settings. Yvonne Yarbro-Bejarano finds this the central problem with identity-based theories and views this problem and its consequences thus:

> The insistence on keeping these analytic categories discrete indicates white people's resistance to perceiving their own gender or sexuality as racially constructed and their tendency to assign the category of race exclusively to people of color, as well as the resistance of people of color to perceiving their own gender or heterosexual privilege. ("Expanding" 127)

Clearly, lesbians of color are situated in both the academic and societal crossfire. This dilemma has important effects on how they construct their own subjectivities. These lesbians not only have special ways of theorizing their identities, but their visions illustrate the importance of questioning all categorizations of self.

One of the most influential theories in feminism and lesbian studies is Judith Butler's well-known performance theory. Butler specifically addresses gender as an identity issue, by way of a Foucauldian genealogy. She attempts to discredit the notion that an essential sexual identity exists and wants to decenter the institutions that posit this view of gender identity (*Gender*, viii-ix), providing a corrective by authorizing the power of performance. According to Butler, parodic performances destabilize the idea of essence and "true" identity (x). Butler sees the subversiveness of parody as the best way to make or be in "gender trouble."

The application of performance theory to the discussion of gender and lesbian identity has merit in that it undermines the view that certain identities are inherently "abnormal." However, I am concerned with how performing identities might affect lesbians of color. Yarbro-Bejarano aptly points out that Butler does not consider how race or ethnic identity affects performance ("Expanding" 129). Butler does not incorporate facets of identity other than sexuality into her paradigm and she therefore implies that either no other elements of identity outside of lesbianism might affect the subject's subversive performance or that the same applies to other aspects of self as regards performance as sexuality does.[1] Using Butler's theory for lesbians of color, therefore, requires a reconsideration of the categorization of identity. In my

view the incorporation of race as performative needs to go beyond an engagement with "passing" because firstly, this option is only available to some and
secondly, successfully passing does not as a matter of course effect any overt
social change but rather continues the perpetuation of racism through existent
hierarchies.

The authors whom I discuss here employ some elements of performative
identity in their work but within important historical and cultural contexts. I
suggest this focus on context is what has the potential to force dramatic
change–for themselves and for ideas of gender identity. This article will focus
on texts that exemplify how lesbians of color can survive within the communities that wish to destroy them and will also explore the strategies they
employ to do so. Each specific work tackles different elements of identity as
well as different cultural and historical contexts. These examples should not
stand as monoliths of the experiences of lesbians of color. Instead, they should
be seen as individual moments when specific characters simultaneously perform a multifaceted identity within sexual and racial frameworks and within
many contexts, including: class, religion, time period, genre, culture, and history. The authors I will look at create a space for survival through re-envisioning
and rewriting cultural traditions by weaving articulations of lesbian identity
into the fabric of inherited cultural (and other) contexts.

I think it is useful to consider first one theory that describes what creative
texts *enact* in order to introduce the value of textual representations as performance. Gloria Anzaldúa's theory of a "mestiza consciousness" articulates an
identity that allows the lesbian of color to exist in a context that continually
wishes to ignore or destroy her. This is an articulated theory of being, of
identity, that has multiplicitous (sex, gender, race, etc.) identifiers at its heart.
Anzaldúa does not "add on" race to an identity theory that speaks from a
white perspective (which is the weakness with most identity theories in my
estimation); rather, she develops her theory from the perspective of a lesbian
of color and therefore accounts for numerous constructions of self and varied,
sometimes contradictory, identifications.

Anzaldúa's discussion of mestiza consciousness is found primarily in her
text *Borderlands/La Frontera: The New Mestiza.* It is useful not just for
discussing representations of genetic mestizas, women of Mexican Indian
and European parentage, but for metaphoric/cultural mestizas as well.[2] Anzaldúa is clearly concerned with the genetic mestiza–the woman who is a
combination of India, Angla, and Mexicana–but she also opens the door for a
broader view of this consciousness. In order to truly live on the borderlands,
and to thereby obliterate the possibility of a center, the inclusiveness that she
constantly speaks of must be applied to the figure that she constructs. Indeed
she thinks that the border psychology is played out in numerous communities. She claims: "the struggle is inner: Chicano, *indio*, American Indian,

mojado, mexicano, immigrant Latino, Anglo in power, working class Anglo, Black, Asian,–our psyches resemble the bordertowns and are populated by the same people" (*Borderlands* 87). Anzaldúa is allowing for multiple embodiments of this paradoxical identity. She also posits a need for connections between theory and material reality to create the possibility of real transformation. She states that

> The struggle [for "border" people] has always been inner, and is played out in the outer terrains. Awareness of our situation must come before inner changes, which in turn come before changes in society. Nothing happens in the "real" world unless it first happens in the images in our heads. (*Borderlands* 87)

Of key importance here, and what differentiates Anzaldúa from other theorists, is that she envisions reality and abstraction as existing on equal planes, working together in order for an individual to conceive of the processes involved in her own transformation (which will ultimately have a wider effect). In my view this is of prime importance because it shifts the focus off the "race for theory," to use Barbara Christian's phrase, and onto the individual's own use of theory, as well as to the larger political consequences of these uses.

The mestiza can be connected directly to Butler's idea, based on Foucault's genealogies, that "natural" gender identities are constructed over time by interactions of subjects with discourses, including compulsory heterosexuality. Similarly, Anzaldúa implies that the concept of a "pure" race (and therefore the solidity of racial identity) is an effect of a white supremacist agenda. This agenda pressures those who are of mixed race to attempt to separate out portions of themselves so that they can fit within that paradigm; one must claim one or the other of the self. Instead, Anzaldúa describes an identity that does not attempt to separate out portions of self (woman, lesbian, white, lower class, Mexican Indian, etc.), but sees the point of confluence of these identities as the border of all and the connection among all. She describes this place as

> That focal point or fulcrum, that juncture where the mestiza stands, is where phenomena tend to collide . . . In attempting to work out a synthesis, the self has added a third element which is greater than the sum of its severed parts. That third element is a new consciousness–a mestiza consciousness–and though it is a source of intense pain, its energy comes from continual creative motion that keeps breaking down the unitary aspect of each new paradigm. (*Borderlands* 79-80)

Anzaldúa also thinks that writing itself is a mode of performing identity–both directly and indirectly. The work lives without her by its side to give it context and so it is interpreted repeatedly. She writes that "My 'stories' are acts encapsulated in time, 'enacted' every time they are spoken aloud or read silently. I like to think of them as performances and not as inert and 'dead' objects. Instead, the work has an identity" (67). This textual existence is important to consider when theorizing identity and performance because it is a unique performance that *escapes the visual*. However, it entails rethinking the object, the written page, or work of art, not as "dead" as is typical of the Western tradition, but in the Aztec way she describes: there is no "split [of] the artistic from the functional, the sacred from the secular, art from everyday life" (*Borderlands* 66).

Anzaldúa has her own notion of performing identities; however, her discussion is centered on a performance of race rather than gender. Here she describes how the mestiza connects to the external forces that wish to see her in categorized sections. She writes: "she learns to juggle cultures. She has a plural personality, she operates in a pluralistic mode–nothing is thrust out, the good the bad and the ugly, nothing rejected, nothing abandoned. Not only does she sustain contradictions, she turns the ambivalence into something else" (*Borderlands* 79). I believe these words can be read as showing how her identity is constructed based both on how others view her, and on how she chooses to present herself to others. In Anzaldúa's example, the outsiders define the mestiza negatively in comparison to themselves. She, though, chooses to allow this negative judgment to make space for the ambiguity of the racial/ethnic identity that she embodies.

Obviously there is an amount of agency involved to operate in this "pluralistic mode," and therefore I suggest, and this is a key point, that choosing to *perform* pluralism within one's cultural tradition can be a useful strategy for the lesbian of color. It is one that potentially allows some of the freedom of movement which Butler describes, while incorporating the understanding of real contexts and racial theory that Anzaldúa details.

This is exactly what some of the lesbian writers have their fictional characters do and what the authors themselves desire to do to successfully articulate their identities while remaining within their communities. This combination forces them to rewrite their cultural traditions to make room for these identities. Performing la mestiza amounts to a choice to identify and play out the paradox of embodying a oneness that is not able to exist within existing categories, thereby challenging many articulated theories of identity.

Women of color have generally been seen as "creative" writers rather than as producers of theory because sometimes their theory tends to be presented differently from the critical theory of white academics. This allows for them to be treated as "exotics" and therefore not as challenges to the status quo. This trend exists in many discourse communities, not just within discursive issues concerned with identity theory. Typically, the writers I have investigated have not been viewed primarily as theorizing their own identities but as telling stories only about and from their authentic and authorized experiences. The fact that these women continue to be erased proliferates the illusion that there need be no consideration of intersecting identities and theories and that the white perspective can "stand" as the monolithic "always already" neutral perspective. Lesbians of color, on the other hand, write from a continually changing perspective, one that is constantly in jeopardy of being both explosive and ignored. It is easy to ignore writers/activists who do not appear to claim a defined "platform" from which to speak. Thus if lesbians of color do not claim a definable identity from which to theorize their experiences it appears they do not theorize at all. Why do these women risk losing their "authentic" voices by not attempting to reify an identity specific to them? Clearly a political agenda is behind the forces attempting to silence them that asks with astonishment: why not organize and speak in a simpler mode, by connecting with a single identity model, to have a more powerful political impact? As I have argued, lesbians of color adopt the strategies they do because to separate out elements of the self is impossible if these women are ever to conceive of themselves as whole. They do not have the luxury of attempting to become free-floating signifiers (to deny any fixed identity) because they already embody this disruption by their very nature. It might also be politically expedient to isolate elements of identity, and therefore to disavow certain elements, to organize under a singular label, but this can be deadly. It has been necessary to risk obscurity rather than buy into the paradigm of hierarchical identity that continues to have the power within academic discourse and society.[3]

Not many authors have been able to negotiate these dangers to articulate a divergent self. The following texts have accomplished a process of negotiating identities that leads to a *sustained* revision of boundaries.[4] Cherríe Moraga's fictional and non-fictional text *Loving in the War Years* is one such example. Moraga strongly connects her love for Chicanas with her feminist politics, and with her own negotiation of her identities as a light-skinned middle class English educated Chicana. After reckoning the forces lined up against her, and by using her experiences "loving in the war years," she connects her identity to the origination of political change within her community. The change she describes necessitates a cultural change in tradition and ideology:

a political commitment to women must involve, by definition, a political commitment to lesbians as well. To refuse to allow the Chicana lesbian the right to the free expression of her own sexuality, and her politicization of it, is in the deepest sense to deny one's self the right to the same. (139)

Moraga asks the political Chicano community to recognize a seemingly simple fact, that lesbians are women and must be included in Chicano politics, and in doing so calls that same community into question. She accomplishes this questioning best through her poetry about her own mother, as within it she weaves together lesbian desire with the recognition of the central importance of her mother (and by extension la Virgen and the myth of "la madre"), as well as her political alliance with working class Chicanas. Moraga writes:

> For you, mamá, I have unclothed myself before a woman
> have laid wide the space between my thighs
> straining open the strings held there
> taut and ready to fight. (140)

Through this physical, political, creative, and revisionist act Moraga is able to "*El regreso a mi pueblo. A la Mujer Mestiza*" (140).[5] It is through connecting the seemingly disparate that Moraga can fashion herself as a lesbian, a perceived threat to her community, successfully *within* her own home community.

Another author who has written both personal and fictional narrative on this subject is Paula Gunn Allen. Much of her work highlights the importance of Native American women for the benefit of both Native and white societies, if not an actual rewriting of cultures specifically for Native American lesbians.[6] However, in her novel *The Woman Who Owned the Shadows* she accomplishes a cultural revision through her main character, Ephanie. Her search is for wholeness; for a liveable identity that blends all the worlds in which she exists: white, Native, feminist, lesbian, traditional, and cosmopolitan. After confronting all the hostilities that wish to eradicate her, she is finally able to connect her identity to that of the woman within the tales her people tell, within her own cultural traditions.

Throughout the text, Gunn Allen continually plays these traditional stories off Ephanie's own story and Ephanie eventually becomes aware of this connection. Gunn Allen shows the direct connection between Ephanie's search for identity and an articulation of a useful theory for lesbians of color. In other words, her use of storytelling is a device both for Ephanie's search and to serve a larger need for identity theory.

The story of "The Woman Who Fell from the Sky" is connected to Ephanie's own remembrance of a fall she took. The woman in the story is forced by her dead father to marry a man, a magician, whom she does not know. The woman obeys her husband and eventually gains a power of sexual self-sufficiency of which her husband is afraid. Her power is symbolized by a flowering tree that impregnates her with its blossom. After the sorcerer has become irrelevant through her power, he also becomes ill; he is certain his wife is to blame so he gets rid of her by encouraging her to leap through a hole in the ground left by the uprooted flowering tree. The woman's fall causes the creation of the earth.

This story is followed by Ephanie's own fall under the heading "A Lot Changed After She Fell." It begins with Ephanie attempting to understand the meaning of the other woman's story. She thinks:

> Was it the sorcerer-chief's jealousy, his fear that betrayed her? Or was it her own arrogance, her daring, leading her to leap into the abyss from which there was no return . . . In her mind laying the question against many memories, against the history, against the tales, against the myths. Against her own life. (195-6)

This is followed by Ephanie's recollection of her fall from an apple tree. Although her friend Elena cautioned her, she was encouraged by her cousin Stephen, fell and ended up in hospital. Afterwards she changed from an adventurous "tomboy" to a cautious "woman" defined by Catholic female-ness. Instead of being free-spirited she becomes invested in an image:

> Instead highheels and lipstick. That she suddenly craved, intently. Instead full skirted dresses that she'd scorned only weeks before. Instead sitting demure on a chair, voice quiet, head down. Instead gazing in the mirror, mooning over lacey slips and petticoats. Curling endlessly her stubborn hair. To train it. To tame it. Her. Voice, hands, hair, trained and tamed and safe. (203)

Not only does she embrace a very "femme" image but also a straight white middle class one that denies her Native self.

> "I never realized what had happened." And now she knew. That what had begun had never been completed. Because she fell she had turned her back on herself. Had misunderstood thoroughly the significance of the event. Had not even seen that she had been another sort of person before she fell. "I abandoned myself," she said. "I left me. . . . " Elena and I, we were going to do brave things in our lives. And we were going to do them together. (204)

She realizes that she blamed Elena for her fall instead of Stephen and there-fore abandoned everything Elena represented: her loving of women. Annette Van Dyke relates Ephanie's original move into western feminization as con-nected directly to Ephanie's mixed race status. She states:

> As a part Guadalupe woman, Ephanie is caught in the erosion of the traditional place of honor and respect in which a Guadalupe woman is

held by her tribe. In the non-Indian world she must deal with both the patriarchal stereotypes of Indians and of women. She is surrounded by forces that work to destroy whatever link she has to the traditional culture in which women were central figures. (19)

As Gunn Allen herself states in an interview, "[Ephanie] keeps expecting men to do her life for her, because she got feminized in the western way instead of the tribal way. She made a terrible mistake and she paid for it until she understood that she had power in her own right" (103).

After this revelation Ephanie has a vision of a traditional woman marked with Spider symbols. The spirit woman connects both the tradition of loving women with Native stories and culture for Ephanie, something Ephanie thought was not possible:

> She understood the combinations and recombinations that had so puzzled her, the One and then the Two, the two and then the three, the three becoming the four, the four splitting, becoming two and two, the three of the beginning becoming the three-in-one . . . First there was Sussistinaku, Thinking Woman, then there was She and two more: Uretsete and Naotsete . . . and so the combinations went on, forming, dissolving, doubling, splitting, sometimes one sometimes two, sometimes three, sometimes four, then again two, again one. All of the stories formed those patterns, laid down long before time, so far. (207-8)

The spirit woman calls upon the tradition of the Native lesbian as prophetess and healer. She shows the centrality of a female tradition within Native culture and stories and tells Ephanie to embrace it to save Native peoples. Ephanie finally understands the rewriting of the tales she heard and misinterpreted, and remembers an erased and hidden tradition which Gunn Allen and other Native lesbians are recovering, and which would include her:

> And she dreamed. About the women who had lived, long ago, hame haa.
>   For those women, so long lost to her, who she had longed and wept for, unknowing, were the double women, the women who never married, who held power like the Clanuncle, like the power of the priests, the medicine men. (211)

By rewriting her knowledge of her own people's traditions, by way of a spirit woman, she realizes that the universe was not only created and fostered by women who have the power to be whatever is needed for the sake of survival, but also that to be a Native lesbian is to be on the pulse of the creative tradition and the survival of the race. The doubleness is what caused Ephanie's confusion; and her own people's attempts to erase her. She thinks her fall is a source of punishment when in fact it is a source of creation. Instead, then, of being a blasphemy, a potentially destructive force within the community, she is the source of power and the upholder of tradition.

Beth Brant writes of how she, as a Native lesbian, fulfills this role that Gunn Allen dramatizes in this novel. She sees Native lesbian writers as starting a new tradition that is a continuance of the old:

> We write not only for ourselves but also for our communities, for our People, for the young ones who are looking for the gay and lesbian path, for our Elders who were shamed or mythologized for the rocks and trees. ("Giveaway" 946)

Like Gunn Allen, Brant describes a Native lesbian existence that incorporates both the importance of writing and a revisioning of cultural traditions that make this woman a natural and integral member of her "home" community.

It is particularly interesting to me that Tom King, a reviewer of this novel, is disgusted with Gunn Allen's "simplicity" in having Ephanie "moralisti-cally" talk about herself as an Indian who is not stereotypical. He is also disappointed in the conclusion of the novel which he sees as too convenient after Ephanie's turmoil (he also implies that Allen is stealing material from Scott Momaday to create the images). He regards the ending as a "fairy [tale] where everyone lives happily ever after" (264). What he sees as a "fairy tale" is this lesbian's successful connection of her identity with her Native traditions. In many ways it is a fantasy; however, King does not make this comment with thoughtful attention paid to the context. He suggests only that her work is oversimplified in its vision and concludes that "Allen may possess a talent that will come into its own place in its own time" (264).[7]

Gunn Allen creates a complex story of a Native American lesbian's exis-tence and struggle to find wholeness within fragmentation. She suggests that the Native lesbian's assuming her position as healer and storyteller is central to the continuation of her race; she has the perspective of the "double woman" who can see the spirit world and the world to come. If this position were to be accepted by the larger Native communities it would cause a rewriting both of culture and of gender constructions to account for her.

Beth Brant rewrites the lesbian into Native American culture and family in her collection of short fiction, *Mohawk Trail.* In her story "A Simple Act," she connects groups of Native women who are making gourds into tools for life and family cohesion with the act of two women loving each other. She starts the story by describing the women with the gourds:

> A gourd is a hollowed-out shell, used as a utensil. I imagine women together, sitting outside the tipis and lodges, carving and scooping.

Creating bowls for food. Spoons for drinking water. A simple act–requiring lifetimes to learn. At times the pods were dried and rattles made to amuse babies. Or noisemakers, to call the spirits in sorrow and celebration. (87)

She then begins a story about two girls, one a Russian immigrant and the other an American Indian. The speaker describes their connection: "We were girls from an undiscovered country. We were alien beings in families that were 'different.' Different among the different" (88). They are different because they fall in love and then are discovered by their parents and separated. The speaker, looking back at this childhood and her relationship with Sandra, the Russian immigrant, connects what could have been between them with the gourds. She therefore connects the simple and profound act of Native women continuing life with two women's love for each other. The Native female speaker describes her imagined relationship with Sandra:

We have a basket filled with gourds. Our basket is woven from sweetgrass, and the scent stirs up the air and lights on our skin . . . Desire shapes us . . . We touch. Dancers wearing shells of turtles, feathers of eagles, bones of our people. We touch. (90)

Brant here connects this lesbian desire with the continuity of Native American life and tradition thereby creating a new space where both culture and lesbianism survive and nurture each other. Lesbian sexuality is directly connected with the survival of her people, both physically and spiritually. Within this framework, lesbian desire is a talisman to keep culture alive, though Brant reinterprets this talisman's power to necessitate the existence and understanding of lesbianism as central to everyone's progression.

Another revision of Native culture is Brant's story "Coyote Learns a New Trick." The coyote figure is generally seen as a trickster within Native American literature and Brant gives this figure a particular twist within her story. Coyote here is a mother who decides to go out in drag to play a joke on everyone. She dresses as a human male, as opposed to a male coyote, and believes that she is convincing in her performance. She is encouraged in the "truth" of her appearance when she runs across the very feminine Fox whom she thinks she can fool easily. It is obvious that Fox sees through Coyote's disguise yet she plays along, flirting with Coyote. Coyote ultimately propositions Fox, planning to reveal her joke at the best moment. Brant writes:

Lying on Fox's pallet, having her body next to hers, Coyote thought maybe she'd wait a bit before playing the trick. Besides, it was fun to be rolling around with a red-haired female. And man oh man, she really could kiss. That tongue of hers sure knows a trick or two. And boy oh

boy, that sure feels good, her paw on my back, rubbing and petting. And
wow, I never knew foxes could do such things, moving her legs like
that, pulling me down on top of her like that. And she makes such pretty
noises, moaning like that. And her paw feels real good, unzipping my
pants. And oh oh, she's going to find out the trick and then what'll I do?
(34)

Fox, sensing Coyote's uneasiness at being discovered, soon says: "Coyote!
Why don't you take that ridiculous stuffing out of your pants . . . And let me
untie that binder so we can get down to *serious* business" (34-5). Brant then
continues to conclude the tale: "So Coyote took off her clothes, laid on top of
Fox, her leg moving between Fox's open limbs. She panted and moved and
panted some more and told herself that foxes were clever after all" (34-5).
Brant here has a wonderful time creating a Coyote story–a traditional form
that she mimics–that varies dramatically in its centralizing of lesbian self-
fashioning. Very simply, she incorporates lesbian desire and sex within Native American tradition and as a natural and enjoyable part of life. Brant also
shows us the slipperiness of performing identity as Coyote performs an
identity in order to disguise herself but actually discovers that her performance leads to her "natural" self. So, instead of using this performance as
parody, Brant uses it to blend culture and lesbian identity. Like Moraga and
Gunn Allen, it is through the insistence on the combination of culture, community and sexual identity that her character becomes whole.

Another example of this dramatic cultural revision occurs within the work
of Audre Lorde. Much of Lorde's life was spent speaking about the realities
of the lives of Black lesbians and how their lives relate to the Black community as a whole. Nowhere is this more apparent than in her "biomythogra-
phy," *Zami: A New Spelling of My Name,* where she writes about the process
of coming out as a Black lesbian, and more importantly, learning to live with
this identity.[8] Because of all the societies that Lorde existed in and passed
through, she has a heightened sense of the performative aspects of not only
roles within the straight world, but racial identities, and roles within lesbian
circles as well. She writes:

> In a paradoxical sense, once I accepted my position as different from
> the larger society as well as from any single sub-society–Black or gay–I
> felt I didn't have to try so hard. To be accepted. To look femme. To be
> straight. To look straight. To be proper. To look "nice." To be liked. To
> be loved. To be approved. What I didn't realize was how much harder I
> had to try merely to stay alive, or rather, to stay human. (181)

This description of the refusal to submit to an identity that is sectioned and
categorized is similar to that of Anzaldúa's la mestiza. Lorde does not present

it as utopian but rather as strategic and necessary for survival. Clearly there are differences between the two women's view of categories and survival tactics; however, I am interested here in how they resonate with one another.

Lorde is rewriting identity to accommodate her own experiences within her social contexts. Within Lorde's story of her relationship with Kitty, short for Afrikete, her rewriting of her community's tradition occurs. Afrikete is it a goddess that Lorde continually refers to in her writing and it is fitting that it is through a woman with this name that Lorde would connect her lesbianism and her heritage.[9] Lorde describes their lovemaking's connection to a plethora of exotic fruits that the women must buy from the West Indian markets. It becomes a ritual to them to buy the fruit, bring it home, and then incorporate it into their lovemaking. It's an interesting connection between Afrikete and the fruit: the fruit from Lorde's mother's homeland is a bridge to the love of a specific woman (named Kitty) and all women (the goddess). She describes the phrase "I got [the fruit] under the bridge" as symbolic of a connection between home and lesbian love. Lorde states about this phrase that it was "an adequate explanation that whatever it was had come from as far back and as close to home–that is to say, as authentic–as was possible" (249). It is after Lorde describes this relationship that she ends her book with a tribute to all the women in her life and her connection with her mother's heritage. This desire to build bridges between females is reminiscent of Adrienne Rich; however, I don't think that Lorde is claiming all of these women as lesbians but rather that she is toppling a male-centered tradition of genealogies by listing all the influential women in her life.

Lorde then incorporates herself into the family, by refusing any sense of the mother being responsible for her "perversion" by the way she was raised, and rather celebrating her lesbianism as a family inheritance–a treasure. As Barbara Christian claims: "Society has tended to blame the mother for the daughter's lesbianism. Lorde sees her mother as her starting point, but she turns the analysis on its head" (199). Indeed, one critic claims that "In her lovemaking with Kitty, Lorde comes full circle; by reclaiming her mythological roots, she reconnects with her matrilineal heritage" (Keating 26). Lorde ends the book with: "Once *home* was a long way off, a place I had never been to but knew out of my mother's mouth. I only discovered its latitudes when Carriacou was no longer my home. There it is said that the desire to lie with other women is a drive from the mother's blood" (256).

AnaLouise Keating describes the importance of Lorde's revisions with women's relationship to patriarchy. She sees the importance of *Zami* as a testament to the "power words give women to redefine themselves and their world" (20) in adding to the work done on women's use of language. She focuses on Lorde's use of Afrikete as a replacement of Judeo-Christian myth to validate her female experiences. She also sees Lorde's claiming a Black

African goddess as the representation of female spirituality as an important expansion on the work done by Mary Daly and Carol Christ, for example. The final element of importance to Keating is the connection of Afrikete to Lorde as poet, trickster, and communicator. Keating believes that with this claiming Lorde "affirms her identity as a Black woman warrior poet" (28). The final affirmation then is Lorde's taking over of Afrikete's identity and "renam[ing] herself and becom[ing] the Black goddess" (29). Keating sees Lorde as making bridges to all of womankind through her revisionism.

While arguably all of these are important consequences for Lorde's revisionism, Keating underestimates the power of Lorde's making Afrikete a flesh and blood lover. This is a relationship that is connected to her community and is accepted by the family. Lorde describes that after she and Kitty would come down off of the roof where they had made love they would come "into the sweltering midnight of a west Harlem summer" that was filled with children and "mothers and fathers" (252-3). She laments that Harlem is not Winneba or Annamabu and yet has consolation in that "It was onto 113th Street that we descended after our meeting with the Midsummer Eve's Moon, but the mothers and fathers smiled at us in greeting as we strolled down to Eighth Avenue, hand in hand" (253). This "family" accepts the women as Black lesbians within their community as just another element of the summer evening along with their irritable children, insomnia, the heat, and their jobs. So, this goddess not only does all the things that Keating describes but also allows Lorde an entrance into her community as a Black lesbian.

Ann Allen Shockley's novel *Say Jesus and Come to Me* also contains a Black lesbian's process of accepting her own identity and ultimately rewriting her community's religious tradition to survive as a minister. Shockley directly confronts a cultural limitation for lesbians within the African-American community: the church. Throughout her novel the main character Myrtle, a lesbian minister, hides her lesbian identity to keep her place within the church and remain respected within the community. She realizes that this separation is killing her, is draining the life force from her. In her mind she actively connects her lesbian desire with God's love, and even seduces members of the church during sermons, but she fears describing herself as a lesbian within the confines of her social contexts.

However, when she falls in love with Travis and wishes to live as an out lesbian she finally decides to connect her ministry with her lesbian self. She tells Travis: "When you leave, I am going to deliver the most important sermon of my life" (277) in which she is going to reveal her lesbian identity. She uses scripture to support an acceptance of homosexuality as natural and as equally loved by God. Shockley illustrates that in order for Myrtle to pave the way for Black lesbian existence within her community she must reinterpret and rewrite Judeo Christian tenets. Only then can she challenge stereotypes of sexuality and gender in order for her to survive as a part of her community. She announces that:

> I am one of those people who imprisoned herself. I *locked* my tongue in silence and carried the weight within my heart. But this morning, I decided to *free-e* myself before you. (281)

She asks her congregation to accept her and they do; by weaving herself into the traditions and beliefs of her culture, instead of completely stepping outside of them, she gains acceptance as a Black lesbian.

It is after this successful presentation of her new self that she and Travis can go "home" together. Myrtle has successfully negotiated the limits of the black church by rewriting the lesbian's importance within it; she says that because "gays are the most rejected by the church" (281) she indicts it as in conflict with God. The home that this black lesbian couple can go to is within the church. By rewriting their "home" culture these Black lesbians can be accepted as such. If they were to subvert the limits to their identities by attempting to perform a racial identity other than blackness, and therefore transcend the Black community's boundaries, they would be perceived as attacking the community and would not be accepted members of it. Shockley reenvisions scripture, something historically used violently against gays and lesbians, to provide wholeness for her characters.

I suggest here that all of these women are metaphoric/cultural mestizas. They occupy a space of paradox, of embodying the impossible and thus making the existence of the lesbian of color possible. Anzaldúa develops her vision of mestiza consciousness in a way that is relevant to many more lesbians of color in her essay "Bridge, Drawbridge, Sandbar or Island: Lesbians-of-Color Hacienda Alianzas." She states:

> Being a mestiza queer person, una de las otras ("of the others") is having and living in a lot of worlds, some of which overlap . . . not comfortable in anyone of them, none of them "home," yet none of them "not home" either. (217-8)

With this kind of generalized language Anzaldúa opens the possibility for the existence of metaphoric mestizas (while still keeping the cultural specificity of the term intact). This is underscored by the similar language used by other lesbians of color to describe their own identities and by the similarity in the way they strive to fashion themselves as whole subjects. For example, in an interview Paula Gunn Allen describes this same kind of mestiza experience. She claims that to survive one "ha[s] to incorporate [all the parts of oneself]. I think that's where you get into alienation, thinking that you cannot have the whole bulk, that you *have* to choose" (103). She further finds that this externally constructed necessity to choose is in fact a weapon in the continuing colonization process. Clearly this idea of incorporating the paradoxical within one's subjectivity is central to the enduring survival of lesbians of color.

I advocate what Anzaldúa refers to as "a symbolic behavior performance made concrete by involving body and emotions with political theories and strategies, rituals that will connect the conscious and the unconscious" ("Bridge" 229). She makes this statement to show how lesbians of different colors can build alliances among their communities. Anzaldúa's desire to include "ritual" as well as the unconscious is similar to Butler's focus on the use of repetition. Both critics advocate individually deployed behavioral strategies. One major difference between them is that while Butler sees this repetition as an external phenomenon, as if one walks onto a stage, performs, and can walk off again unharmed, Anzaldúa insists on a change in one's internal psychology. The external nature that Butler describes also accounts for the neat packaging of the one facet identity; the identity that is antithetical to these lesbians' existence. This consideration of the limitations of Butler's strategy of performance should not equate to a simple "inclusion" of racial identity but rather to an acknowledgement of the power that contexts have for all subjects. The question soon becomes: how can persons with multiplicitous identities perform them as multiplicitous in a way that will affect societal change? Anzaldúa constantly refers to states of being, perspectives on life, but she does not discuss how exactly one might use these states and perspectives as strategies for survival. I suggest here that this consciousness needs to be focused into a strategy, or strategies, of survival which can be deployed by individual agents to negotiate their identities. It calls for *performing* the paradox, the slipperiness that has recurred among these women's narratives–"performing la mestiza."

NOTES

1. Other recent theorists, such as Kath Weston and Sagri Dhairyam, have also made this point. Butler attempts to account for this in her more recent text *Bodies that Matter*. However, I find that even within her discussion of Black and Latino drag queens she still does not adequately discuss the historical and cultural significance of race/ethnicity and their very real (and sometimes fatal) consequences.

2. I consider a metaphorical mestiza to be a subject whose identity can be described as an embodiment of paradox. In the case of lesbians of color I find that the use of the mestiza metaphor is appropriate, as is the description of their mestiza-ness originating in their negotiation of the conflict between specific cultural positions and their lesbian identity. Therefore, when I refer to lesbians of color throughout I equate the metaphoric and cultural use of "mestiza" as an equal to "biological" mestiza.

3. Clearly, many women have not been published because of this risk. For example, in an interview, Paula Gunn Allen describes her experiences with publishing her

work: "the people who are in the small press world, or in the big-press-but-liberal-radical world want a certain kind of Indian, just as much as Harper and Row does, just as much as Random House does or anyone else does. They want a 'sellable' Indian. That's what the big ones are after. What the little ones are after is a 'pathetic' Indian, an Indian they can relate to, put back in the damn grave, and say, 'well it's been nice talking to you. I've gotten my goodies. I've used you in my speech. I've used your bodies to make my point'" (16).

4. I want to mention a fascinating essay by Yvonne Yarbro-Bejarano wherein she discusses various Latina lesbians who make a space for themselves within their cultures by using elements of popular culture. She argues that they use cultural icons to reclaim a space that dismisses them. She describes this as "working simultaneously within and against dominant cultural codes" ("The Lesbian Body" 181). She explores their methods within Latina camp shows, photographs, paintings, and stand-up comedy.

5. "I return to my pueblo. A Mestiza woman."

6. Probably most famous is her book *The Sacred Hoop: Recovering the Feminine in American Indian Traditions,* as well as her essay "Who is Your Mother? Red Roots of White Feminism." Neither of them focuses specifically on Native lesbians.

7. This comment is a perfect example of how the works of many women of color are treated. Because many readers don't pay attention to the important cultural and historical contexts, the authors are seen as describing their emotions, experience or a utopian perspective instead of well-developed and purposeful ideas.

8. In an interview Lorde herself described this form as fiction with "elements of biography and history of myth. In other words, it's fiction built from many sources" (115). I consider the "Audre" in the text to be the author and a fictional character simultaneously.

9. Judy Grahn describes what she learned of Afrikete from Lorde: "Audre Lorde kindly took the time to tell me more about Oya and the other Orisha of the Yoruba/ Macumba religion. . . . As for the trickster god Eshu, Lorde says in Yoruba ceremonies he is always danced by a woman who straps on a straw phallus and chases the other women. He is also called Elegba. Originally he was a female, Afrikete. . . . Eshu/Afrikete is the rhyme god, the seventh and youngest in the old Mawulisa pantheon, Mawulisa being male/female, sun and moon. As the trickster, he/she makes connections, is communicator, linguist, and poet. Only Afrikete knows all the languages of all the gods. Afrikete always appears in guises, so it is wise to be nice to stones and bees, for instance or anything at all that might be the mischievous Afrikete" (124-5).

WORKS CITED

Allen, Paula Gunn. 1983. MELUS Interview: Paula Gunn Allen. Melus 10.2: 3-25.

_____. 1991. *The sacred hoop: Recovering the feminine in American Indian traditions. Boston: Beacon, 1992.*

_____. 1989. *The woman who owned the shadows.* San Francisco: Spinsters/Aunt Lute, 1989.

_____. 1984. Who is your mother? Red roots of white feminism. *Sinister Wisdom* 25: 34-45.

Anzaldúa, Gloria. 1987. *Borderlands/La Frontera: The new mestiza.* San Francisco: Spinsters/Aunt Lute.

_____. 1990. Bridge, drawbridge, sandbar or island: Lesbians-of-color *hacienda alianzas.* In *Bridges of Power: Women's Multicultural Alliances.* Ed. Lisa Albrecht and Rose M. Brewer. Santa Cruz, CA: New Society. 216-33.

Brant, Beth. 1985. Coyote learns a new trick. In *Mohawk Trail.* 31-6.

_____. 1985. A simple act. In *Mohawk Trail.* 87-94.

_____. 1993. Giveaway: Native lesbian writers. *Signs* 18.4 (Summer): 944-7.

_____. 1985. *Mohawk trail.* Ithaca, NY: Firebrand.

Butler, Judith. 1993. *Bodies that matter: On the discursive limits of "sex."* New York: Routledge.

_____. 1990. *Gender trouble: Feminism and the subversion of identity.* New York: Routledge.

Christian, Barbara. 1985. *Black feminist criticism: Perspectives on black women writers.* New York: Pergamon.

Dhairyam, Sagri. 1994. Racing the lesbian, dodging white critics. In Doan 25-46.

Doan, Laura, ed. 1994. *The lesbian postmodern.* New York: Columbia UP.

Grahn, Judy. *Another Mother Tongue: Gay Words, Gay Worlds.* 1984. Boston: Beacon, 1990.

Keating, AnaLouise. "Making 'our shattered faces whole': The Black Goddess and Audre Lorde's Revision of Patriarchal Myth." *Frontiers: A Journal of Women's Studies* 13.1 (1992): 20-33.

King, Tom. 1984. Review of *The woman who owned the shadows,* by Paula Gunn Allen. *American Indian Quarterly* 8 (Summer): 261-64.

Lorde, Audre. 1983. Interview. *Black women writers at work.* In Claudia Tate, ed. New York: Continuum.

_____. 1982. *Zami: A new spelling of my name.* Freedom, CA: Crossing Press.

Moraga, Cherríe. 1983. *Loving in the War Years: lo que nunca pasó por sus labios.* Boston: South End.

Naylor, Gloria. 1980. *The women of Brewster Place.* New York: Penguin.

Shockley, Ann Allen. 1987. *Say Jesus and come to me.* Tallahassee, FL: NAIAD.

Van Dyke, Annette. 1992. *The search for a woman-centered spirituality.* The Cuttin Edge: Lesbian Life and Literature. New York: NY UP.

Weston, Kath. 1993. Do the clothes make the woman? *Genders* 17 (Fall): 1-21.

Yarbro-Bejarano, Yvonne. 1995. Expanding the categories of race and sexuality in lesbian and gay studies. In *Professions of desire: Lesbian and gay studies in literature.* Ed. George E. Haggerty and Bonnie Zimmerman. MLA: New York. 124-35.

_____. 1995. The lesbian body in latina cultural production. In Emilie L. Bergmann et al., eds. *¿Entiendes? Queer readings, Hispanic writings.* Q ser. Durham, NC: Duke UP. 181-200.

Entre Nous, Female Eroticism,
and the Narrative of Jewish Erasure

Terri Ginsberg

SUMMARY. Although grounded in wartime and immediate postwar contexts, *Entre Nous* has been critiqued primarily for its portrayal of ambiguous female eroticism to the exclusion of how such eroticism is linked via the film's narrative structure to the Jewish Holocaust, the French collaboration, and U.S. transnationalist hegemony. This paper takes up an examination and explication of this narratological linkage as well as theorizes the determinants of its persistent critical ignoring. *[Article copies available for a fee from The Haworth Document Delivery Service: 1-800-342-9678. E-mail address: getinfo@haworthpressinc.com <Website: http:// www.haworthpressinc.com>]*

KEYWORDS. Lesbian film, anti-Semitism, Judeo-Christianity, Holocaust, French feminism, allegory, narrative theory, hermeneutics, tanakh, Jewish history, transnationalism

Terri Ginsberg has taught film and literature at New York University, Rutgers University, and The New School. Her publications include *Perspectives on German Cinema* (co-edited with Kirsten Moana Thompson) and 'Holocaust Film Criticism and the Politics of ([Judeo-]Christian) Phenomenology' (in the Routledge reader *Violence and American Film*).

Address correspondence to: Terri Ginsberg, Department of English, Rutgers University, New Brunswick, NJ 08901.

This paper is based on work the author did for her dissertation, *Regarding the Holocaust: Politics of Hermeneutics in Four Contemporary Holocaust Films* (New York University, 1997).

[Haworth co-indexing entry note]: "*Entre Nous*, Female Eroticism, and the Narrative of Jewish Erasure." Ginsberg, Terri. Co-published simultaneously in *Journal of Lesbian Studies* (Harrington Park Press, an imprint of The Haworth Press, Inc.) Vol. 4, No. 2, 2000, pp. 39-64; and: *'Romancing the Margins'? Lesbian Writing in the 1990s* (ed: Gabriele Griffin) Harrington Park Press, an imprint of The Haworth Press, Inc., 2000, pp. 39-64. Single or multiple copies of this article are available for a fee from The Haworth Document Delivery Service [1-800-342-9678, 9:00 a.m. - 5:00 p.m. (EST). E-mail address: getinfo@ haworthpressinc.com].

In 1983 *Entre Nous* (dir. Diane Kurys, France) opened to international acclaim across Europe and, a year later, North America. Distributed first in France and other Euroamerican Francophone regions such as Belgium and Québec under the title *Coup de foudre* (literally, 'thunder clap'; figuratively, 'love at first sight'), and in the United Kingdom as *At First Sight, Entre Nous* presented French actress Diane Kurys' cinematic rendition of the dissolution of her parents' marriage and her mother's entry into an erotically charged, commercially lucrative bond with another woman, seven years after her parents' return to France from Italy, where, as Jews, they had hidden from the Nazis and their Vichy collaborators for two and one-half years. Unlike her previous film, Prix Louis Delluc recipient *Diabolo Mentha* [*Peppermint Soda*] (France, 1977), which also was autobiographical but which focused on the more local, French suburban, quasi-provincial schoolgirl milieu of Kurys' own pubescence, *Entre Nous* dealt with the more complex, globally extended, generationally distanced milieu of her parents' early adulthood, a milieu in which the Kuryses, following their persecution in the Holocaust, were compelled to begin their lives anew, eventually building a successful small business and starting a nuclear family in the provincial city of Lyon. Due partially to this broadened scope, *Entre Nous* received significant press coverage in the United States and Canada, where, echoing French praise for its supposed exemplary aesthetic sensibility, it was lauded as masterful, mature, accomplished, humane, civilized, enlightening, and representative of a giant leap forward in French filmmaking. In France, *Entre Nous* was highly celebrated, and in the United States, it won a 1983 Academy Award nomination for Best Foreign Language Film.[1] By way of these rewards, *Entre Nous* was catapulted to critical heights unprecedented for a female-directed, woman-centered film, as it became one of the first of its kind to be recognized and formally rewarded by the Hollywood film industry.[2]

The fact of *Entre Nous*' popular and industry success did not shield it from widespread criticism and debate. At the same time that the film won accolades for being formally accomplished, dramatically consistent, thematically coherent, and aesthetically evocative (all qualities considered meritorious and praiseworthy on the Euroamerican art cinema circuit), *Entre Nous* sparked a lively and polemical press debate across the North American public sphere. The crux of this debate was the ethical question of whether or not the erotic female bond portrayed in the film represented a socially responsible alternative either to the traditional heterosexual or male homosocial bonding usually depicted in the cinema, and whether or not the representation of that alternative, as ambiguous and non-physical, was ideologically consistent with the political agenda of lesbian-feminism as this was then gaining acceptance as a topic of public discourse. This debate, which took place across the pages of mainstream North American newspapers and magazines, had a lasting effect on how *Entre Nous* came to be characterized and understood in cultural circles–as a female bonding film whose major problematic concerned the sexual orientation of its female relationship and, in turn, the question of what it meant to define such an orientation as 'sexual,' not to mention 'lesbian,' in regard to a film which consistently refused to portray that relationship as physically consummated.[3]

The debate over *Entre Nous*'s 'sexual orientation' opened a number of critical questions, including those inquiring into its concomitant class orientation and, more formalistically, its structuring. Despite the intellectual space opened by these questions, an overwhelming discursive focus on the ambiguous figuration of the film's female bond has given the erroneous impression that the question of female relationships *per se* is central and primary to *Entre Nous*, and that larger, potentially more far-reaching questions must be sidelined to how the depiction of such a relationship intersects with and comes to signify in relation to the non-sexual, non-erotic issues with which the film is heavily concerned and which compel one to characterize it more broadly and complexly as *a Holocaust film*.

This critical exclusion of political and historical questions is more evident in scholarly than popular press reviews, where one is least likely to find even a mention of the diegetic-historical placement of *Entre Nous'* narrative in the Holocaust or post-Holocaust contexts or into the associated, political-economic and ideological problematics of (post-) Vichy France. This despite the fact that approximately one-quarter of *Entre Nous'* running time is devoted to depicting significant events from both women's wartime experiences, which include vivid portrayals of one of the women, Hélène ('Léna') Korski (née Weber) [Isabelle Huppert], interned at the Rivesaltes deportation camp, where she, a Belgian Jew, is rescued from certain shipment to Auschwitz by agreeing to marry one Mordeha Isaac Simon ('Michel') Korski [Guy Marchand], a French-Jewish *légionnaire* not yet subject to Nazi racial decrees; and the other, Madeleine Segara (née Vernier) [Miou-Miou], caught in the midst of a violent shoot-out between *Résistance* fighters and pro-fascist *miliciens*, during which her newlywed husband, Raymond Klinger [Robin Renucci], is killed by a ricocheting bullet, and after which she suffers a debilitating nervous breakdown which confines her to convalescence at her parents' country estate for the duration of the war. During this early portion of the film, parallel sequencing suggests a metonymic symmetry between the two women which is then provisionally sutured by their first meeting. Following this meeting, the film traces a narrativized 'working-through' of the ostensibly analogous choices the women have been compelled to make during the war and which now have landed each woman in similarly dissatisfying, indeed stifling, circumstances to which the other seems to hold the crucial, liberatory, and–not insignificantly–entrepreneurial key.

Instead of acknowledging and elaborating these matters and concerns in ways that might at least call into question the structured symmetry between the women's wartime experiences, not to mention the representation of the Holocaust, World War II, and Jewish-Christian relations, popular press reviews of *Entre Nous* have generally provided only brief and incipient references to these matters.[4] Scholarly reviews have effectively replaced these albeit limited references with descriptive analyses and normative criticisms of the film's formal-structural properties (the gaze, frame composition) and authorial-contextual influences (the Kurys *oeuvre*).[5] Any ethical, political, or ideological criticism concomitant with the recognition and critique of the inscription of *history* in the film has thus been relinquished to the designs of aesthetic appreciation.[6]

The progressive absenting by critics of the significance of the women's wartime choices and experiences for the development of their erotic relationship is perhaps as glaring and consistent as is *Entre Nous*' ambiguous sexualization of that relationship itself. In considering it, one comes inevitably to the question of why such an absenting has occurred, for whom, and to what purpose. How is it that a film with such explicit diegetic-historical contextualization of the Holocaust and World War II could be received with international acclaim and debated prolifically in the North American public sphere with hardly a mention of how that contextualization signifies for the film's narrative-compositional structure and for the erotic female bond which is that structure's thematic locus? How is it, furthermore, that focus on the film's erotic female bond has taken what may be considered an almost obfuscatory precedence over focus on its historical, including political and ideological, aspects *during a socio-cultural period in which female eroticism and lesbianism themselves not only are still relatively taboo subjects for mainstream discourse but in which the Holocaust and World War II increasingly have become topics of widespread interest and debate?*[7]

Answers to these questions lie first and foremost in the particular way in which *Entre Nous* positions itself as a Holocaust film–that is, how it depicts the Holocaust/World War II and post-Holocaust/-World War II periods as an irruptive issue of erotic female bonding, and how its portrayal of the erotic female bond comes to figure as a primary and overdetermining signifier of both holocaustic catastrophe, or, *holocausticity*, and a particularly dubious mode of liberation therefrom. First it must be conceded that the public debate which developed around *Entre Nous* attests to the fact that it is an atypical Holocaust film: considering its limited depiction of the Holocaust/World War II period in the first twenty minutes of its narrative, it is not wrong to read that aspect as mere background to the film's more obvious portrayal of erotic female friendship. Indeed only after the narrative shifts from the depiction of the wartime 'past' to the postwar 'present' does *Entre Nous* even become what might be called dramatic: significant plot interaction between the Korski and Segara families occurs only after the shift, marked by the initial, erotically charged encounter between the women, at which point these women quickly begin to understand their predicaments and start engaging in certain questionable, even unethical practices (lying, cheating, stealing) which soon carry their marriages into ruinous dissolution and their erotic relationship into an uncertain, if promising, even redemptive, entrepreneurial future.

Precisely because this shift and its ensuing plot developments are marked dramatologically by the introduction of an erotic female bond, however, neither its significance nor that of the bond itself can accurately or reasonably be theorized without also to some degree theorizing the diegetic-historical context–the Holocaust and World War II–in which are situated the initiation of that shift and that bond and against which the latter develops into a simultaneously catastrophic and liberatory relationship. This essay will ana-lyse the initial encounter between Léna and Madeleine in which the theoreti-cal connection between their erotic bond and *Entre Nous'* historical discourse on the Holocaust and World War II is evidenced in a paradigmatic and revealing way. This will entail both a narrative-compositional analysis of that particular moment in the film and, in keeping with the theme of past-present relationality, a critical elaboration of the conceptual framework functioning across the film such that its development of erotic female bonding comes to represent and, moreover, epitomize the sort of narrative discourse on lesbian-ism, coined appropriately but uncritically by Straayer as 'hypothetical lesbian narrativity.' This discourse ironically reproduces some of the very perspec-tives on the Holocaust and World War II–antisemitism, economic imperial-ism, historical fatalism–which many of these critics, especially feminists and lesbian-feminists, would oppose. After all, such perspectives are thought generally to have contributed to the conception and perpetration of Nazi atrocities themselves, including the persecution and murder of lesbians.[8]

Before continuing, however, it is important to note that the question of *Entre Nous'* past-present thematic has not been entirely absent from the discourse surrounding the film–especially not from the popular press debate over the sexual orientation of its erotic female bond. In keeping with a general, implicit recognition of the film's ambiguous figuration of that bond, many reviews of *Entre Nous* have insisted that its sense of the 'past,' while not the film's central focus, is one of its persistent, underlying motifs, a theme that resonates synoptically across its narrative and textual layers and registers tropologically, in varying allegorical modalities, during the post-historical portion of the narrative.[9] In numerous interviews from the time of *Entre Nous'* North American release, Kurys encouraged interpretations of her film which took into account her parents' experience of the Holocaust. Her memoir, *Coup de foudres* ['Love at First Sight'], published in tandem with the film's French release, implies that such readings are not to be detached from the ethno-religious and socio-economic aspects of her parents' characters and beliefs as portrayed in the film.[10] These encouragements and insistences highlight the theoretical absenting performed by other critics vis-à-vis the film's hermeneutic and philosophical registers, that is, those aspects of its Holocaust cultural discourse whose recognition, acknowledgment, and rigorous analysis are crucial to an *anti*-holocaustic comprehension not only of the film but of the Holocaust and World War II in general.

Indeed crucial to an understanding of *Entre Nous*, its holocausticity and its 'hypothetical lesbian narrativity' is a recognition and acknowledgment of one of its outstanding hermeneutic layers, the Judeo-Christian allegorization of Jewish history. This theological layer, I shall argue, rather dubiously serves in the film to subsume the questions *Entre Nous* raises about the Holocaust and French wartime history into an historically, politically, socially disengaged problematic of female sexual (non-)expression whose critical ignoring is undeniably implicated in the perpetuation of the antisemitism associated historically with the Christian world view and exploited during the Third Reich to holocaustic ends.

The Judeo-Christian interpretation of Jewish history has traditionally lacked both accuracy and rigor. Most notorious is its imposition of a teleological reading onto Jewish genealogy, which it traces selectively across the Hebrew Bible (the *tanakh*) and thereby casuistically reduces the significance of that geneaology to a mystical prefiguration and, in turn, epiphenomenal residue of the christology.[11] During the post-Enlightenment period, this Judeo-Christian misreading was deployed oppressively and exploitatively to confine the 'Jewish' to the esoteric domains of theological and ethno-cultural knowledgeability, whereupon Judaism became divested of its Talmudically overdetermined social-worldly ethic and was reinscribed as a faith-based locus of Christian confession and gnosis. The paradigmatic characterological signifier of this locus was the *juif errant*, or, Wandering Jew.[12] During the medieval period, this Judeo-Christian myth of inherent Jewish indigence and moral decripitude, as both fated retribution for presumed Jewish culpability for the death of Jesus and fulcrum of redemptive wisdom accrued as a result of having led an existence presumably mired in sin, came to stand as one of the most prevalent and enduring means by which the social cleavage between Jews and Christians has been rationalized.[13] As far back as the Biblical era, Christian appropriation of the subtly but significantly distinct Talmudic analytic, prompted initially by this mythological rationale and characterized *inter alia* by an iconic hypostatization of the Talmud's critical–but ultimately only provisional–undecidability as well as by its dialectical praxis of interrogation (i.e., *le-didakh*, or, according to that opinion which is yours), led James,

father of Catholicism, to proselytize the Jews of Roman Jerusalem by reflexively allegorizing the christic martyrdom to holocaustic prophecies of *tanakh*. As with later, Enlightenment and post-Enlightenment confinements of
Judaica to esoterica, these attempts to construct the 'Jewish' as at once
symmetrical to the 'Christian' and transcendent of the material histories of
either discourse came to position the 'Jewish' as signifier of perpetual suffering analogizable to the (self-)sacrificial suffering of Jesus. This positioning
would only intensify as the Roman Church Fathers seized upon this allegori-
cality as an ideological lynch-pin of imperialism. Importantly, insofar as the
resulting demonization of the Jews was prompted by a reflexive reading
practice heavily indebted to Talmudic analytics, this Christian allegorization
carried with it the *appearance* of *Jewish* authorship and, in turn, a rhetorical
compulsion to Jewish answerability in the form confessional conversion.[14]

In consonance with this mythology, *Entre Nous* is organized rather overtly–*and precisely by way of its ambiguous female bond*–to affirm the moral
reduction of the 'Jewish' to a locus of christological confession; and it is on
this basis that the film reconstructs the post-Holocaust era which is its primary diegetic setting as a period of *post*-sacrificial, *post*-confessional, even
post-*national* salvation for both its Jewish and Christian characters, who
henceforth are construed erroneously and, notwithstanding their other and
extenuating, ethnic and class differences, as having sustained comparable
treatment by the Nazis during the likewise christologically understood Holocaust. The Holocaust is relegated to the status of sublimity, and by characters
who, perceiving their respective wartime experiences as somehow analogous,
end up ceaselessly deferring the critical social and self-interrogation necessary to real historical mourning-work over those experiences. Instead they
engage in the ironically uncritical, socially divisive, partially self-destructive
economy of a mutually supportive, erotically charged entrepreneurism–an
economy associated historically less with the facilitation of female bonding
than with large-scale, patriarchal corporate entrepreneurism (i.e., transnationalism) that, at least since the release of *Entre Nous*, has implicated France
alongside the U.S. in the implementation of numerous Third World holo-
causts.[15]

At its most schematic, the film's christo-allegorical development may be
broken down into the following pattern: (1) a spatio-temporal dislocation of
the film's narrative present from its diegetic past; (2) a present-tense subla-
tion of the film's diegetic past into a (dis)continuous, ambiguous and sometimes disorienting narrative-textual configuration which symptomatizes but
does not repair this dislocated quality; and (3) an ideological *re*location of the
narrative, thus disfigured, to its diegetic past, such that any future (re)articu-
lation of that past becomes apparent only as a highly privatized, imaginal,

aestheticized banalization, a dissimulation of what ostensibly is meant to pass as its comparative and relative historicization.

The initial meeting between Léna and Madeleine is particularly significant for the narrative's christo-allegoricality, because of its rhetorically overdetermined construction and the function it serves as such in hyperbolizing the editorial segue between the film's diegetic-historical and present-tense portions, that is, between the Jewish-historical, Holocaust-oriented portion and the post-Holocaust, post-Judaic portion. It therefore stands, especially vis-à-vis the latter portion's ambiguity and asymmetricality, not simply as a syntagmatic node of spatio-temporal transition but as a paradigmatic hapax of the erotic female bond's christo-redemptive potentiation.

À *propos* of the complex layering of the narrative, this paradigmatic quality is discernible in multiple registers, the first of which is the dramatological one of plot. In this initial aspect, one notes that several plot discoveries are elicited across the scene about what has transpired since the period of Léna's wartime exile in Italy and, concomitantly, Madeleine's 'exile' at her parents' home during the period of her nervous breakdown. For instance, we learn that Léna and Michel not only have survived their secret exile in Italy but have returned to a rather successful, regenerated life in France. We see an extremely well-dressed, embourgeoisified Léna, proud of the talents of her two daughters, Florence [Patricia Champagne] and Sophie [Saga Blanchard], who are performing in a school play, and altruistic enough to oversee the child, René [Guillaume le Guellec], of a complete stranger (who turns out to be Madeleine's husband, Costa [Jean-Pierre Bacri]), although it costs her time. Her acts and deportment reveal no trace of her and Michel's wartime travails; she is exceedingly gracious and ebullient. We then learn that Madeleine, too, has survived her wartime trauma and now, likewise, is married, but to a man clearly frustrated with her capriciousness and lack of traditional motherly instinct. She no longer dresses in the black mourning clothes she'd worn during her 'exile' but instead has gone to the opposite extreme, sporting bright colors and clothing styles quite daring for the socially conservative postwar French milieu (slacks, stockingless legs and feet). Unlike Léna, she shows little if any interest in her child and instead identifies with his shyness and melancholia vis-à-vis an impatient and unsympathetic father/husband. She, like Léna, bears no visible scars from her wartime travails, having seemingly overcome them via immersion in a romantic passion for fortune-telling and other sensual-mystical experiences. All in all, however, the rather superficial flightiness she displays throughout the scene, both toward her son and Léna, indicates her more difficult readjustment to postwar, post-traumatic life and elicits an intensity of longing, or loss, strangely absent from the characterology of Léna.

Alongside these plot discoveries, there is a destabilization of the spatio-temporal framework contextualizing them, which I suggest is Judeo-Christian in orientation. This second, poetical register, which makes the scene's paradigmatic quality even more discernible, contextualizes both an incipient undermining and a prefigurative rationalization of the characterological features and relationality evinced between the women at the dramatological register of plot, features and relationality which henceforth are re-organized in such a way that their ostensible symmetricality–that is, the historically mediated analogy they articulate between Léna's and Madeleine's experiences of World War II–becomes at once, and in perfect Judeo-Christian fashion, a structural facilitator for the alterior-symbolical repetition of those experiences and a dissimulation of the ideological reversal of Léna and Madeleine's characterology necessary thereto. The shot immediately preceding the scene and contextualizing it within the parameters of the historical diegesis epitomizes, via the device of narrative ellipsis, this christological destabilization and rationale. For this reason, I shall now analyze its formal construction and effectuality before continuing to investigate its effect on the erotic representation of the two women as it develops across the scene into an ostensibly complementary, if asymmetrical, trope of christic allegoresis.

At the commencement of this shot, we are presented with a frontal view of the Lyon art academy where Madeleine studied painting and sculpture before the war and is now encountering her wartime lover, Roland Carlier [Patrick Bauchau], who has just been released from a Vichy prison where he was incarcerated for his participation in the *Résistance*. It is VE-Day, and rowdy American soldiers dance and drink to blaring Glenn Miller music. As the shot continues, the camera, following the path of a helium balloon released into the air by one of the soldiers, moves parabolically and in a rightward direction into an extended overhead shot of the sky above the celebration, and it does not regain perspectival equilibrium until several seconds later, when it comes to frame what shortly afterwards is revealed as an elementary school almost identical in architectural structure to that of the art academy we have just been shown. During the initial course of the shot, little if any indication is provided of a shift in spatio-temporal context: clouds depicted via the pan remain undistorted by any cut, the color of the sky remains constant. As equilibrium is regained, however, an alteration in both the soundtrack and the appearance of two signs, one diegetic, the other non-diegetic, inform us that, despite the initial semblance of continuity, a major shift has taken place. As the camera comes to focus on the elementary school, for example, a sign appears carved into the latter's facade which reads, '*L'École des Fils*' ['Elementary School'], thus identifying the structure as something other than an art academy. As the camera comes to focus more specifically on a window of the school, moreover, the parodic voice of Maurice Chevalier replaces the celebratory Glenn Miller music, and an intertitle flashes up which reads

'Lyon 1952,' recalling but altering a much earlier, introductory intertitle, 'Pyrénées 1942.'

The christo-allegorical quality of this elliptical shot becomes especially discernible when one considers the peculiarly reflexive way in which it has signified the passage of time. Of course by the very definition of ellipsis, the shot is already imbricated with a certain chronological reflex: on the one hand, it facilitates temporal movement; on the other, it qualifies that movement as movement *per se*. This strictly formalist sense of the shot's reflexivity is trivial, however, when compared to the larger sense associated with its iconographical and semiotic qualities, for only in their regard does the historical and ideological meaning of the shot's temporality, necessary to the theological designation of its hermeneutic, become available.

In the first, iconographical, instance, one notes the effect produced by the shot's unusual parabolic formation and prolonged duration on the dramatological aspect of the temporal passage: a concern is produced for the fact that time has passed and for the reason why such a passage has occurred. Dramatological questions are prompted as to what actually has transpired since the Korskis' treacherous climb up the Madonna Pass and since Madeleine's mournful showing at the VE-Day celebration, and as to why, moreover, it has even been necessary to ellipsize rather than depict the periods immediately proceeding those events. There is thus the construction of an enigma, a narrative secret meant to produce suspense and hence suture the spectator to a greater or lesser degree into the ensuing drama.

In the second, semiotical instance, the starkness of the change in musical soundtrack and the uncanny similarity in the two intertitles produce an effect on potential solutions to this very enigma. These devices foreground the mimetological layer of the drama, where the particular events framing the ellipsis are seen to refer back to other, earlier events, so that it becomes possible to ascertain reasons for the particular mode and quiddity of this temporal passage that are grounded less in dramatological pragma than in semiotic and discursive signification. The depiction of the architectural facade of the elementary school partially repeats, via visual resemblance, the depiction of the pre-elliptical Lyon art academy. This suggests that Madeleine's current, post-elliptical situation, which has developed out of the horrific shooting that had occurred in the earlier locale, may at least partially be explained in terms of how notions invoked by the later locale (e.g., education, childhood, and the "elemental") qualify the meaning and significance of those notions invoked by the earlier (e.g., romantic love, violent death, eros-thanatos). Likewise, as the intertitling over the first shot of the elementary school partially repeats the intertitling over Léna's deportation camp-bound bus ride across the southern French landscape at the beginning of the film, a similar suggestion is made about the Korskis' post-exilic situation, namely, that it, too, is explainable via an intertextual cross-fertilization of notions–in this case, of those mentioned above invoked by the elementary school and those (such as fate, pragmatism, and the pastoral) invoked by Léna's holo-caustic internment. One might also consider the possibility that, with the ellipsis itself placed just subsequent to shots of an abject Madeleine, duly fallen from her prewar aristocratic security, juxtaposed with shots of a rowdy American soldier, risen from the mass melting pot ('That's for my mother in Jersey!') to the status of world conqueror, a suggestion is made that what has thus far been elided by the film, and what thereby perhaps is being culled into the construction of its enigma, may be explained by reference to the notion of global politics invoked via this juxtaposition as it not only forms the matrix of the narrative jump to the diegetic present-tense but is reconfirmed in its potentially ideological significance by the hindsight afforded from within that present-tense–which as we know from history marks a watershed in the development of U.S. political-economic hegemony on the European conti-nent.[16]

In effect, each of these instances encourages through the typically allegori-cal mode of strategic intertextual, alterior repetition a reflexive questioning not simply of the formal-cinematic but contential-contextual layers of the ellipsis and, by extension, the narrative, one that promotes the sort of alert-ness and attentiveness to multiple hermeneutic layering that has frequently been considered characteristic of the Judeo-Christian appropriation of Talmu-dic narrative discourse.[17]

In saying this, of course, it also must be recognized that the characteristics we have just explicated are also potentially interpretable from a strictly Juda-ic perspective, as constitutive of a Judaic allegorical inscription, especially as regards the way in which the relationship between past and present they help map invokes the hermeneutic patterning associated with *tanakh*, that central text of Jewish history as explicated and interpreted by Talmud and related commentaries. Differential textual devices predominate across the sequence such as semiographic patterning, syntactical repetition and hyperbole, and phonetic polysemantics, which produce a reflexive interpretive layer familiar from Talmudic reading praxis. These in turn enable the grafting onto the narrative of a likewise Talmudic, extended series of questions about the meaning and significance of the film.[18] The ostensible Judaic structuring of *Entre Nous* is oriented, like that of *tanakh*, toward the narration of (a) Jewish *history*, that is, toward the telling of a story that involves the Jewish experi-ence and recovery from social catastrophe, and that, from its very inception, places the inscription of that experience and its recovery into narrative-textu-al dialogue with its non-Jewish component. In marking its narrative shift from the diegetic past to the present tense, the film frames that spatio-tempo-ral movement in terms mediated by an abstractly structured, schematic relationality between two women, one Jewish, the other non-Jewish, both of whom are first shown respectively experiencing, and in the latter case, surviving, holocaustic events, then coming together to form a postwar, interreligious, inter-ethnic relationship, itself marked formally by an ellipsis whose allegoricity would seem to invoke Talmudism by its textual differentiality and, by extension, suspension of narrative movement pending questions about the meaning and significance of that relationship to the film as a whole, including the post-Holocaust context in which it emerges and is received.

If one considers the differences between (Judeo-)Christian and Judaic allegory, especially between their tanakhic(-exegetic) articulations, as gauged against the particular construction of this ellipsis, however, the ascription to it and to the film of a strictly Judaic determination becomes difficult, if not impossible, to support. In the first instance, the rearticulation of Talmudic textuality–or, of the peculiarly Judaic relationship between the various hermeneutic layers of language and discourse–onto tanakhic narrativity is, at least from the Judaic perspective, quite similar to the articulation of Talmudic discourse itself. The layers of tanakhic narrative are understood as interpretive *extensions* rather than *abstractions* of one another, related tropologically in various, syntactico-metaphorical, or, *metonymic*, ways to the broader and more significant articulation of the project of Jewish genealogical redemption. These include inference by syntactical juxtaposition or association (*smuchin*), which finds its Judaic narratological apogee in the organizational lay-out of the Talmudic page;[19] apprehension and cross-narrative association of the phonetic properties of vowel sounds (*al tikrei*), which traditionally are not included in Hebraic texts and whose insertions and alterations by the reader can significantly alter the meaning of a narrative passage (the most well-known example of this is the polysemic reading of names); and apprehension and allegorical association of the graphical form of (Hebrew) letters themselves (*gematria, notarikon*), which also propose a polysemic, often numerical and/or acrostic-acronymic alteration in narrative significance.[20]

The Judeo-Christian appropriation of tanakhic narrative history is basically respectful of these complex hermeneutic practices, yet in typical christological fashion, it contains them along the inversive and subsumptive lines pointed out during the general discussion of Judeo-Christianity. More specifically, and as regards the detailed character of Judaic tanakhic exegesis, Judeo-Christian appropriation of tanakhic narrative history recognizes and overtly acknowledges its differential, metonymic, polysemic character and in some cases goes to great lengths to prove this, but in the end, it always manages to foreclose that character via the (re)assertion of typically Christian qualifications thereof–as, for example, incessantly ambiguous, or, asymptotic, figurally metaphoric (i.e., iconic), and morally reducible to a christic etymological mapping.[21]

It is perhaps out of concern that any textual(ist) re-reading of *tanakh* undertaken in the wake of an imposition such as this one will become co-opted into this sort of christological perspective that recent Judaic tanakhic exegesis has shied away from extending interpretation to the intertextual and allegorical, potentially historical and political layers of tanakhic referentiality. The unfortunate result is that New Testament moralism has had interpretive dominance in recent tanakhic scholarship and its more secular, including cinematic, articulations.

To return to my analysis of the parabolic ellipsis, I can now argue that, if read with this hermeneutic distinction in mind, the shot under inspection cannot be considered Judaic, but supports, in fact, a Judeo-Christian reading. Firstly, while accessing a multilayered textuality, and while promoting a reflexive, self-conscious comprehension of the relation between *Entre Nous'* diegetic-historical and present-tense narrative sections, the syntactical metaphor it extends across the narrative gap between these sections takes the graphical form of (Judeo-)Christian allegory (i.e., the asymptotic parabola). Secondly, through phonetic, semiotic, and intertextual associations back and forth across the gap, it qualifies that form as a rhetorical proponent of Judeo-Christian historicity. Indeed, 'history' as charted in this shot does not comprise, as it does in Talmud-*tanakh*, a narrative of temporal movement grounded in the social and institutional conflicts and struggles overdetermining necessary material concerns such as resources, land, knowledge, privilege, and control, even though its diegetic background involves an event, the Holocaust, brought about in relation to all of these concerns. 'History' as charted via this shot extends a christological, phenomenological presumption that social movement is strictly an effect of heavenly, teleological compulsion leading gradually, while unevenly, across the 'debased' realm of the material and physical world toward apocalyptic, transcendental resolution. Hence the temporally prolonged depiction of the sky between depictions of the two buildings, which signifies via its duration the theological notion of eternity; the spectatorial non-knowledge of the Korskis' survival despite knowledge of Madeleine's, which signifies the asymmetricality of Jewish and Christian historical knowledgeability; and the parabolic framing and propulsion of these aspects, which itself graphically figures an asymptote and signifies the formulaic image, or icon, of the irruptive while historically unfounded christo-allegorical projection.

Moving past the elliptical shot, moreover, toward the ensuing scene of Léna and Madeleine's first meeting, one finds this apparent christo-allegoricality realized, insofar as that meeting *per se* resolves anagogically the ethno-national and religious divide which previously had separated the women (and bound them to their men) in the diegetic-historical portion of the narrative. This was figured narratologically via the parallel construction of their respective wartime experiences, and collocated selectively, but with intertextual overlap, up until the moment of this very elliptical shot, the ostensibly analogous circumstances without which the women might never have met.

It is precisely this structural aspect of the relationship between the two women that was neglected by reviews which chose to focus their attentions on the erotic quality of that relationship, its sexual (in)definability and (un)ethicality. This in turn contributed to their failure to view *Entre Nous* as both a Holocaust film and a Holocaust film with dubious, Judeo-Christian overdetermination. Instead of extending such a critique, reviews by Weiss, Straayer, and Wattelier, for instance, have taken the limited and rather facile position that the bond's ambiguous sexual constitution is itself sufficient means for so doing, that its undecidability signifies an erotico-aesthetic or onto-libidinal 'subversive' excess that renders it structurally resistant to containment or definition. The transgressive or ambiguous quality of the women's relationship is the source for alternative, including lesbian, responses to patriarchal containment in that it upsets, while not necessarily overturning, traditional cultural hierarchies.

In their attempts to show the erotic female bonding in the film reflexively resistant to and/or imminently transcendent of patriarchal appropriation, these reviews overlook the long-established social fact that patriarchy is more than simply a cultural or aesthetic phenomenon, and that the confinement of its analysis to the formal and/or thematic level of interpretation runs the risk of reinscribing the very deep-structural problematic of heterocentrism they would ostensibly oppose and in contradistinction to which they attribute such an emancipatory, subversive potential to erotic female solidarity.

This is not, of course, to deny claims made by these reviews regarding either the ambiguity and undecidability of that solidarity as articulated in *Entre Nous*, or the possibility of such solidarity coming to serve an emancipatory, feminist function. Despite, indeed because of, these claims, however, *Entre Nous*' deployment of ambiguity and erotic solidarity does not lend more than rhetorical lip-service to the problems of gender oppression and heterosexism in feminism, film theory, or the socio-cultural arena at large. For just as the ambiguity inscribing the women's relationship and its narrative effectuality maintains a characterological differentiation between them, such that their bond does not come to signal a totalizing drive toward irenic homogeneity, so likewise does it leave untouched the deep-structural patterns and conventions, especially those of ethno-religious and socio-economic orientation, which previously had been established as conditioning each woman's relationship to (her) gender and, in turn, the possibility that an economically lucrative, culturally daring friendship be considered as a means of liberation therefrom. Whereas sexuality and gender are destabilized throughout the film, the distinction between Léna and Madeleine as Jew and

(French-)Catholic is cursorily emphasized to the point of its stereotypification. As the relationship between the women tightens, they begin to adopt certain of each other's characterological, especially gender-oriented, traits, such that the traditional typological polemus, Jew-Christian, appears significantly deconstructed. Vis-à-vis her exposure to Madeleine, for instance, Léna's deportment alters drastically from conservatively clad and enculturated, assimilated Jewish bourgeoise to fashionable neo-bohemian–an alternation signified most overtly by her adoption of a more strident, masculinized disposition. As the friendship is realized economically, this disposition is further enhanced, in its non-Jewish, Christianized aspect, as Léna, characterized previously as verbal-linguistic by her ability to compose letters, deploys visual-artistic knowledge gleaned from Madeleine in order to design and supervise the construction of a fashion boutique, Magdalena, to be co-managed by her and Madeleine. In this regard, Léna adopts a certain feminized aspect that both complements her newly acceded masculinity and adds to its stridency. As for Madeleine, however, the adoption of 'Jewish' traits vis-à-vis Léna are strictly stereotypically based and, while inscribed along the same destabilized gender axis, stop short of equitable reciprocity in the ethno-religious, socio-economic regard. In the first place, from the moment of her traumatic 'victimization' during World War II to her divorce from the inept and bungling Costa, any Judaization Madeleine undergoes presumes an undeniably Judeo-Christian understanding of the Jewish and, by extension, gender, one that is in fact prefigured by the initial, pre-marital, pre-exilic characterization of Léna. There, a dual construction of Léna is formulated that appropriates the axes of gender and ethno-religiosity toward what only can be described as an ironically *anti*-feminist position.

Noting the former of these axes, numerous of *Entre Nous*' Lacanian-inflected critiques have recognized the early construction of Léna in terms of what Lacan might have designated a cinematic inscription of the classic figure of Woman. To them, Léna is portrayed both as a subject of and without, or, outside of, knowledge. On the one hand, her gaze often goes unreturned, which positions her as subjectively stable or self-possessed; on the other hand, the objects of her gaze are pastoral scenes and scapes whose idyllity, following the same tradition, suggests an alignment of her subjectivity and, in turn, her desire with that of an imaginal, even originary, ineffability which cannot return a gaze and, therefore, cannot be known because it does not function, much less exist, on the same ontological plane. For Lacan, this sort of dual(ist) construction bespeaks the very essence of Woman, which he designates *jouissance*, the silent, unattainable, unspeakable dynamic of male-masculine (phallic) desire for both transgression of and conciliation to the primordial 'Law of the Father,' and which subsequently is identified with its ostensive opposite, the female-feminine absenting of desire, 'aphanisis.'

For the reputedly feminist reviews of *Entre Nous*, this neo-romantic theoriza-
tion translates as the proverbial 'desire that dare not speak its name'–lesbianism–which poses such a threat to male-dominated society that it has to be
idealized, and thereby defused, in the form of mystical, non-knowledgeable,
gnostic opacities such as *ekstasis, yichud*, 'beatitude,' *jouissance, jeu*, even
divinity itself. In these reviews, the recognition and naming of lesbianism as
an erotic, if not sexual, possibility for woman–as well as a means of suspend-
ing and redirecting any such possibilities for men–is one of the first steps
toward demystifying it and, in turn, overturning the (hetero)patriarchal sche-
ma. From their perspective, *Entre Nous*' construction of Léna as (un)know-
ing female subject–what Irigaray has in another context referred to as an
'awoman'[22]–is a first, clever, and effective means toward realizing such an
end.

While these critiques are prolific on the almost epitomical quality of
Léna's engendering, they do not follow the Lacanian theory on which their
analyses are based to the theological level which other reviews have
broached[23] and which Lacan himself enters unabashedly, enabling him to
liken the dual(ist) dynamics of *jouissance* (i.e., the heteropatriarchal containment of lesbianism) to the dissimulatory phenomenology of *Christian trini-
tarian belief.*[24] For the latter reviewers, *pace* the Lacanian tradition, the
philosophical function of *jouissance* and/or Woman, like that of the Jew on
the christo-theological register,[25] is as an ethical exemplar, a model illustra-
tion of what is possible and what must be conceded, or, confessed, vis-à-vis
the (hetero)patriarchal (or, in the case of the Jew, christological) status quo.
Indeed for Lacan, who differs significantly from Freud in this respect,[26]
acceptance of this exemplary function is key to psychological equilibrium
pursuant to one's analytically-wrought realization of how provisional and
unstable is worldly existence and how necessary therefore are the conventions of language and interpellation to one's functional continuation in the
world. On this basically Christian line, the realization and enactment of
lesbianism is tantamount to madness–to an hysterical suspension and uproot-
ing of ideologico-linguistic conventions (i.e., the Symbolic), with the result
that one's relation to the worldly becomes divested of the cognitive-discur-
sive means by which the possibility of intersubjectivity and socialization is
realized.

The elliptical-asymptotic, chronicle-like aspect of the *Entre Nous* narrative, which figures a discursive undecidability, and which, as such, facilitates
a French feminist-inflected refusal to depict the women making any fixed
decision regarding the direction of their actions and desires, including their
sexual orientation[27]–this structural aspect can henceforth be read by *Entre
Nous*' quasi-Lacanian critics only in terms of a certain formal, lesbian-feminist aesthetic, not in terms of what also should be seen as its secular reinscrip-

tion of Judeo-Christian theology's selective and subsumptive reading of *ta-nakh*. Indeed apropos the Judeo-Christian designation of *tanakh* as rhetorically anomic, or, endlessly interpretable and undecidable, the uncertainty projected by *Entre Nous* regarding the sexual nature of the women's erotic bond would have to go without saying. To decide either way on the matter would signify a drive toward masculinist mastery in the French feminist sense and also, ironically, a negative invocation of the very Judaica which the Judeo-Christian perspective, in its (re)turn to *tanakh*, would seem interested, at least cursorily, to emulate and support. Hence the narrative's constant oscillation with respect to the women's sexuality, to their portrayal as (non-)decision-makers, and even to the depiction of their bond as at once cathartic and salvific. All of this must be seen as a structural, Judeo-Christian means toward resisting the (post-Holocaust) persistence of a Jewishness understood (erroneously) as wholeheartedly and monolithically masculinist, as inscribed across the financially controlling figure of the Jewish husband, Michel–an observation lost on critics who see this means of resistance only through Lacanian eyes, as an arbitrarily wrought, formal-aesthetic device for maintaining an "hypothetical" sex-gender distinction between the two women and, in turn, a sense of sex-gender pluralism among the film's community of spectators.

From this perspective, the narratological significance of Madeleine's turn toward Léna's 'Jewishness' can only be interpreted rhetorically, the overdetermination of this apparent turn by Judeo-Christian discourse, much like that of the diegetic-historical paralleling of the women's wartime experiences, chalked up to a seductively sensual subversiveness. Read from the Judaically-inflected perspective elided by this essentially Christian view, however, Madeleine's 'subversive' turn to Léna's 'Jewishness' must be seen in its reinforcement of the asymmetricality, nay, theoretical exploitativeness, inscribed across the film's characterological and, in the cases of the parabolic ellipsis and the parallel sequencing, narratological registers. It is no surprise, for example, that throughout the development of the erotic female bond, it is Madeleine, the narrative antagonist, who actually inspires, instigates, even provokes all the actions which together will culminate in both women's divorces and, more importantly for her, will lead to her winning over Léna. The women are never portrayed as making fixed decisions; their choices are always undercut, either by the enigmatic quality of their subsequent behaviors and expressions or by the consequences for the further development of the erotic bond. The possibility that the women become entrepreneurs, that they open a clothing boutique, for instance, arises only as a result of Madeleine's albeit inadvertent bungling of an adulterous affair she has with Roland, which Léna, the Jew, is then compelled to repair. Indeed, the idea of using a boutique in order to gain financial and, in turn, social and legal independence from (their) men occurs to them *only after* Michel, jealously enamored of Madeleine, walks in on her and Roland in bed together at his apartment while Léna is away on holiday, and a potential rift is thereby effected between the two families which threatens to keep the women apart indefinitely and thus to destroy any of the early, unexpressed liberatory hopes. The actual contracting of Magdalena, its financing and construction, also occurs at a 'subversive' moment–following the newly-divorced Madeleine's rather capricious announcement to Léna during their secret weekend together in Paris that she plans to remain in Paris to eke out her living there, thus leaving Léna, now planning the boutique, to proceed with the project alone. At this stage, as with Madeleine's bungled affair, it becomes incumbent upon the Jewish Léna to make good–in this case, to do all the footwork, finagle a start-up loan from Michel, and implement the design ideas presumably suggested by Madeleine in order to make the boutique a reality. This particular, economically mediated articulation of asymmetricality is itself anticipated by an earlier scene in which Madeleine, who admits ignorance of monetary matters, must rely on the apparently natural business savvy of Léna to figure out how to prevent a somewhat more gullible, money-lending (*auri-fière*) Michel from discovering that Costa is unable to pay back a loan from him. Léna's decision finally to abandon the Lyonnaise boutique and divorce Michel is neither arbitrary whim nor blind necessity brought about solely on account of the latter's destructive violence, but the result of a 'subversive' act by Madeleine, who steps boldly into full view from behind a wall at the boutique, where she'd been hiding from Michel, knowing full well Léna's promise to him and seeming not to mind that her act will provoke his volatile temper. The practiced timing and highly staged character of her emergence suggests that her act is deliberate, that she intended to call Michel to a challenge for the favors of Léna, that she even had been resentful of the apparent early success of the boutique, since instead of being more a product of her influence, it had been financed and morally nurtured by Michel, who is designated as her rival on all fronts–sexual, ethno-religious, and socio-economic.

This narratological subversiveness is also inscribed at the structural level. When Léna and Madeleine first meet, for instance, the stage quite literally has been set for an encounter that signifies much more than the scene's face-value. Their encounter is overdetermined by a diegetic context in which the gender-sexual and ethno-national oppressions which both women, in various ways, have endured have subtly been subsumed under a revisionist rubric that retains a hold on Christian antisemitism even while its critique of these former oppressions would appear to orient it otherwise, and even while (or perhaps because) that reorientation would seem at least to proffer a philosemitic appreciation of the 'industrious-but-suffering' notion of the

'Jewish' implied by allegorical reference to both these oppressions. The key device of this resituation is a superimposition effected only seconds before the depiction of Madeleine's entrance into the school auditorium and only seconds after an impatient Costa has left René behind with Léna, who has agreed to watch over him until Madeleine's arrival, and who is now in the process of asking him his name. Just as the depiction of Madeleine's entrance is about to occur, a shot is provided of a closing stage curtain taken from the perspective of Léna and René seated beside one another in a now-empty auditorium which is itself then shot from the perspective of the now-empty stage. The immediate effect of this superimposition is to destabilize the spatio-temporal dimensionality of the scene, but unlike an earlier alternation between the stage and the audience, which conveyed a sense of Léna's spatio-temporal transgressiveness in relation to her daughter, the Kurys prototype, Sophie, this destabilization results, via its utter overlapping of spatial and temporal, existential and proairetic, registers, in a *transcendence*, not merely a *transgression*, of these dimensions. Blending the 'real' and 'imaginary' fields of the auditorium and stage produces a hybrid image in which the two fields are at once distinct and interchangeable and thus together signify the very definition of transcendence.

Madeleine's arrival is figured under the rubric of this superimposition, as she is portrayed entering the auditorium toward the conclusion of the long-shot. That very arrival, as well as the desiring gaze she casts shortly afterwards at an ostensibly objectified Léna, take on the character of this transcendence, this hybridity, so that they, too, are seen as ontologically destabilized, and the erotic relationship they prefigure is enabled to accrue a qualitatively different meaning than that signified earlier by the purely filial alternation between Léna and Sophie. Yet for all the difference it signifies from the pre-superimpositional portion of the scene, the proscription of this relationship via the transcendent gaze of one of its members, as cast at the subjective expense of its other, indicates an ideological limit to the ontological resituation which has prefigured it. Indeed, Madeleine is not constructed as the conventional owner of her gaze but, instead, as its phenomenological agent. Through the ordering of its constitutive reverse-shots into blocks of two-shots of the women seated beside one another on the same spatial plane, the typical Hollywoodian, male-centered structure associated with the male characters in the film is disallowed her. Whereas one might view this ordering as a welcome opening of the gaze onto a plural, even ecumenical, community of spectators, such a reading would not negate the fact that the ordering of this gaze would seem to locate a matrix of emergence largely beyond the figure of Madeleine, in an 'imaginary' field signified first by the stage from which she initially is portrayed, then by the expenditure of excessive screen-time during her casting of that gaze and the commencement shortly thereafter of a tender, poignant, if not romantic melody over the soundtrack.

Seen in this way, it is apparent that neither the 'awoman,' Léna, nor the seemingly subjectivized Madeleine figures as a subject of her (own) desiring gaze. Yet this fact does not render the women homologous. Only moments following their meeting in the auditorium, at which point Léna knows little more about Madeleine than that she is capricious and prone to mysticism, Léna is already relating to her the story of her own holocaustic exile and return, as though receipt of the latter's desiring gaze had been enough to establish the requisite degree of trust for such a confession. At this point, Léna not only recalls but relives her concentrationary internment, as she momentarily takes on the character of her concentrationary friend–named, not incidentally, Sarah [Christine Pascal]–who also confessed her woes 'at first sight,' and whose thoughts on Michel's marriage proposal had been instrumental in what soon was to become Léna's liberation. This recollection/re-enactment may be read as an effect of *gilgul*, a kabbalistic term designating a consensual, even erotically-tinged relationship based in the occasioning of metempsychosis, the passing of the soul of a dying person into the body of one who still lives. In this case, Madeleine might be understood as the literal embodiment (not only the allegory) of 'Sarah,' and Léna, having taken on the latter's confessionalism, as Madeleine's figural complement. Recalling christology, we might say that the relationship, its desiring gaze and verbal enunciation are *salvific*, that they *instantiate* the Holocaust that is otherwise not represented directly but, instead, by an indirect, textually mediated reference to the memory-concept, 'Sarah.' As such they facilitate the phenomenon of remembrance necessary to the Judaic reparation (*tikkun*) of that event. The meeting between Madeleine and Léna is as much an initiation of a friendship as an occasion for mourning the loss of Sarah, or, metonymically speaking, the dissemination of the Jewish(-Abrahamic) legacy up to and including the Holocaust. Madeleine's desiring gaze is less autonomous than mnemonic, and Léna's recognition thereof, signaled by her ensuing confession, the means by which its allegorical referent, the *pathos* of the Holocaust, may be re-experienced and, thusly, properly mourned. As this is accomplished, the women are suddenly awakened to the various ways in which they have not yet shed the chains of the past, and as in a perfectly wrought prolepsis, intuit one another as the necessary tools with which to do so. It is not for nothing that Madeleine, for instance, will soon after confess her 'holocaustic' history to Léna, or that her illicit affair with Roland will take place in Léna's own bed.

This consensuality between Léna and Madeleine is so privatized, so genealogically dislocated, so resistant to symbolization, moreover, that its manifestation as *gilgul*, like much else in this film, is ultimately more akin to that concept's Christian rather than Judaic interpretation. In the Christian reading of Kabbalah, metempsychosis entails an extra-historical, apolitical emanation, a manifestation of force above and beyond the material development of the social.[28] On this transcendental perspective, a metempsychosis whose ostensive referent is the *pathos* of the Holocaust would require for its realization the diversion (*détournement*) of that *pathos* into sheer *aesthesis*, that is, the denial of the Holocaust as an event, an occurrence with a political, economic, ideological and cultural *history*, followed by its ontotheologistic substitution as an experiential, gnostic 'happening,' an extra-social, eschatological, catastrophic epiphany. In such a case, the pathetic experience required for the process of mourning would no longer be understood to signify a material, but rather an ideal, referent, and the process of mourning itself, a never-ending, aphanisic, universalizable struggle which neither broad investigation nor close analysis may forestall or bring to closure. Like a New Testamental narrative, the *pathos* of the Holocaust thus understood is, despite appearances, both evoked and projected outside the register of what is known from the Judaic perspective as *le-didakh*–an analytic praxis always binding to the imperative of critical answerability. Around it is a hermeneutic silence bespeaking reverence, gnostic transparency, and awe, a silence implying that what is being recollected is not only devoid of answerability but, like the matrix of the (female) gaze throughout *Entre Nous*, emptied of discrete subjectivity: something sacred, untouchable, ineffable, omniscient; something which cannot be located in a material particularity; something which is applicable to a transhistorical range of traumatic experiences; something whose perpetuation, not permanent cessation, is the key to liberation from its devastating effects.

This would explain why, at the moment of their exchange of erotic glances, Madeleine and Léna speak no words, not even those inquiring into one another's name (something which otherwise has marked, and will continue to mark, the introduction of characters throughout the film), and why, when Michel relates his Holocaust experience to the Segaras one night over dinner (also during the acquaintanceship sequence), he is basically dismissed, despite his socialist sympathies, as a petit-bourgeois boor, and the humorous aspect of his tale is received in uncomprehending, disinterested silence. The interpellation into the covenant by the Judaic act of (mis)naming (i.e., misrecognition), as well as the physical practice of (hetero)sexuality and the adherence to a social code of ethics, both signified by the Jewish husband/father, socialist/capitalist Michel, are neither ingredients for transcendence nor the sustained positing of a 'sinful,' cataclysmic, holocaustic world against which such a transcendence may be gauged. In the hyperreality of *Entre Nous'* "hypothetical" structure, only an erotic, unnamed, antinomian bond is so geared, one based in an *entrepreneur*ial ethic of private individual, not social, progress (what Straayer correctly but strangely, affirmatively, refers to as 'isolation,' the 'opportunity' of the film, p. 21), and operative only insofar as its own, cultural and economic advancement occurs at the expense of a certain well-known typology of 'Jewishness' stubbornly resistant to adopting the dominant (albeit secularized) Christian ethic.

With this in mind, the rationale for the critical silence around *Entre Nous'* Jewishness and holocausticity takes form. For although the three historically most attuned, if journalistically limited, reviews of the film note that something about ethno-nationality, about class, and about gender-sexuality is missing from *Entre Nous*, none of them mention the fact that the structural device for such an absenting is, in fact, the Jewish Holocaust, which itself is absented, or, more correctly, displaced, throughout the film, and which in turn becomes the basis of its ideological call for Jews and Christians, gay and straight alike, to engage in the advancement of transnational capitalism. Seligsohn notes that, 'for all its fragile truths, *Entre Nous* has a tendency to wilt sometimes for a lack of light in some of its obscure corners,' but as for the connection of this obscurity, which for him concerns the 'Jewish,' to the ideological displacement of the Holocaust in the film, he is silent. Quart likewise is unable to draw connections between the phenomenon of (Judeo-Christian) Holocaust displacement and what she criticizes as *Entre Nous'* lack of "interest in what seems to be the wealth of Madeleine's background and Léna's having a maid and nouveau riche furs";[29] and Denby, for all his insightfulness, confines his almost anomalous recognition of this diplacement to a commentary on personal ethics: "Kurys is not saying that Léna is wrong to leave [Michel], only that personal liberation can also be a form of murder" (59).

If critics remained silent on this issue, it is not simply for fear of opening the Pandora's box of 'Jewish self-hatred,' or because doing so would have delivered a blow to the expanding canon of female-directed films and, in relation, the growing field of lesbian/feminist public and scholarly discourse. It is because recognizing and speaking to the film's Judeo-Christian displacement of 'Jewish Holocaust' onto an entrepreneurial trajectory would have meant having also to recognize and speak to something no film at that time, or for many years thereafter, was willing to confront: the religious hermeneutic expropriation of the Holocaust as a rationale for a form of political-economic imperialism, transnationalism, which at once recruits the collaboration of formerly oppressed Jews, women, homosexuals, and workers, and denies them the very history, intelligibility, and materiality which made it possible for them to become so 'victimized' and, in turn, so 'redeemed,' in the first place.

NOTES

1. One of its three running competitors was the Hungarian Holocaust film, *The Revolt of Job* (dir. Imre Gyongyossi and Barna Kabay, 1983). The winner was *Fanny and Alexander* (dir. Ingmar Bergman, Sweden, 1983). See Richard Shale, *The academy awards index: The Complete Categorical and Chronological Record* (London and Westport, CT: Greenwood Press, 1993), p. 642.

2. Prior to *Entre Nous*, only one female-directed film had received this degree of formal acclaim: in 1976, *The Seven Beauties* (dir. Léna Wertmüller, Italy), a Holocaust film, was nominated for both Best Director and Best Foreign Language Film. To date, only one female-directed film has actually received an Academy Award– *Antonia's Line* (dir. Marleen Gorris, Belgium/Netherlands/UK, 1995) in the Best Foreign Language Film category; and only one woman has been nominated for a Best Director award–Jane Campion for *The Piano* (Australia/France, 1993), which lost to Steven Spielberg for his *Schindler's List* (a Holocaust film par excellence). Not incidentally, *Antonia's Line* is a self-consciously post-Holocaust film and, like *Entre Nous*, both it and *The Piano* were concerned, *inter alia*, with the politics of gender and sexuality. Shale ibid., p. 287; Ronald Bergan et al., *Academy Award Winners* (London: Prion, 1994), p. 681.

3. Typifying the negative side of the debate was the review by Carole Corbeil, film critic for the *Toronto Globe and Mail*, for whom *Entre Nous'* female bond epitomized the superficiality and elitism of Euroamerican art cinema, as well as its social evasiveness. For her,

> There is nothing particularly endearing in having the beautiful Miou Miou and Miss Huppert run around in beautiful and imaginative retro dresses while bemoaning the stupidity of their husbands. It all seems redundant, somehow, as if a pretty-pretty French art director had thrown a bell-jar over the proceedings . . . [The film] is unbearably coy, incidentally, on the subject of just how physical this friendship gets. In France, the movie was called *Coup De Foudre*; *Entre Nous*, the title of the North American release, desexualizes the friendship . . . What could have been authentic–and there is no doubt in my mind that many spirited women used fashion in the fifties as a springboard to independence, becomes too self-consciously aesthetic. ('Star Quality Burdens *Entre Nous*,' *Toronto Globe and Mail* 17 Feb. 1984: E9)

Pauline Kael's review appears sweeping and all-encompassing and yet, in its frankness, must also be counted as the most politically pointed of the *Entre Nous* critiques:

> [*Entre Nous*] has a political commitment to women's friendship, and it comes very close to having a political commitment to lesbian sex . . . but Kurys doesn't develop that. She just keeps it lurking in the air, though the film's title in France was *Coup de foudre*–love at first sight . . . Léna and Madeleine are what used to be called soul mates; *Entre Nous* is about spiritual lesbianism . . . sexual politics without sex. ("The Current Cinema," *The New Yorker* 3 May 1984: 133-4)

For other examples of reviews involved in the debate over the sexual orientation of *Entre Nous'* female bond, see David Ansen, 'More than good friends,' *Newsweek* 6 Feb. 1984: 81; Molly Haskell, 'Women's Friendships: Two Films Move Beyond the Clichés,' *Ms.* Dec. 1983: 23, 25; David Hughes, 'A Subtle Hymn to Women's Love,' *The Sunday Times* (London) 9 Oct. 1983: 39; David Sterritt, 'Building Bonds of Friendship and a Filmmaker's Career,' *Christian Science Monitor* 3 Aug. 1984: 21-2; David Denby, 'Les Girls,' *New York Magazine* 23 Jan. 1984: 57-9; *Playboy* Feb.

1984: 28, Rev. of *Entre Nous*; Gary Arnold, 'Notions of Love: "Entre Nous"': Men and Women Apart,' *Washington Post* 24 Feb. 1984: B1-2; Maureen Peterson, '"Coup" Strikes Blow for Female Friendship,' *Montréal Gazette* 10 Sept. 1983: C-4; Patricia Bosworth, 'Some Secret Worlds Revealed,' *Working Woman* Oct. 1983: 202-4; Andrea Weiss, 'Passionate Friends,' *New York Native* 13-26 Feb. 1984: 34-5; Peter Wilson, 'What Exactly Is This Film Trying To Say?' *Vancouver Sun* 24 Feb. 1984: B1; Stanley Kaufmann, 'All For Love,' *The New Republic* 27 Feb. 1984: 22-4; John Simon, 'Dishonesty Recompensed,' *National Review* 4 May 1984: 54-6; John Gillett, *Monthly Film Bulletin* Nov. 1983: 301; Leo Seligsohn, *Newsday* 25 Jan. 1984: 51; Rex Reed, *New York Post* 25 Jan. 1984: 19; Richard Corliss, *Time* 30 Jan. 1984: 78; Vincent Canby, *New York Times* 25 Jan. 1984: C17; and *New York Times* 4 Feb. 1993: C20.

4. At most, popular press engagement with the Holocaust-oriented aspects of *Entre Nous* was limited to the provision of background information on the film's plot, by which only the most abbreviated commentary was made possible on the social problematicity of this issue. The only review even to have hinted at the specific questions of antisemitism and the 'Jewish' was that of a French critic, Marie Cardinal, in *Le Nouvel Observateur* (22 April 1983: 96).

5. Barbara Koenig Quart, *Women Directors: The Emergence of a New Cinema* (New York: Praeger, 1988) 3; Susan Hayward, *French National Cinema* (London and New York: Routledge, 1993), 5; Chris Straayer, 'The Hypothetical Lesbian Heroine in Narrative Feature Film,' in idem., *Deviant Eyes, Deviant Bodies* op cit., 4; and Hervé Wattelier, '*Entre Nous*: Gender Analyzed,' *Jump Cut* 32 (April 1986): 8, 32, 37. Even Andrea Weiss' *Vampires and Violets: Lesbians in Film* (New York: Penguin, 1993), which discussed *Entre Nous* amply, oddly cited in relation thereto only texts whose central foci are films *other* than *Entre Nous* (123-24, 172n 27 & 28), and did so abstractly, as did Straayer, in formalist terms of the gaze. The very recent Guy Austin, *Contemporary French Cinema: An Introduction* (Manchester and New York: Manchester University Press, 1996) simply mimics the Weissean perspective (88).

6. Exceptions include Annette Insdorf, *Indelible Shadows: Film and the Holocaust*, 2nd ed. (Cambridge and New York: Cambridge University Press, 1989), 86, which notes *Entre Nous*' depiction of the Holocaust while denying bluntly its status as 'Holocaust film'; and André Pierre Colombat, *The Holocaust in French Film* (Metuchen, NJ: Scarecrow Press, 1993), 95.

7. Examples of this proliferation of cultural discourse and contestation include Hollywood television's *Holocaust* (dir. Marvin Chomsky, NBC, 1978) and *Playing for Time* (dir. Daniel Mann, CBS, 1980), along with the 1970s Nazi *rétro* film phenomenon and the Holocaust historiography debates begun in France and continuing into Germany at the time of *Entre Nous*' release.

8. For books on the Nazi persecution of lesbians, see Erica Fischer, *Aimée and Jaguar*, trans. Edna McCown (New York: HarperCollins, 1995); Claudia Schoppmann, *Days of Masquerade: Life Stories of Lesbians During the Third Reich*, trans. Allison Brown (New York and Chichester, West Sussex: Columbia University Press, 1996); and Günter Grau, *Hidden Holocaust? Gay and Lesbian Persecution in Germany, 1933-45* (London and New York: Cassell, 1995).

9. As Andrea Weiss has suggested, for instance, 'Madeleine's and Léna's stories are intercut in such a way as to offer shrewd insight into how the war so profoundly shaped their adult lives and later their relationship with one another' ('Passionate Friends,' 34); likewise Maureen Peterson notes that '[t]his tale of 'love at first sight' is inextricably linked to its time in history, the years from 1940-1954 . . . In essence these women might well have chosen other mates in other times . . . That fact is important enough to take on an almost symbolic significance' (Peterson op cit.).

10. Olivier Cohen and Diane Kurys, *Coup de foudre: Le rêve des années 50* (Paris: Éditions Mazarine, 1983). For instance, in an interview she gave in *Film Comment*, Kurys makes explicit reference to the legacy of the Holocaust recounted in *Coup de foudre*'s preface, and its effect on her understanding of the 'Jewish': 'Our ambitiousness [that of children of survivors and, generally, the Wandering Jew] is a kind of revenge,' but also a kind of protection against ever becoming the victims our parents were' (qtd. Marcia Pally, 'World of Our Mothers,' *Film Comment* 20.2 [1984]: 17).

11. Arthur A. Cohen, T*he Myth of the Judeo-Christian Tradition* (New York: Harper and Row, 1970); Mark Silk, 'Notes on the Judeo-Christian Tradition in America,' *American Quarterly* 36 (Spring 1984): 65-85; and Robert Boston, *Why the Religious Right Is Wrong: About Separation of Church and State in America* (Buffalo, NY: Prometheus, 1993).

12. See Galit Hasen-Roker and Alan Dundes, *The Wandering Jew: Essays in the Interpretation of a Christian Legend* (Bloomington and Indianapolis: Indiana University Press, 1986), esp. Hyam Maccoby, 'The Wandering Jew as Sacred Executioner,' 236-260.

13. For an interesting critique of this age-old tack, see John Dominic Crossan, *Who Killed Jesus? Exposing the Roots of Anti-Semitism in the Gospel Story of the Death of Jesus* (San Francisco: HarperSanFrancisco, 1995).

14. For conservative instances, see William J. Courtenay, ed. *The Judeo-Christian Heritage* (New York: Holt, 1970); and J. H. Hexter, *The Judaeo-Christian Tradition*, 2nd ed. (New Haven and London: Yale University Press, 1995). For a rabidly reactionary version, see Gary North, *The Judeo-Christian Tradition: A Guide for the Perplexed* (Tyler, TX: Institute for Christian Economics, 1990).

15. Ward Churchill, *A Little Matter of Genocide: Holocaust Denial in the Americas, 1492 to the Present* (San Francisco: City Lights Books, 1998); William K. Blum, *Killing Hope: U.S. Military and CIA Interventions Since World War II* (Washington, DC: Common Courage Press, 1995); and Frank Chalk and Kurt Jonassohn, *The History and Sociology of Genocide: Analyses and Case Studies* (New Haven: Yale University Press, 1990).

16. Arno Mayer, *Why Did the Heavens Not Darken? The 'Final Solution' in History.* Rev. ed. (New York: Pantheon, 1990); and Noam Chomsky, *The Fateful Triangle: The U.S., Israel, and the Palestinians* (Boston: South End Press, 1983).

17. A relevant example of such an appropriation is Eugene Kaelin's ontotheology of the 'parabola,' in 'Poesis as Parabolic Expression: Heidegger on How a Poem Means,' *Art and Experience: A Phenomenological Aesthetics* (Lewisburg: Bucknell University Press, 1970), pp. 234-80.

18. For Talmudically-inflected and/or rabbinical readings of *tanakh* which are particularly attuned to the *textual* layering of its narrative logic, see, for example, Susan Handelman, *The Slayers of Moses: The Emergence of Rabbinic Interpretation in Modern Literary Theory* (Albany: SUNY Press, 1982); Daniel Boyarin, *Intertextuality and the Reading of Midrash* (Indianapolis: IUP, 1990); and, from a theoretical perspective, Edmund Jabés, *The Little Book of Unsuspected Subversion* (Stanford, CA and London: Stanford University Press, 1996).

19. For an example of this lay-out, see Jacob Neusner, *Talmudic Thinking: Language, Logic, Law* (Columbia, SC: University of South Carolina Press, 1992).

20. For an elaboration of these practices, see Handelman op cit., 74; and Daniel Boyarin, 'Dual Signs, Ambiguity, and the Dialectic of Intertextual Readings,' *Intertextuality* op cit., 57-78.

21. Examples include Robert Alter, *The Art of Biblical Narrative* (New York: Basic Books, 1981); Crossan op cit.; Geza Vermès, *Jesus the Jew: A Historian's Reading of the Gospel* (London: William Collins, 1973).

22. Luce Irigaray, *This Sex Which Is Not One*, trans. Catherine Porter with Carolyn Burke (Ithaca: Cornell University Press, 1985), 113-14.

23. Hughes, op cit.; and David Robinson, 'Richness of Moral Speculation,' *The London Times* 14 Oct. 1983: 11.

24. This is especially evident in the essay, 'God and the *Jouissance* of The Woman: A Love Letter,' in *Jacques Lacan, Feminine Sexuality: Jacques Lacan and the école freudienne*, trans. Jacqueline Rose (New York and London: W. W. Norton; Pantheon, 1982), 135-49.

25. Hence the phonetic likeness often foregrounded between '*jouissance*' and 'Jewishness,' '*jeu*' and 'Jew.' Cixous literalizes this phonetic slippage with her pun, *juifemme*, meaning 'I am a Jewish woman,' in *La fiancée juive: de la tentation* (Paris: Des Femmes/Antoinette Fouque, 1995). For a discussion of the usage and significance of *juifemme*, see Elaine Marks, *Marrano as Metaphor: The Jewish Presence in Writing* (New York: Columbia University Press, 1996), 143-53; and idem., '*Cendres juives*: Jews Writing in French "after Auschwitz,"' Lawrence D. Kritzman, ed., *Auschwitz and After: Race, Culture, and "the Jewish Question in France"* (New York and London: Routledge, 1995), 35-46.

26. David H. Fisher, 'Introduction: Framing Lacan?' In Edith Wyschogrod et al., eds. *Lacan and Theological Discourse* (Albany: SUNYP, 1989), pp. 1-25.

27. For cinema studies discourse on French feminist undecidability, see Sandy Flitterman-Lewis, *To Desire Differently: Feminism and the French Cinema* (Urbana: U of Illinois P, 1990); Patricia Mellencamp, *Indiscretions: Avant-Garde Film, Video, and Feminism* (Bloomington and Indianapolis: Indiana University Press, 1990); and Susan Rubin Suleiman, *Subversive Intent: Gender, Politics, and the Avant-Garde* (Cambridge, MA and London: Harvard University Press, 1990).

28. Joseph Leon Blau, *The Christian Interpretation of the Cabala in the Renaissance* (New York: Columbia University Press, 1944), 15.

29. Barbara Quart, rev. in *Cinéaste* 13:3 (1984): 46-7.

The Dispersal of the Lesbian, or Re-Patriating the Lesbian in British Writing

Gabriele Griffin

SUMMARY. Based on an analysis of Kay Summerscale's (1997) biography *The Queen of Whale Cay,* Jeanette Winterson's (1997) novel *Gut Symmetries* and Patricia Duncker's novel *Hallucinating Foucault* (1996), I argue that the emergence of postmodernism and queer has led to a re-positioning of 'the lesbian' in a number of contemporary texts whereby the once taken-for-granted notions of women and their relation to each other have become subsumed under an interrogation not so much of gender, the queer term, but of textuality, the postmodern turn. The result is a dispersal and simultaneously a re-patriation of 'the lesbian'[1] which obliterates her within the in/difference of the text. *[Article copies available for a fee from The Haworth Document Delivery Service: 1-800-342-9678. E-mail address: getinfo@haworthpressinc.com <Website: http://www.haworthpressinc.com>]*

KEYWORDS. Queer theory, gender bending, postmodernism, lesbian writing

---

Gabriele Griffin is Professor of English at Kingston University, Kingston upon Thames, Surrey, UK. Her publications include *Straight Studies Modified: Lesbian Interventions in the Academy* (co-edited with Sonya Andermahr, Cassell, 1997); *Gender Issues in Elder Abuse* (co-authored with Lynda Aitken, Sage, 1996); *Feminist Activism in the 1990s* (Taylor & Francis, 1995); *Heavenly Love? Lesbian Images in 20th Century Women's Writing* (Manchester University Press, 1993). She is currently completing a book, *Visibility Blue/s: AIDS and Representation* (Manchester University Press). She is also co-editor of *Feminist Theory*, a new academic journal (Sage, 2000).

Address correspondence to: Gabriele Griffin, Department of English, Kingston University, Kingston-upon-Thames, Surrey KT1 2EE, United Kingdom.

[Haworth co-indexing entry note]: "The Dispersal of the Lesbian, or Re-Patriating the Lesbian in British Writing." Griffin, Gabriele. Co-published simultaneously in *Journal of Lesbian Studies* (Harrington Park Press, an imprint of The Haworth Press, Inc.) Vol. 4, No. 2, 2000, pp. 65-80; and: *'Romancing the Margins'? Lesbian Writing in the 1990s* (ed: Gabriele Griffin) Harrington Park Press, an imprint of The Haworth Press, Inc., 2000, pp. 65-80. Single or multiple copies of this article are available for a fee from The Haworth Document Delivery Service [1-800-342-9678, 9:00 a.m. - 5:00 p.m. (EST). E-mail address: getinfo@haworthpressinc.com].

INTRODUCTION

Before the outbreak of postmodernism, and more specifically queer,[2] lesbian identity was debated as a material and political reality in which the questions concerned degrees of (sexual) involvement and politico-emotional affiliations, viewed from a perspective informed by a notion of differences among women.[3] The Radicalesbians' (1970) assertion that 'A lesbian is the rage of all women condensed to the point of explosion' (17), Adrienne Rich's (1980) lesbian continuum, and Catherine R. Stimpson's (1981) definition of the lesbian as 'a woman who finds other women erotically attractive and gratifying' (97) all took for granted the idea of woman[4] and of women's relation with each other, as well as the notion of man as other from, and traditionally more powerful than, woman. Intersexual difference seemed a problematizable but unproblematic given. As in the feminist debates of the 1980s,[5] the focus on *women* rather than on women's relation to men was at the centre of lesbian writing and criticism.

The 1990s have seen a significant shift in this position. In *Sexual Practice/ Textual Theory* (1993) Susan J. Wolfe and Julia Penelope express their sense of threat by pointing to the way in which 'We live in the postmodernist, poststructuralist (and, some would say, postfeminist) era, during a period when the term *Lesbian* is problematic, even when used nonpejoratively by a self-declared Lesbian' (1). They take issue with the ways in which lesbian cultural criticism such as that of Diana Fuss (1990) has asserted the textuality and constructedness of lesbian identity, maintaining that such a stance 'seems to us to threaten the erasure of real (or, as the postmodernists would say, "material") Lesbians' (2). The relation between the material and the textual is a complex one in which the subordination of the one to the other is endlessly at stake. In the discussions of that shifting hierarchy intra-textual considerations often become secondary. From a materialist lesbian perspective this is an issue since the fashioning of lesbians from/through texts is well documented[6] and one might therefore expect an interest in the kinds of lesbians portrayed in lesbian texts, meaning texts depicting lesbian characters. It is the pursuit of that interest which governs this article since, it seems to me, that whilst the debates about the relative merits of postmodernist or queer and materialist or radical lesbian positions have stimulated much debate, the new figures that seem to emerge in lesbian writing get lost. More specifically, some critical questions concerning the implications of the representations of the lesbian in women's writing of the 1990s need to be asked.

In this article I shall concentrate on three recent British texts: Kate Summerscale's (1997) biography of Joe Carstairs entitled *The Queen of Whale Cay*; Jeanette Winterson's (1997) novel *Gut Symmetries*; and Patricia Duncker's (1996) novel *Hallucinating Foucault*, to examine a phenomenon which is increasingly prominent in British lesbian writing and which I shall term the 're-patriation' of the lesbian in texts. This 're-patriation' which I shall explain below is associated with the dispersal of the lesbian referred to in the title of this article. When I visited a major bookshop in Leeds recently to buy the texts under consideration here, none of them could be found in the section on lesbian and gay writing. Lesbian writing, as classified in that bookstore, is very specific. It means publications by the Naiad Press, the novels of Katherine V. Forrest and Sarah Dreher, genre fiction, 'easy reads.' It seems to mean specifically, and virtually exclusively, pulp fiction and does not appear to include many of the so-called lesbian classics such Radclyffe Hall's *The Well of Loneliness* or the writings of Jeanette Winterson, for example. For these you have to go to the main 'Fiction A-Z' section. Such placement effects a dispersal of lesbian writing which simultaneously mainstreams and obliterates lesbian writing. A reader without specific knowledge of what she is looking for might be inclined to go to the 'Lesbian Writing' section, thus missing out on the texts that have (been) migrated to the main 'Fiction A-Z' section. The lesbian reader is thus no longer offered the full range of lesbian writing now in print but only a particular set thereof. If she has no direct knowledge of the other texts, she (like all other readers) may come across other lesbian writing in mainstream bookshop sections or she may not. This new mainstreaming of lesbian writing and its dispersal does not facilitate the search of lesbian readers for lesbian work. It is a means of invisibilizing lesbian writing and it newly contains the amount of space given over to what is specifically termed lesbian writing. In the 1990s lesbian book space is thus contracting rather than expanding in a context where the rise of lesbian studies and the increasing proliferation of lesbian texts should mean expansion. This means, *inter alia*, that there exists now a kind of dispersal of lesbian writing in the context of its display in some mainstream bookshops which impacts on how it is available.

'I WAS NEVER A LITTLE GIRL.
I CAME OUT OF THE WOMB QUEER.'

This assertion, 'I was never a little girl. I came out of the womb queer' (18) is one of several which frames the depiction of Joe Carstairs in Kate Summerscale's biography of her. Carstairs was a woman who 'had been famous in the 1920s': 'Always dressed in men's clothes, she had raced for Britain and established herself as the fastest woman on water. In 1934 she all but vanished when she left England to become ruler of the Bahamian island of Whale Cay . . . ' (1-2). In Summerscale's biography Carstairs epitomizes a certain kind of lesbian idea/l of the modernist period, inhabiting a masculinized role from a position of wealth and privilege which allows her to take the risks and liberties 'ordinary' women or lesbians could and can only dream of.

What interests me, however, is not so much Carstairs' extraordinary history but the way in which her life is represented in Summerscale's biography. The biographer, it has to be remembered, makes choices about how to present her subject.

Summerscale made, it seems, a considered decision to create a biography which was 'not a book about lesbianism' because, as she puts it, 'Joe Carstairs was too singular and strange to be representative of anything other than herself' (6). This celebration of individualism,[7] which is interestingly pursued throughout the construction of the biography, at once points to and obliterates the notion of Carstairs as lesbian on the basis that Carstairs is beyond anything but self-representation and that she is in a sense stranger, even, than lesbians. Lesbians here function as a domesticated category which Carstairs exceeds in her self-sameness, itself beyond comparison. In Summerscale's account, this excess of self is linked to the idea that 'the principle by which [Carstairs] defined herself was male' (6). Throughout the biography Carstairs' assumed masculinity[8] is foregrounded. Comments such as 'years later, her niece reflected that "she should have been a boy"' (45) abound. This assumed masculinity is underscored by how Carstairs' relations with other people are depicted. Gestures towards promiscuity (her display of 120 photos of girlfriends; p. 218) and a seeming inability to commit herself to one person; her emotional investment in objects rather than in people;[9] her love of machines (predominantly boats); her financial quasi-patriarchal support of other people as a function of a certain kind of loyalty on her part; her tyrannical, despotic, authoritarian rule of her island and its people;[10] her cruelty and sadism towards others; her nasty pranks;[11] her continuous attempt to be in control[12]–all suggest the image of an autocratic patriarchal figure.[13] Tellingly, Summerscale writes: 'her perpetual supply of money robbed her of the opportunity to be–as her maternal grandfather had been, and as she longed to be–a self-made man' (9). Summerscale neatly displaces Carstairs' inability to fulfil a particular masculine role, that of the 'self-made man' from Carstairs' anatomy to her property, suggesting by implication that without an unearned income Carstairs might, indeed, have become a 'self-made *man*.' She ignores the fact that Carstairs was *a woman* and, as far as the biography indicates, never, for example, contemplated or undertook a sex-change operation.[14] In other words, physically Carstairs remained a woman all her life despite having enough money, for instance, to have such an operation should she have wished to do so. In Summerscale's account of Carstairs' life, however, the body and hence the anatomically material, is conveniently obliterated to create a person who is ontologically constructed to be that which she is not, a man, through the representation of a queer enactment of quasi-masculine roles. This enactment is reinforced through a vocabulary of the performative: in Paris she '[learns] to live like a man' (35). According to Summerscale,

> confusion of status appealed to Joe. She was a woman in the guise of a man . . . such ambiguities not only played to her sense of theatre, they were also tools to disconcert and outwit. (59-60)

Simultaneously, Summerscale's representation of Carstairs' assumed masculinity is undercut or repositioned by her assertion that Carstairs 'loved to dress up as a woman' (143). All Carstairs' dressing, whether as man or as woman, is in Summerscale's view performative. In this sense Carstairs is constructed as queer.[15] However, her queerness is one of appearance rather than of sexual practice. Discussion of the latter is avoided in the biography other than in terms of a fleeting reference to Carstairs' competent performance (*sic*) in bed–a boast attributed directly to her and reminiscent of male boasts of sexual prowess.

Repeated references are made to Carstairs being mistaken as a male.[16] However, it is also clear that Carstairs delighted in such mistakes and retold them with great glee. The significance of this retelling depends on the teller's and the audience's appreciation of the discrepancy between what is perceived and what is real. The delight is in the unmasking, in the mistake, not in the disguise or its letdown. Carstairs in this sense never seems to have wanted to be a man in the ways that Summerscale's biography implies; rather, Carstairs enjoyed the performance of diverse gender roles but from a position which did not evacuate her status as a woman. Summerscale never investigates what it might mean for a woman to enact masculine roles but without wanting to be a man–her early refusal to construct a text about lesbianism and supposedly instead, in keeping with the conventional idea of biography as being about a unique and extraordinary individual (as opposed to a type), to cast Carstairs as singular, enables Summerscale to elide the issue of Carstairs as a lesbian. Carstairs is instead effectively re-patriated. Both geographically (through Prospero-like becoming a 'patriarch' on her very own island) and ontologically, she is situated in a masculinized framework which refuses the fact that she was both a woman and a lesbian. One cannot but have sympathy with Wolfe and Penelope's position here when they argue that 'the existence of real Lesbians has been denied, once again, this time by those theorists and practitioners who would regard Lesbians as mere discourse constructs, the product of textuality, undetermined by sexuality' (5). This is precisely the image of Carstairs which emerges from Summerscale's biography. It is reinforced through the ways in which Summerscale utilizes textual analogies to interpret her presentation of Carstairs' assumed masculinity.

Summerscale constructs an intertextual relation between the biography and these texts. She thus moves Carstairs from the realm of material reality into one of textuality. The analogies drawn encompass references to J.M. Barrie's *Peter Pan*,[17] Virginia Woolf's *Orlando*, Djuna Barnes' *Nightwood*, and Arthur Ransome's *Swallows and Amazons*. What these texts share is a preoccupation with theatricality, performance, dressing up and disguise. Such queerness, in the contemporary sense of the word, enhances Summerscale's perception of Carstairs as someone quite literally 'out of this world.' Summerscale details a story which Carstairs apparently wanted to have her biography begun with: 'Her genesis, by this account, was of her own making: she was not born of human flesh but of her own will, and sprang forth fully formed, a creature of her desire' (8). Such self-fashioning, *sui generis*, ignores the reality of the contexts in which creation takes place. Its anti-originary stance and suggestion of an arrival *ex nihilo*, close to many myths of masculinity such as those of the 'self-made man,' the 'Romantic genius,' etc., feeds into a queer cultural mythology but denies the interconnections necessary to sustain any material (as opposed to textual?) reality. As Halberstam writes:

> The postmodern lesbian body as visualized by recent film and video, as theorized by queer theory, and as constructed by state of the art cosmetic technology breaks with a homo-hetero sexual binary and remakes gender as not simply performance but also as fiction. (210)

This is not always and entirely the case. As regards Carstairs' biography, there is no body to speak of. Gender is certainly re-made as a fiction but a fiction with a very particular slant. Summerscale re-uses Carstairs' 'genesis' story later in the biography when she establishes a link to Greek mythology: 'Like the armoured goddess Athena, who emerged fully formed from Zeus' head, both Dolly [Wilde] and Joe strove to give the impression of being invented rather than born' (33). The invention here is one based on male procreation, a further re-patriation of Carstairs. The slant, in other words, is towards the re-patriation of the lesbian, towards situating her within a patriarchal framework. As I shall detail below, a similar scenario is presented in Winterson's *Gut Symmetries*.

This repatriation denies, in the instance of the biography, Carstairs as a woman and a lesbian. The texts Summerscale activates on Carstairs' behalf serve to reinforce Summerscale's view that Carstairs 'seemed to believe that masculinity and youth were powerfully linked, that by casting off her femininity she might also cast off her mortality. She would try to restore the spent manhood of the Great War in her own person' (40). The kind of masculinity evoked in the biography is that of 'the boy who would not grow up,' epitomized in Carstairs' doll Lord Tod Wadley, described by Summerscale as Carstairs' 'male *alter ego*' (34). The opening image of the biography is of an elegantly dressed woman–the closing images are of the doll. Both are images, of course, but their sequencing suggests a transformation from life into death, from a sexually identifiable being into the sexually unclassifiable which mirrors the curious absence, in this biography, of any sense of the daily life which Carstairs, the woman who loved women, lived with her lovers and friends. The analogy Summerscale sets up with *Peter Pan* enables the presentation, to use Marjorie Garber's words, of 'a regendered, not-quite-degendered alternative persona who can have adventures, fight pirates, smoke pipes, and cavort with redskins' (168).

Garber also details the ways in which the effect of women wearing men's clothing, as evidenced in 'self-help books,' can create the image of a boy rather than a man. She quotes one such text which states:

> The 'imitation man look' does not refer to looking tough or masculine. The effect is more like that of a small boy who dresses up in his father's clothing. He looks cute, not authoritative . . . The same thing applies to women. (41)

Summerscale utilizes similar views in her analysis of Carstairs' life in that she focuses on the notion of Carstairs as an imitation boy, doubly imitating since she herself dressed like a boy[18] and had as her alter ego a male doll. Summerscale writes:

> By dressing as a man, it seemed, a woman could elude the constraints both of gender and of age. As she slipped on her costume she slipped off her maturity, and the public saw her not as sexually doubled but as unsexed. (89)

Through casting Carstairs as a boy and coupling her with the boy doll Summerscale effectively desexes Carstairs by making her into a figure who inhabited and was expressive of a particular kind of prepubescent fantasy. She quotes Djuna Barnes in support of this position: 'The doll and the immature have something right about them, the doll because it resembles but does not contain life, and the third sex because it contains life but resembles the doll' (Summerscale 81). Carstairs is transmuted from materiality into textuality, a move which re-patriates her within a sexual economy which denies lesbians a lived reality. As Garber puts it in her discussion of *Peter Pan*: 'This discontinuity, oddly, produces not consternation but reassurance. Love for–or cathexis onto–a 'boy' turns out to be love for or cathexis onto a woman, after all' (175). The reassurance, one assumes, is for a heterosexual audience. The boy disguise, according to this reading, unmasks Carstairs as a woman, thus effacing her assumption of a masculine position and reinstating the patriarchal economy. Summerscale asserts: 'For all her sexual exploits, Joe seemed to hanker after a sexless, pre-pubescent kingdom. In her fantasy land, there was no breeding, only self-invention' (190). Summerscale does not engage with the fact that the association of sex with breeding points to heterosex rather than lesbian relations. She systematically ignores that difference.

The reinstatement of a patriarchal economy at the end of Carstairs' life is reinforced by the fact that when Summerscale was first notified of her death, she as well as all others at the *Telegraph* obituary desk had never heard of the woman and that Whale Cay, Carstairs' island, is reported as having fallen into disrepair: 'I had merely glimpsed the ruins of the kingdom Joe had built. As she had predicted, without her the island had returned to jungle' (6). The absence of a lasting impact, as mapped by Summerscale, allows for the construction of Carstairs as a fantasy figure almost, as one who had no material reality. This is reinforced through the association of Carstairs with timelessness: 'Joe stayed young by forgetting the past, and with it the future' (186). The idea of living in and for the present is reiterated again and again, fixing Carstairs in an ahistorical space which acts as a time capsule, insulating her from the lesbian community of which she was a part, lesbian traditions within which she operated and re-patriating her through extrusion. Carstairs' insertion into a masculine economy is thus assured. In different ways, a similar process can be observed in Winterson's *Gut Symmetries*.

THE DRAMA OF OUR BEGINNING

When Jeanette Winterson first shot to fame with her novel *Oranges Are Not the Only Fruit* (1985), queer had not yet reached British shores and lesbian identity seemed less fluid than it has become since. In *Oranges* Winterson constructs a world in which lines are clearly drawn, women and men are infinitely and unproblematically different, and lesbian identity is something to be found and retained as life for life. Notwithstanding the assertion:

> that is the way with stories; we make them what we will. It's a way of explaining the universe while leaving the universe unexplained . . . Everyone who tells a story tells it differently, just to remind us that everybody sees it differently (93)

there is a clear sense in *Oranges* that some stories have more 'truth' value than others. The central character's lesbian identity is found and embraced without reservation though not without struggle: 'I would cross seas and suffer sunstroke and give away all I have, *but not for a man*, because they want to be the destroyer and never the destroyed. That is why they are unfit for romantic love' (170; emphasis added). As Laura Doan writes: 'The problem, as Jeanette sees it, stems not from her exquisite longings for women, but from others' inability to recognize and acknowledge the loveliness of sexual love shared between women' ('Jeanette . . . ,' 137). The certainty which informs the protagonist's choice of a lesbian identity operates within a structure which recognizes binary divisions between women and men and in which the assumption of a 'true' lesbian identity is permanent. But, as Doan states:

> Winterson clearly presents lesbianism as the only viable and intelligible alternative for Jeanette; yet, on a fundamental level, Winterson remains (albeit unwittingly) in the realm of parody, of imitation, in the unproblematic reversal of binary terms–a strategy that privileges the status of the lesbian over that of the heterosexual but doesn't facilitate an ongoing critique of compulsory heterosexuality or patriarchal control. (146)

That was in the 1980s. Since then Winterson's writing has undergone many changes.[19] The situation in *Gut Symmetries* (1997), her most recent novel, is very different from *Oranges*. No longer is the protagonist a lesbian, just waiting to find her identity. The issues which concern Winterson and which to some degree were summarized in the quotation from Doan cited above still remain, however, cast in quasi-essentialist terms:

> It may be that here in our provisional world of dualities and oppositional pairs: black/white, good/evil, male/female, conscious/unconscious, Heaven/Hell, predatory/prey, we compulsively act out the drama of our beginning, when what was whole, halved, and seeks again its wholeness. (*Gut Symmetries* 5)

The question, if one accepts all the premisses presented here (and it has to be understood that these binarisms are conventionally viewed as representing a male world view), is what is the drama of our beginning. I shall return to this point.

The storyline of *Gut Symmetries* concerns a woman who falls in love with a married man and is then seduced by his wife. The three attempt to come to terms with their situation through temporarily sharing each other but this triangle is doomed as the man's jealousies and the women's interest in each other call for a refiguration which ultimately ends with the man being extruded and the women uniting. At the beginning of the novel the identity of Alluvia Fairfax as either heterosexual or gay is not engaged with. Her falling in love with Jove, a man, seems to cast her as heterosexual but this is undercut when the text states: 'I said there was a love affair. In fact there are two. Male and female God created them and I fell in love with them both' (16). The novel then goes on to suggest that if, unlike the usual heterosexist notion of the 'eternal triangle' which works because 'Everyone knows the score, and the women are held in tension, away from one another' (16-17), wife and mistress meet, the result will be the expulsion of the male. The novel works away from an idea of lesbian types to create a scenario in which the relationship between wife and mistress is presented as unexpected to them both. But it does not result in an investigation of what lesbian identity means. Rather, underlying the novel is the notion of a 'human condition' which exists outside the categories in which we conventionally operate such as female and male, or homosexual and heterosexual:

> The human condition seems to be one of waiting to be rescued. Will it be you? Will it be today? . . . What are my chances of choosing well? We court each other in elaborate masks and ballgowns. I clothe myself in conversation, money, wit. Whatever will win you, I become. I disguise myself as your rescuer so that you will be mine. (177)

This human condition, couched in the postmodern terms of masquerade, disguise and performance, and utilizing pronouns ('I'; 'we'; 'you') which are devoid of, or conceal, the sexual identities of those referred to, supersedes notions of individual identity, and identity within the fixed frames of time, class, gender, geography that have become the preoccupation of so much feminist and lesbian feminist writing. This novel is in this sense humanist, not lesbian. Interestingly, and like the Carstairs biography as well as like Duncker's novel to be discussed below, *Gut Symmetries* takes place on boats, is preoccupied with journeys, water, change and beginnings. These resist the closing, fixing narratives which take categories such as class or geography as determining structures. But they also create a sense of removal from such embeddedness, which then reinforces the primacy of fantasy and desire in the stories and in a sense, denies any rootedness in material reality. As in *Oranges*, so is Winterson in *Gut Symmetries* preoccupied with the issues of story-telling, fantasy and reality, and the relationship between past and present: 'It is just as likely that as I invent what I want to say, you will invent what you want to hear. Some story we must have' (25). This undermining of certainty is part of the postmodern project of framing insecurity. But simultaneously the story presents one narrative as more resistant to uncertainty than another.

Alluvia thinks of Jove that 'he made me fully human. I did not think of us as one man and his dog' (104). However, the seemingly god-like qualities embodied in Jove's name and in his ability, apparently, to make her fully human, are denied in the second sentence which already carries with it the recognition of a problematic power structure as operating within their relationship. Its doom seems pre-determined. A similar problem is observed in Alluvia's parents' generation: '[My mother] completed [my father]. She manifested him at another level. He absorbed her while she failed to absorb him. This was so normal that nobody noticed it. At least not until much later, when things began to change' (59). The reality of Alluvia's parents' relation-ship is mapped onto Greco-Christian myths which replay the idea of woman's dependency on, and inferiority to, men. Winterson writes: 'Hus-band and wife. Man and rib. What could be more normal than that? And now they were having a baby. That is, my mother was bearing my father's child. It was different when my sisters were born but I was Athene. Athene born fully formed from the head of Zeus' (59). Here is the repetition of the Greek myth already found in Summerscale's representation of Carstairs and referred to above. But Winterson, in contrast to Summerscale, produces a meta-dis-course which links this myth to other patriarchal structures: 'Sex and procre-ation easily fit in with the body's plans for Empire: it wants to extend its territory, needs to reproduce itself. It resists invasion. Love the invader com-promises the self's autonomy. Love the rescuer is the hand held out across the uncrossable sea' (26). Here the body is constructed as an agent in its own right, assailed only by love. Alluvia's love for Stella, Jove's wife, leads her not only to find and rescue Stella when she and Jove have been lost at sea but that love also outlasts the relationship between Jove and Alluvia and between Stella and Jove. This, however, is not constructed as the apotheosis of lesbian love. The word 'lesbian' is never mentioned in the text. While Stella has decided to divorce Jove, he is already 'surrounded by Italian nurses listening to his extraordinary story of survival' (215). The wife who leaves him is already replaced by other females occupying the traditional feminine roles of carer and attention-giver. Alluvia and Stella remain together. So is this the end of the drama of our beginning?

If one is to understand that beginning as the separation of mother from child, then the search for wholeness is the search to be reunited with a woman–for both women and men. In that sense the female as the object of everybody's desire is celebrated in this novel. Winterson asks: 'Can anybody deny that we are haunted? What is it that crouches under the myths we have made? Always the physical presence of something splitting off' (4). In the course of the novel this physical presence becomes embodied in Alluvia for Stella and Stella for Alluvia. When Stella and Jove are reported missing at sea Alluvia asks herself which one she would prefer to have remained alive if only one of them survived. From a dream in which she sees 'stars in an upturned hod, tipping out over me' (202) she wakes up crying, 'Stella! Stella!' (202). This scene is oddly reminiscent of other similar scenes in nineteenth-century fiction such as *Jane Eyre* where, in a moment of crisis, the protagonist has a vision in a dream of a maternally positioned face (i.e., looking down from above as into a baby's cot) and cries for the mother or a quasi-maternal female figure. It reinforces the idea of the quest for, support by, and alignment with an unconscious feminine. In that sense Winterson continues the representation of the world as conventionally binary in the terms suggested in Doan's reading of her work. It accounts for the re-patriation of which her female characters are, in some respects, object. Even the meeting of Stella and Alluvia is constructed by Winterson as having been engineered by Jove who writes an anonymous letter to his wife telling her of his affair. In reflecting on this Jove thinks: 'Oddly, I never thought that they would really *do* anything, the sex was a surprise. I made the mistake of thinking that I could control the experiment. I won't make that mistake again. This time it nearly cost me my life' (193). He does not decide not to marry again or not to have any more affairs but simply to try and exercise better control. The impossibility of that is both demonstrated and reiterated throughout the novel. The novel's subversive impulse lies in precisely that assertion.

HALLUCINATING MASCULINITY

Patricia Duncker's novel *Hallucinating Foucault* (1996) is another tale of a quest, the quest of a male PhD student for the gay French writer on whose work he is doing his thesis. The PhD student is picked up by a female fellow researcher who thinks that one should love the object of one's research and that 'if you love someone, you know where they are, what has happened to them. You put yourself at risk to save them if you can' (24). As the narrator finds out that the object of his study is incarcerated in an asylum for the mentally ill, he, goaded by his girlfriend, decides to find the writer and free him from his imprisonment. This he does. He falls in love with the writer, Paul Michel, and they have a summer of love before Michel kills himself, devastating the narrator.

At the centre of this novel then is an affair between two men[20] but what prompts this affair is a woman–a woman who, herself the child of a gay father, loves Michel whom she met when she was a child. In a story critical to this text Michel, who to all intents and purposes has always been gay, tells the narrator about this meeting and about the fact that he mistook the girl, with whom he too fell in love, for a young boy. Over a long period of time Michel thought of the girl as a boy: 'The moment of reversal, of revelation if you like, came that night on the steps of the hotel . . . His ambiguity suddenly broke over me with all the force of the sea against the great rocks. I had not mistaken the nature of this child. But I had certainly been deceived in her sex' (161). It is during that evening when Michel discovers her 'true' sex that she says to him: 'If you love someone–you know where they are and what has happened to them. And you put yourself at risk to save them if you can. If you get into trouble I promise that I'll come to save you' (162). This is the imperative she subsequently imposes on the narrator whom she effectively–as he belatedly realizes–sends to save Michel.

In Michel's narrative of his encounter with 'the boy' cited above, a distinction is made between 'nature' and 'sex.' The former here refers to 'the boy's' personality; the latter to his sexual identity about which Michel is mistaken. In *Gut Symmetries*, too, a distinction is made between love and sex; Alluvia states: '[Jove] had one virtue; he did not call sex, love' (205). Sex and love are differentiated, with the latter being cast in a humanist universalizing form which exists outside sexual frameworks. The same is also almost true of Summerscale's biography of Carstairs where sex and being (rather than love) are separated out so that the former is represented as insignificant in relation to the latter. In Duncker's novel, the fact that the narrator falls in love with a man when he has had no previous homosexual experiences may be viewed as evidence of–to use a cliché–the power of love. Again, as in Winterson's text, there is no sense that the narrator becomes gay as a consequence of this encounter or that he finds his 'true' self or sexual identity as a consequence of this relationship. The relationship seems more powerful than that with his fellow PhD student, the girl–they drift apart after Michel's death.

Within the text, the girl occupies at once a marginal and a central role; she is the prime mover behind the key actions which take place. The relationship between the narrator and Michel is framed by her relationship with the narrator. She is described as solitary. As in Summerscale's and Winterson's texts, here too we find a reference to the Athene myth. The girl, never identified by name, has two fathers: her biological one, the gay man, and the man whom her mother lived with subsequently. When the narrator explains that she has two fathers to his flatmate, the latter says, 'I suppose one of them is Zeus' (19). Due to her scholarly interests she is continuously described as 'the Germanist'; as in her 'real' life her closest relationships seem to be with gay men, so her intellectual interests are focused on two male writers, Goethe and Schiller, who enjoyed a close relationship.

One might ask why I write about this last novel at all within the context of discussing lesbian writing since the only significant female character seems heterosexual and embedded in what appears to be a male homoerotic culture. But this, in a sense, is precisely my point: we see emerging, in the context of lesbian writing, a phenomenon which I can only describe as the re-patriation of the lesbian, the subsumption of the female character in a male world in which gender specificities have given way to a humanist notion of an idea of love or living which is seemingly independent of the particularities of bodies. In a striking piece in *Sinuosities* (1996) Jeffner Allen analyses the impact of the postmodern on writing by women. She begins by positing two tales of the positioning of women as difference, one 'the tale of the amazon,' the other 'the tale of the feminine, the lesbian, and the feminist.' Within the former tale, the amazon lives far away and is wealthy but elusive. This is rather reminiscent of the way in which Summerscale casts Carstairs and is also somewhat like Stella in Winterson's *Gut Symmetries*. This version of woman as other, according to Allen, has given way to the second tale:

> The 'Tale of the Feminine, the Lesbian, and the Feminist' is a postmodern tale in which the amazon, a transcendental ideal of modernity, is split and recast. The 'Tale of the Amazon' is displaced by this new romance of the margins, a romance that entails a twofold discipline of woman as difference: the domestication of difference, represented as 'the feminine,' and the outright dismissal of difference which would take the form of the 'lesbian' or 'the feminist,' she who would defy the postmodern power of representation. (95-6)

This romance of the margin, which Allen suggests is characteristic of the postmodern, creates a scenario where 'difference, the harbinger of postmodernity, vanish[es] in the indifference of the text' (98). Something like that, I would suggest, happens in the three texts I have discussed. The indifference in question though is not gender-neutral, as the term 'indifference' might indicate, but powerfully gendered within the conventions of masculinity. The romance, as in *Hallucinating Foucault*, is between men–woman has retreated into a textuality which denies her. This problematic, the evacuation of both women and lesbians in one strand of current women's writing, needs to be addressed because

> However, unless a narrative recognizes women as individuals who inhabit distinctive histories, unless a narrative moves with a certain intimacy and proximity to tangible events, unless a narrative questions the privilege of its own discursive requirements, that narrative may make little difference for women's lives. (Allen 98)

NOTES

1. 'The Lesbian' is here deliberately used in a grammatically ambiguous fashion to denote both a substantive and an adjectival noun.

2. In the UK many would date the emergence of queer and postmodernism in lesbian criticism from the publication of Judith Butler's *Gender Trouble* (London: Routledge, 1990). This does not mean that 'queer' tendencies could not be discerned in lesbian writing (theoretical and other) before that date.

3. A good example of this is Sidney Abbott and Barbara Love's *Sappho was a Right-On Woman* (1972; rpt. New York: Stein and Day, 1985) which details, *inter alia*, the fraught relationship between lesbian and heterosexual women in the US feminist movement.

4. This does not detract from debates carried on mainly outside the UK, and epitomized by the works of Simone de Beauvoir and Monique Wittig, for example, about questions of 'woman' as a construct within heteropatriarchy.

5. One key and typical text here is bell hooks' *Feminist Theory: From Margin to Center* (Boston: South End Press, 1984).

6. There have been a number of texts such as Lee Lynch's 'Cruising the Libraries' which suggest that some women come to their sense of lesbian identity via texts in which lesbians are portrayed.

7. In *Subjectivity, Identity, and the Body* (Bloomington: Indiana UP, 1993) Sidonie Smith speaks of 'normative (masculine) individuality' (3) to describe the celebration of individualism within the malestream tradition of writing (auto)biography.

8. I use the word 'assumed' to denote both the idea of performance (as in: assuming a role) and to suggest an assumption on Summerscale's part that the most appropriate way to deal with Carstairs as a subject is to cast her in terms of an underlying masculinity.

9. Summerscale writes, for example: 'Joe could now afford to marry her two loves–machines and the sea. In 1925 she used her new riches to commission the best motorboat money could buy' (63). The vocabulary of heterosexist patriarchy, which conjoins ownership of objects with ownership of women, as indexed in the word 'marry,' is striking and deliberate.

10. There are interesting parallels in this representation to Sarah Scott's *Millennium Hall* (1762; rpt. London: Virago, 1986), perhaps the first novel in English centering on a utopian world governed by females.

11. See, for instance, pp. 192-3, 206.

12. Quasi-reminiscent of Coriolanus' line 'I banish you' to Rome in Shakespeare's *The Tragedy of Coriolanus*, Summerscale has Carstairs, who was sent to boarding-school in America supposedly because of cruelty to her half-siblings, take the position: 'her banishment, she tried to suggest, was not a mark of her powerlessness but of her power . . . In a one-page autobiography she compiled in her nineties, she effected this inversion neatly with a single phrase: "Left family aged 11"' (21).

13. According to Summerscale, Carstairs 'modelled herself on a colonial ruler. The persona she constructed drew on old-fashioned models of manhood: she stood for Empire, Britishness, cleanliness, hard work, physical bravery, moral fibre' (178).

14. I do not wish to suggest that a sex-change operation is the only way a woman can be(come) a man. Kate Bornstein's *Gender Outlaw* (London: Routledge, 1994) provides an interesting account of the (im)possibilities of achieving gender euphoria through a sex change.

15. In a useful chapter, Judith Halberstam describes the range of queer identities now available in culture: 'guys with pussies, dykes with dicks, queer butches, aggressive femmes, F2Ms, lesbians who like men, daddy boys, gender queens, drag kings, pomo afro homos, bulldaggers, women who fuck boys, women who fuck like boys, dyke mommies, transsexual lesbians, male lesbians' (212). Significantly, these are based on sexual practice rather than on appearance. However, Summerscale avoids all discussion of sexual practice in her depiction of Carstairs.

16. See, for instance, pp. 23, 24, 43, 71.

17. In an interesting essay Marjorie Garber produces a reading of *Peter Pan* which suggests that Peter Pan as a construct is a woman rather than a man, hence the congruity between that figure and him being played predominantly by women.

18. Repeated references are made to Carstairs having looked like a boy (e.g., pp. 81, 89, 90).

19. Laura Doan's essay 'Jeanette Winterson's Sexing the Postmodern' provides a good analysis of this.

20. The novel very self-consciously constructs another relationship as the simultaneous centre of the text–that between reader and writer. However, I shall not pursue this further here.

WORKS CITED

Allen, Jeffner. 1996. *Sinuosities: Lesbian poetic politics*. Bloomington: Indiana University Press.

Doan, Laura, ed. 1994. *The lesbian postmodern*. New York: Columbia University Press.

_____. 1994. Jeanette Winterson's sexing the postmodern. In Laura Doan, ed. *The lesbian postmodern*. New York: Columbia UP. 137-55.

Duncker, Patricia. 1996. *Hallucinating Foucault*. London: Picador.

Fuss, Diana. 1990. *Essentially speaking: Feminism, nature and difference*. London: Routledge.

Garber, Marjorie. 1992. *Vested interests: Cross-dressing and cultural anxiety*. London: Routledge.

Halberstam, Judith. 1994. F2M: The making of female masculinity. In Laura Doan, ed. *The lesbian postmodern*. New York: Columbia University Press. 210-28.

Lynch, Lee. 1990. Cruising the libraries. In Jay, Karla and Joanne Glasgow, eds. *Lesbian texts and contexts*. New York: New York University Press. 39-48.

Radicalesbians. 1970. The Woman identified woman. Rpt. in *For lesbians only: A separatist anthology*. Eds. Sarah Lucia Hoagland and Julia Penelope. London: Onlywomen Press, 1988.

Rich, Adrienne. 1980. Compulsory heterosexuality and lesbian existence. Rpt. in *Blood, bread and poetry: Selected prose 1979-1985*. London: Virago, 1986. 23-75.

Stimpson, Catherine R. 1981. Zero degree deviancy: The lesbian novel in English. Rpt. in *Where the meanings are: Feminism and cultural spaces*, London: Routledge, 1989. 97-110.

Summerscale, Kay. 1997. *The queen of Whale Cay*. London: Fourth Estate.

Winterson, Jeanette. 1997. *Gut symmetries*. London: Granta.

_____. 1985. *Oranges are not the only fruit*. London: Pandora.

Wolfe, Susan J. and Julia Penelope, eds. 1993. *Sexual practice/textual theory: Lesbian cultural criticism*. Oxford: Blackwell.

The Intimate Distance of Desire:
June Jordan's Bisexual Inflections

AnaLouise Keating

SUMMARY. Through an exploration of June Jordan's poetry and prose, this essay questions contemporary definitions of bisexuality and lesbian writing, and attempts to enact a nonbinary bisexual reading praxis. I argue that Jordan employs several tactics–including ambivalently gendered pronouns, oscillations among apparently distinct categories of meaning, shifting referents, and performative speech acts–to resist restrictive identity politics. These bisexual inflections enable Jordan to replace conventional Enlightenment-based concepts of isolated, self-enclosed identities with open-ended models of identity formation that transform both herself and her readers. Moving between sameness and difference, Jordan's bisexual inflections destabilize the binary system structuring sexual, gender, and ethnic categories, creating an intersubjective matrix where new commonalities can arise. *[Article copies available for a fee from The Haworth Document Delivery Service: 1-800-342-9678. E-mail address: getinfo@haworthpressinc.com <Website: http:// www.haworthpressinc.com>]*

KEYWORDS. Bisexuality, Jordan, June, reader response criticism

AnaLouise Keating teaches at Aquinas College. Her book *Women Reading Women Writing: Self-Invention in Paula Gunn Allen, Gloria Anzaldúa, and Audre Lorde* (Temple, 1996) examines the revisionary techniques and the transformational epistemologies developed by these writers. She has also published on queer theory, feminist theory, gender issues, Latina/Chicana writers, and pedagogy.

Address correspondence to: AnaLouise Keating, 1607 Robinson Road SE, Grand Rapids, MI 49506.

Poetry appearing in this essay is taken from *Naming Our Destiny: New and Selected Poems* (Thunder's Mouth Press, 1989). © June Jordan. Used by permission.

[Haworth co-indexing entry note]: "The Intimate Distance of Desire: June Jordan's Bisexual Inflections." Keating, AnaLouise. Co-published simultaneously in *Journal of Lesbian Studies* (Harrington Park Press, an imprint of The Haworth Press, Inc.) Vol. 4, No. 2, 2000, pp. 81-93; and: *'Romancing the Margins'? Lesbian Writing in the 1990s* (ed: Gabriele Griffin) Harrington Park Press, an imprint of The Haworth Press, Inc., 2000, pp. 81-93. Single or multiple copies of this article are available for a fee from The Haworth Document Delivery Service [1-800-342-9678, 9:00 a.m. - 5:00 p.m. (EST). E-mail address: getinfo@ haworthpressinc.com].

These poems
they are things that I do
in the dark
reaching for you
whoever you are
and are you ready?

These words
they are stones in the water
running away

These skeletal lines
They are desperate arms for my longing and love.

I am a stranger
learning to worship the strangers
around me

whoever you are
whoever I may become.

June Jordan

In both her poetry and her prose, June Jordan enacts a complex process of interactional identity formation where self-change occurs only in the context of other people. Throughout her writing, Jordan uses her own self-naming process to illustrate the interrelational nature of individual and collective social change. Drawing connections between her personal experiences as a twentieth-century bisexual U.S. woman of Jamaican descent and the experiences of women from all ethnic backgrounds, colonized nations, gay men, and other oppressed groups, Jordan demonstrates that each person's self-determination entails recognizing and affirming both the commonalities and the differences between self and others. As she incorporates this mobile self-naming process into her poetry and prose, Jordan rejects restrictive notions of isolated, self-enclosed individual identities and creates intimate dialogues between herself and her readers. She invents an intersubjective, potentially transformational space that she invites her readers to share. Thus in the poem I have borrowed for my epigraph, Jordan employs ambiguous, shifting pronouns to generate new forms of identification and desire that break down without entirely erasing the boundaries between writer, readers, and the words on the page. Flesh becomes text (her poems are '*desperate arms for my longing and love*') as she infuses the desire for connection and transformation into her words, embodying them.

I begin with this poem because it offers me a map, a model for interacting with Jordan's complex self-naming process. She adopts an opening, questioning position that she invites her readers–invites me–to adopt. In the first stanza as her words become concrete acts reaching outward, towards her readers–towards *'you / whoever you are'*–I identify with this 'you' and accept Jordan's challenge to change. Her words–tangible yet elusive (like *'stones in the water / running away'*)–seduce me, draw me into the poem, invite me to re-examine my own subject position. As I read her words on the page, I become the stranger Jordan describes, and this process of becoming-stranger begins to transform me, compels me to reach out, so that I too begin *'learning to worship the strangers / around me.'* Yet this worship of strangers–strangers who include both Jordan and me–entails an openness and, by extension, a willingness to take risks. By concluding this poem with two open-ended questioning statements that shift from second person to first, Jordan interpellates her readers–interpellates me–into a transitional place, where identification and desire converge, partially merging while remaining in some ways distinct.

As she inscribes herself into the words on the page, Jordan creates a transformational space–an intimate distance of desire–between herself and her readers. More specifically, by identifying both herself and her readers as strangers, she mobilizes new constellations of sameness and difference that make the development of commonalities possible. It is these new constellations I describe as an intimate distance of desire–a transitional place where the acceptance of differences leads through transformation to new forms of connection. I borrow the phrase *intimate distance* from Jordan, where it indicates open-ended potential, a meeting point between self and other. As she explains in her essay on Walt Whitman, 'the intimate distance between the poet and the reader is a distance that assumes that there is everything important, between them, to be shared' ('People's Poetry' 8). This shared space of difference acknowledges the separation between writer and reader yet redefines this potentially dualistic relation, creating a place where commonalities can arise. Inscribing this shared space of difference into her words, Jordan invites her readers to do so as well.

For Jordan, this intimate distance of desire opens up a bisexualized, intersubjective matrix–a nonspecific but gendered, sexualized space where new modes of identity can occur. Thus in the poem I began with she reaches out, through the darkness, toward her readers, reaches with *'longing and love,'* towards you–*'whoever you are.'* By oscillating between self and other, she enacts a bisexual inflection–an ethical, highly erotic vision that deploys mobile configurations of identification and desire to challenge restrictive labeling. These oscillations between sameness and difference (between 'I' and 'you') destabilize the binary system structuring sexual, gender, and ethnic categories, thus creating a space where alterations in consciousness and different modes of desire (can) occur.

But why describe this ethical vision and the shifting inflections Jordan employs as 'bisexual'? After all, in the poem I have adopted for my epigraph gender seems to be entirely irrelevant; the 'I' and the 'you' she refers to are unmarked by gender, sex, ethnicity, or any other system of difference. Moreover, other theorists who most definitely do not identify as bisexual express similar desires but use different terms. (Take, for example, Elizabeth Meese's (sem)erotics and lesbian:writing, or Gloria Anzaldúa's new mestiza queers: two theories of boundary-crossing invented by self-identified lesbian writers.) Is the bisexual inflection I find in Jordan's words simply the product of my own (bisexual) desires, reinforced by Jordan's open affirmation of *her* bisexual identity? Would other readers, who tell different stories about their lives, read Jordan's words differently? The concept of bisexuality is, itself, highly problematic–constantly evoked only to be ignored, erased, or in other ways dismissed as too ambivalent, elusive, and transitional to matter.[1] So why use the term 'bisexual'?

At this point, so many directions open up, many paths I could take in this essay: should I define and justify my use of the phrase bisexual inflections? (I could explain the ethical dimensions in the ambivalently gendered pronouns these inflections deploy.) Or should I continue with this personalized, self-reflective style of writing and tell you about my particular bisexual interactions with Jordan's poetry and prose? (I could narrate my personal experiences and explain how Jordan's self-declared bisexual politics speaks to my own, previously inarticulated desires and offered me a position–shifting, slippery, and elusive though it is–from which to think, speak, act, and love.) Or should I adopt a more scholarly approach? (I could begin by exploring Jordan's shifting identifications, draw on theoretical interpretations of bisexuality as an epistemological position, and argue that Jordan enacts an alternate mode of thinking that deconstructs binary oppositions from within.)

Perhaps, in the conclusion, I will return to my own story and to the questions I have raised concerning the (in)effectiveness of bisexual labels. Or perhaps I won't. But first I want to explore the transformational ambiguously gendered, multiply sexualized possibilities opened up by the intersubjective matrix Jordan's bisexual inflections create. More precisely, I want to examine the ways in which Jordan uses language to break down conventional boundaries between subject/object, writer/reader(s), and the material/psychic dimensions of writing and life. As she inscribes her self, her desires, and the intimate events from her life into her work, Jordan goes beyond dyadic relationships between 'me' and the words 'I' write to encompass 'you' as well–you reading me as I read Jordan. Together we (the at-least-three of us) enter into an intersubjective space, transformed by Jordan's textualized self-inscriptions.

As she writes her self, her desires, and the intimate events from her life into her work, Jordan develops an intricate interplay between sameness and difference that blurs the boundaries between writer, reader, and text. She challenges her readers–no matter how we identify, whether as male, female, heterosexual, homosexual, bisexual, lesbian, gay, black, white, or brown–to reexamine our own subject positions. Take, for example, 'A Short Note to My Very Critical Friends and Well-Beloved Comrades' where she enacts a mobile self-naming process that challenges restrictive labeling. After defiantly outlining the numerous ways her well-meaning friends and comrades have tried unsuccessfully to classify her according to color, sexuality, age, and ideology, Jordan confidently reaffirms her ability to define herself as she sees fit:

> Make up your mind! They said. Are you militant
> or sweet? Are you vegetarian or meat? Are you straight
> or are you gay?
>
> And I said, Hey! It's not about *my* mind. (*Naming* 98)

The implications of this final line are clear. Rejecting restrictive labels and the binary forms of thinking they so often entail, Jordan throws the responsibility back on her well-meaning questioners: they must reexamine their own desire for fixed labels and static categories of identity. These lines have a similar impact on readers; as Peter Erickson explains, 'Having aroused our irritation, the poem dares us to examine it, to probe our discomfort at being unable to pin down the poet's identity' (222). (What about you, reader: Do you agree with Erickson's statement? Are you, too, irritated with Jordan's flippant refusal to situate and name herself?) As she oscillates between apparently distinct categories of meaning, Jordan disrupts the boundaries between fixed identity locations. By destabilizing her own subjectivity, she destabilizes her readers' as well. She replaces the conventional, Enlightenment-based belief in isolated, self-contained identities with open-ended models of identity formation.

In the above lines, it is the way Jordan depicts sexuality that intrigues me. To begin with, by associating the binary opposition between straight and gay with political styles ('Are you militant / or sweet?') and eating habits ('vegetarian or meat?')–two aspects of life that we shape and change according to our needs, circumstances, and desires–she implies that sexuality also involves a degree of choice. And, by refusing to identify as either straight or gay, she refuses the limited choices we are generally offered, exposing the limitations in binary modes of thinking. She calls into question the conflict model of sexual identity that posits an irremedial difference between homo-sexual and heterosexual identities. This conflict model erases the middle ground and denies the possibility of hybrid sexualities that combine yet exceed hetero and homosexuality. (But what might these possibilities be? Jordan leaves that to us–to you and me–to decide and live out for our selves.)

As she goes beyond specific gender and ethnic categories of meaning, without denying their temporary historic significance, Jordan redefines iden-tity as a constantly shifting internal process. As she asserts in 'Civil Wars,'

> Neither race nor gender provides the final definitions of jeopardy or refuge. The final risk or final safety lies within each one of us attuned to the messy and intricate and unending challenge of self-determination. I believe the ultimate power of all the people rests upon the individual ability to trust and to respect the authority of the truth of whatever it is that each of us feels, each of us means. (187)

In emphasizing the messy, intricate, unending nature of this self-naming process, Jordan replaces conventional identity politics–or the tendency to base political actions on restrictive definitions of gender-, ethnic-, or sexual-specific identity categories–with her own fluid politics of self-determination. She points to the possibility of new types of identification based on each individual's interests and desires. Her words invite readers–invite me and (perhaps) you–to establish different ways of connecting with others, shaped by the particular situations we enter into and the specific individuals with whom we interact.

This fluid, open-ended politics of self-determination plays an important role in the bisexual inflections I find in Jordan's words. As she writes herself and particular events from her life into her poetry and prose, she oscillates between apparently distinct identities and locations. She employs open-ended pronouns that extend her experience outward, inventing a space her readers can share–an intimate distance of desire.

Jordan's bisexual inflections move the reader–move this reader, move me (and, perhaps, you?)–into and beyond an erotics of physical, heterosexual or homosexual pleasure and stimulate a desire for different connections. At this point, however, I won't even try to describe the particular forms these new connections might take (for you); they must be invented and lived out by each reader. All I can say is that the fluid–yet gendered–oscillations between sameness and difference open up new grounds for interchange and (e)merg-ing desires.

Even love poems apparently addressed to male subjects–love poems pre-sumably coded 'straight'–incorporate these bisexual inflections. Thus in 'For Dave: 1976' Jordan briefly describes an afternoon of lovemaking between herself and another person named 'Dave,' a person I–and probably other readers as well–assume to be male. Yet this assumption is based solely on the title. There are no gender-specific markers in the text itself. Throughout this short poem Jordan employs ambiguous nongendered pronouns; nothing in her description definitively positions this afternoon lover as a man: there's 'the Army cap that spills your / hair below those clean-as-a-whistle ears nobody / knows how to blow so you hear them honest-to / God' and the '(red shirt / new shoes / the shower shining everywhere about you).' Unmarked by gendered labels, these references to 'you' are open to multiple interpretations. 'You' could be male or female, black, white, or any shade of brown; it could be me or you, reader. But to my mind, the important thing here is not the lover's gender but rather the intimate distance Jordan depicts between herself and 'you.' As in the poem I borrowed for my epigraph, she acknowledges the differences between 'me' and 'you' but uses the intimate distance this acknowledgment opens up to create new points of connection. Thus she concludes by stating

> And I accept again
> that there are simple ways of being joined
> to someone
> absolutely different from myself (*Naming* 30)

It's this acceptance of simple interconnections despite–or at times perhaps because of–tremendous differences that makes possible the new forms of identification and desire I read in Jordan's words. But as in the poem I used for my epigraph, Jordan does not tell us what these simple ways of being joined to someone absolutely different might be; she simply points to the possibility of new types of connection through difference but leaves the specific details for readers–for us–to imagine and (perhaps) to begin living out with the bodies we encounter.

Significantly, 'For Dave' is followed in *Naming Our Destiny* by 'Meta-Rhetoric,' a poem addressed to an unnamed but most likely female subject, a potential lover referred to only as 'you.' Again Jordan employs shifting referents to blur the boundaries between reader and writer, between 'my' body and 'yours': 'your mouth on my mouth / your breasts resting on my own.' Each time I read this poem, identifying both with the 'I' and the 'you,' I oscillate between subject positions (Is it my mouth on yours? yours on mine?). To be sure, these lines can be read as an expression of lesbian desire. (After all, both 'I' and 'you' have breasts.) To my mind, however, this lesbianized reading is too restrictive and simplifies the ambiguously gendered pronouns Jordan employs. Take, for example, the opening scene she describes between 'us':

> we sit apart
> apparently at opposite ends of a line

and I feel the distance
between my eyes
between my legs
a dry
dust topography of our separation (*Naming* 31)

Once again, Jordan opens up an intimate distance between herself and her reader, between 'me' and 'you.' However, by locating 'our separation' both within herself and between herself and 'you'–her potential lover–Jordan doubly embodies this intimate distance of desire, unsettling the binary opposition between self and other. As I identify both with the 'me' and the 'you' in Jordan's words, I too draw on my own memories of internal and external separation and experience the desire for connection through difference.

As in 'For Dave,' Jordan's oscillations between 'me' and 'you' indicate bisexual inflections that trigger new forms of identity and desire. And again, Jordan concludes by pointing to an intimate distance of desire between 'me' and 'you':

My hope is that our lives will declare
this meeting
open (*Naming* 32)

These lines defer closure, shifting responsibility partially onto the reader, onto me or (perhaps) onto you. We are invited to enter into this shared embodied space of difference. If we do so, we too experience this partially expressed, perhaps only partially speakable desire.

In both poems, then, Jordan's pronouns create scenes–interactions between 'me' and 'you'–that seem gendered yet move beyond specific categories of identity. Her words are performative and move (us) from the page, from the fixed categories in our minds, into new ways of thinking and acting. If, as Marjorie Garber suggests, 'language can function *as* a sexual act, not just as a way of naming one' (144, her emphasis), Jordan's bisexual inflections seduce readers–seduce me and (perhaps) you. No matter how we label ourselves–whether as male, female, heterosexual, homosexual, bisexual, lesbian, gay, brown, black, white, or any variation among these terms–Jordan invites us to enter into this intersubjective matrix and enact new, sexualized encounters that go beyond familiar self-definitions, beyond conventional interactions between writer, reader, and text. She develops flexible models of subject positioning that enable her to establish points of similarity and difference with readers of diverse backgrounds. In these new constellations of reading/desire, gender becomes far less important than the desire for connection, for alternate forms of communication.

Do I read these poems–one (apparently) addressed to a man and one (apparently) to a woman–as bisexual because I read myself–my erotic attractions and desires–as bisexual? Would other readers who tell different stories about their lives read these poems differently? Or, do these questions even matter? After all, one of the points I want to make in this essay is that identity categories and labels can become far too restrictive, preventing us from establishing commonalities and points of connection with people who seem very different from ourselves. All too often, the labels others impose upon us, as well as the names we select for ourselves, shape the ways we perceive others and the ways we interact. This name-driven mode of perception compels us to read a poem (ostensibly) written by a woman to a man as 'heterosexual.' And this name-driven perception compels us to read a poem (ostensibly) written by a woman to a woman as 'lesbian.'

By reading 'For Dave' and 'Meta-Rhetoric' against their apparent codings, I attempt to resist this label-driven perception.

INTERLUDE; OR, THE PROBLEMS WITH NAMING

To be sure, this theory of bisexual inflections I try to invent as I read and interact with Jordan's words could be dismissed as what some might call my own over-identification with this openly bisexual writer. Remember: I write these words about this self-identified bisexual woman poet 'as' a bisexual. But what does it mean to desire bisexually, or to identify myself as 'bisexual'? Am I simply telling you that I have had both women and men as my lovers? Does bisexuality imply desiring–physically hungering for (lusting after) both women and men and doing so (hungering, lusting, desiring) in both masculine and feminine fashion or terms? When I identify myself as bisexual am I telling you that I incorporate both masculine and feminine energies within myself? Yet which of these definitions cannot also be applied to many people who identify as 'lesbian,' 'gay,' or 'straight'? Yes, this word–'bisexual'–disturbs me. With its reference to two it can easily–no matter how inadvertently–reinforce binary thinking and useless, dualistic definitions of bisexual identity–two sexes in one body, two sexual desires–one for women, one for men. Is it possible to escape these multiple forms of duality? These questions have no easy answers. Perhaps they have no answers at all.

To make matters even more confusing, as I seek alternate definitions for this sometimes dualistic term, I am torn between my own conflicting desires–no, not my erotic attractions to women and men. Rather, I am split by my desire for a politics of visibility–an affirmation of this elusive, so often erased bisexual identity–and my desire to break the categories, to demonstrate the limitations that define/confine us as 'heterosexual,' 'lesbian,' 'man,' 'woman,' and so on. In our label-driven thinking, each label becomes a restriction, a limit to the many ways identification and desire (can) flow. For example, when I read Elizabeth Meese's description of the lesbian/body, must I limit myself to totally female encounters, to lesbianized interactions? Borrowing from Catherine Stimpson, Meese asserts that

> 'Lesbianism represents a commitment of skin, blood, breast, and bone' ([Stimpson] 164). But the literal body, however powerfully evoked, is a referential one, the 'skin' and 'bone' of textuality's absent lesbian, 'there,' and, literally speaking, not there at all, whose 'being' depends on the word's evocation. She is called forth, in the way that I see your figure on the page, make you present for me as I write my letter to you. Your body is only as 'literal' as the letter, the shade and angle of the marks on a page. (2)

Who is this 'you' Meese addresses? If I read this statement with the labels intact, I must visualize a female body, feminized letters sprawled out on the page. But these textualized marks say different things to me than they do to Meese (and probably to you). To be sure, the 'lesbian' body she refers to, the 'lesbian' bodies I have known, remain absent, 'not there at all.' Yet even in this absence these bodies are far more present than the bisexual body I know so well but so rarely, so very rarely, meet in print.

So how do I react? What do I read when I see *lesbian/body*? How do I embody, change, or desire these terms? Here, for example, is sidney matrix's take on lesbian/bodies and words:

> Writing embodied lesbian:theory means assembling myselves, not into a whole self, but into integrated selfhoods, encompassing all the scraps I was taught to overlook, lay by the wayside (un)necessarily. The notions of what a lesbian can be shape the way I think through myselves. Sometimes I rebel, resist, reject the ideal(s) of lesbianism, and sometimes I camp it up, flaunt it, work it for all it's worth. Within webs of cultural discourses–religious, medical, parental, heterosexist, feminist, lookist, intellectual, erotic, racist–I exist as a lesbian like this, lesbian like that. The lesbian *I* has always already been discursively constructed/constituted, and writes (re-writes / un-writes) according to what has been written, said, and imagined about lesbian experience(s). (71)

Like matrix, when I think about personalized inscriptions I assemble myselves, pulling together the scraps I was taught to overlook, as well as the scraps that have no name(s). However, I cannot say the same thing about 'the bisexual *I*.' This '*I*' does not–yet–exist. Not in print, anyway. It has not 'always already been discursively constructed/constituted.' It does not write (re-write / un-write) according to what has been written, said, and imagined about bisexual experience(s). Perhaps it will never exist. And maybe it shouldn't. Very little has been written about this bisexual *I*, or about bisexual bodies, bodies that can be male or female, mine or (maybe?) yours. And the small amount of material out there in print is so highly personal, so very body specific, that I must say 'No. That's not me.' Over and over again I say it.[2]

BISEXUAL INFLECTIONS: EMBODYING A MIDDLE GROUND

Let me emphasize: my goal in this essay, my goal in theorizing bisexual inflections, is not to negate the importance of developing a body of lesbian criticism. Nor am I adopting a 'me too' position–a defensive call for increased representation and respect for bisexuals. (At this point I could go into a diatribe on bi invisibility, but I'll spare you.) Rather, I want to break down the categories even further, and as I stated pages ago, I think Jordan's words provide one way to do so.

Jordan offers the clearest statement of the categorical breakdown she and I desire in 'A New Politics of Sexuality' where she emphasizes the contextual, action-based nature of all self-naming:

> I will call you my brother, I will call you my sister, on the basis of what you *do* for justice, what you *do* for equality, what you *do* for freedom and not on the basis of who you are, even so I look with admiration and respect upon the new, bisexual politics of sexuality. This emerging movement politicizes the so-called middle ground: Bisexuality invalidates either/or formulation, either/or analysis. Bisexuality means I am free and I am as likely to want and to love a woman as I am likely to want and to love a man, and what about that? Isn't that what freedom implies? If you are free, you are not predictable and you are not controllable. To my mind, that is the keenly positive, politicizing significance of bisexual affirmation: To insist upon complexity, to insist upon the validity of all of the components of social/sexual complexity, to insist upon the equal validity of all the components of social/sexual complexity. (193)

The middle ground: a space often reserved for wishy-washy moderation. Straddling the fence, so to speak. Refusing to identify, refusing to take a stand. Jordan enters into and politicizes this ambivalent space without denying the ambivalence. She embodies it in her texts. By so doing, she loosens the labels that define–and, in defining confine 'us'–whoever this 'us' might be, whoever 'we' might become. Jordan's bisexual inflections create the sexualized, politicized middle ground she envisions, reminding us–reminding me, anyway–that we are all interconnected.

My point is not to argue that this intimate distance/bisexual inflection is *really* 'bisexual'–assuming that we could even agree on a single meaning for the term. Rather, I want to underscore the transformational dynamics that (can) occur in reading and writing, and I believe the bisexual inflections Jordan enacts in her poetry and prose provide a space (a nonbinary middle ground, perhaps?) in which to do so. It is the ambivalence generally associated with bisexual modes of identity and attraction that I find so appealing, for the oscillations between 'me' and 'you' disrupt existing categories of meaning. Bisexual inflections open multiple readings which in turn open multiple channels of desire. They break down without erasing conventional boundaries in sexually-specific labels and texts, leaving the next step to me and (perhaps) to you, reader: '*whoever you are / whoever I may become.*'

NOTES

1. See, for example, Jo Eadie, Clare Hemmings, and Kenneth MacKinnon.
2. See, for example, the anthologies edited by The Bisexual Anthology Collective; Loraine Hutchins and Lani Kaahumanu; Naomi Tucker; and Rebecca Weise.

WORKS CITED

Anzaldúa, Gloria. 1991. 'To(o) queer the writer–*Loca, escritora y chicana*. In *Inversions: Writing by dykes, queers, and lesbians*. Ed. Betsy Warland. Vancouver: Press Gang. 249-64.

The Bisexual Anthology Collective, eds. 1995. *Plural desires: Writing bisexual women's realities*. Toronto: Sisters Vision.

Eadie, Jo. 1993. Activating bisexuality: Towards a bi/sexual politics. In *Activating theory: lesbian, gay, bisexual politics*. Eds. Joseph Bristow and Angelia R. Wilson. London: Lawrence & Wishart. 139-70.

Erickson, Peter. 1986. The love poetry of June Jordan. *Callaloo* 9: 221-34.

Hemmings, Clare. 1995. Locating bisexual identities: Discourses of bisexuality and contemporary feminist theory. In *Mapping desire: Geographies of sexuality*. Eds. David Bell and Gill Valentine. London and New York: Routledge. 41-55.

_____. 1991. Resituating the bisexual body: From identity to difference. In Bristow and Wilson 118-38.

Hutchins, Loraine and Lani Kaahumanu, eds. 1991. *Bi any other name: Bisexual people speak out*. Boston: Alyson.

Jordan, June. 1981. *Civil wars*. Boston: Beacon P.

_____. 1989. *Naming our destiny: New and selected poems*. New York: Thunder's Mouth P.

_____. 1987. For the sake of people's poetry: Walt Whitman and the rest of us. In *On call: Political essays*. Boston: South End P. 5-15.

_____. 1993. *Technical difficulties: African-American notions and the state of the union*. New York: Pantheon.

MacKinnon, Kenneth. 1993. Gay's the word–or is it? In *Pleasure principles: Politics, sexuality, and ethics*. Eds. Victoria Harwood, David Oswell et al. London: Lawrence & Wishart. 109-23.

matrix, sidney. 1995. Experiencing lesbian:theory, lesbian:writing: A personalist methodology. *Critical matrix*: 67-78.

Meese, Elizabeth A. 1992. *(Sem)Erotics theorizing lesbian: writing*. New York: New York UP.

Tucker, Naomi, ed. with Liz Highlyman and Rebecca Kaplan. 1995. *Bisexual politics: Theories, queries, and visions*. Binghamton, NY: Harrington Park P.

Weise, Elizabeth Reba, ed. 1992. *Closer to home: Bisexuality and feminism*. Seattle: Seal P.

Loose Talk:
Lesbian Theory, Hysteria, Mastery
and the Man/Woman Thing

Wendy Leeks

SUMMARY. In order to be a radical political activity, lesbian theory has to resist heterosexual dominance and the terms in which that dominance and mastery are inscribed. How can this be done? This paper uses Jacques Lacan's theory of the Four Discourses to examine the discursive and subject positions involved in critical analysis of psychoanalytic theory itself. Feminist cultural analysts have attempted to adopt the position of the hysteric in critiquing the master narrative of Freud. As Jacobus (1986) shows, Freud was himself subject to hysteria in producing narratives of women and femininity. Feminist and lesbian critiques, in their attachment to woman, risk repeating the oversight of the hysteric and the analyst (and reinforcing mastery) by continuing to view sexuality in terms of a bisexuality composed of masculine and feminine components. Perhaps what is needed is an attempt to produce a discourse of perversion–not produced by Lacan–beyond the phallus and beyond the constructions of the man/woman thing. *[Article copies available for a fee from The Haworth Document Delivery Service: 1-800-342-9678. E-mail*

Wendy Leeks is Head of Academic Development in the Media/Arts Faculty at Southhampton Institute, UK. She trained as an art historian, specializing in feminist and Lacanian psychoanalytic approaches to spectatorship, developed through film theory. Her doctoral thesis investigated lesbian spectatorship of paintings by the artist J. A. D. Ingres, and included an analysis of Freud's interpretation of an instance of female 'homosexual' spectatorship in the Dora case. She has published on this subject. Her current research, mainly on popular film, concerns issues of transference and queer viewing, reading, and teaching.

Address correspondence to: Wendy Leeks, Media/Arts Faculty, Southampton Institute, East Park Terrace, Southampton SO14 0YN, UK.

[Haworth co-indexing entry note]: "Loose Talk: Lesbian Theory, Hysteria, Mastery and the Man/Woman Thing." Leeks, Wendy. Co-published simultaneously in *Journal of Lesbian Studies* (Harrington Park Press, an imprint of The Haworth Press, Inc.) Vol. 4, No. 2, 2000, pp. 95-114; and: *'Romancing the Margins'? Lesbian Writing in the 1990s* (ed: Gabriele Griffin) Harrington Park Press, an imprint of The Haworth Press, Inc., 2000, pp. 95-114. Single or multiple copies of this article are available for a fee from The Haworth Document Delivery Service [1-800-342-9678, 9:00 a.m. - 5:00 p.m. (EST). E-mail address: getinfo@haworthpressinc.com].

address: getinfo@haworthpressinc.com <Website: http://www.haworthpressinc.com>]

KEYWORDS. Bisexuality, lesbian theory, perversion, hysteria, Dora case, Lacan: Four Discourses, transference

HER BREAST FULL OF SORROW, HER HEAD FULL OF DOUBT[1]

My concern is with the practice of teaching and writing lesbian theory; with the ins and the outs of the doing of it. However much I feel hard put to do it, this teaching and writing, the question is, in doing it how am I fixed? And furthermore, what might be the consequences, not just for me? The concern, my concern, with this issue is certainly a matter of a personal fixation, but it has also a political and theoretical dimension that makes it supra- though not im-personal. If establishing and developing lesbian theory and lesbian studies in education is a political necessity, then so is the examination of what this placement might be and/or do. It is also a theoretical necessity given, for one thing, that lesbian teaching and writing involves, on one side or the other, the assumption of an identity and a level of reiteration. Might this not serve to construct a regulatory norm? For another thing, the performances of writing and teaching, reading and studying, must entail libidinous investments. Could these not subvert or perhaps even foreclose any conscious subversive or radical intent of the enterprise? Performativity and psychoanalysis make the examination of the practice unavoidable.

Many heads have already sweated over similar questions, about feminism in the academy, for instance–intervention or incorporation? A slightly different tilt to an old hat is probably academic business as usual. The present tilt, then, is can lesbian studies, lesbian teaching, lesbian writing be prevented from becoming a usual part of the business, if this is the business of mastery? If outlaws are necessary to make the law real, and 'in-laws' service it, how do you break the Law? These are questions of subjective and discursive positions. If lesbian teaching and writing aims to be a practice of resistance to inscription by the dominant, how is this aim to be achieved? These lesbian concerns look like a woman/woman thing, so this resistance must have its specificity as a distinct form of 'women's resistance' since, after all, 'women's resistance' can often be a woman/man thing. Nevertheless, I want to examine a discursive realm that has been characterised as an arena of specifically feminine resistance–the hysterical–by investigating its operation within psychoanalytic practice and theory. Does this mode offer the potential for subversion and resistance that should form a basis for lesbian teaching, writing and theory? And if not, why not?

THE TEASINGLY TIME-OLD RIDDLE

In his lecture 'Femininity' (1933, *PFL, 2*) Freud quotes Heinrich Heine to indicate how

> through the ages heads have sweated under a variety of different hats over the riddle of the nature of femininity. But this is 'a question in masquerade' (Doane, 1982, 75), as the one posed by Heine later on in the poem is actually, 'Tell me, what signifies Man?'

Freud's reiterative question of the other, woman, which has contributed so much to legitimising the positioning of woman as other, was, as Doane and others have amply demonstrated, his own, subjective, ontological question in objective disguise. And it is relevant to look at how much this theoretical, perhaps academic, posing not only arose from but also structured his clinical practice. It was worked out very largely on women, through a process of talking with women and writing for and to men. One might even say that it was a process of writing *with* the men, since in inscribing woman as 'the problem' (Freud, op. cit., 146) he insistently positioned himself within that community of male questioners and observers that he addressed. The question of femininity–'What does the woman want?'–is based on Freud's questioning of the hysteric. In the preface to her analysis of Freud and Breuer's case history of Bertha Pappenheim (Anna O.) Mary Jacobus quotes Juliet Mitchell: 'Hysteria . . . is simultaneously what a woman can do both to be feminine and to refuse femininity, within patriarchal discourse.' And later: 'I do not believe there is such a thing as female writing, a "woman's voice" . . . there is the hysteric's voice which is *the woman's masculine language*' (Jacobus, 1986, 201). In her complex analysis Jacobus draws out the connections between the hysteric's enactment of bodily symptoms, her disjointed speaking of a history (disrupted by reminiscences, forgettings, repetitions), the analyst's reading of symptoms and speech, and his writing of an apparently coherent narrative–the case history. However, a psychoanalytically-based, feminist literary criticism of the case history reveals both the incoherences in it and how the very operations of reminiscence, forgettings and repetitions that produced the patient's symptoms and storytelling also produce the analyst's account.

> The tales which Breuer and Freud retold and reread (reminisced and repeated) compel them to re-enact the hysterical processes they describe; forgetting the meaning of the stories they tell, analytic listeners are themselves turned into hysterical tellers–'turned,' that is, by the transferences of hysteria, the 'intimate connection' that seems inescapable, even uncanny . . . The case histories included in *Studies on Hysteria* are at once narratives generated by hysteria, and narratives that

> generate hysterical reading–a form of reading which might even be
> called theoretical. (Jacobus, 198-9)

At one level, the structure and mechanisms of the analyst's account appear to
be determined by those that the hysteric presents; in other words, the hysteric's condition seems to set the terms both of the analyst's reading of what the
hysteric does and says and his writing of the narrative of the treatment. The
hysteric hystericizes the analysis. Subsequently, these terms are redoubled in
the (feminist, literary) analysis of the case history, hystericising this re-reading and its record. Thus the hysteric generates narrative and theory as hysterical discourse, against the will, you might say, of the analyst who wants to
generate 'science' in contradistinction to this hysterical proliferation. Jacobus
reveals another level, however. In the transferential relation of the analysis, it
is hysteria, not simply the patient's but also the analyst's, which generates
hysterical reading, speaking, writing, theory. The unconscious desires that the
patient brings to the analysis drive her to cast the analyst in the roles of
characters from her psychic history, and to re-enact through the analyst her
entanglements with these characters. Similarly, the analyst's unconscious
desires enter the space of analysis, the countertransference producing its
affects, particularly if the doorway is not 'properly' guarded by technique.
Jacobus demonstrates the operations of countertransference (the analyst's
libidinal investments in the case) in Breuer and Freud's treatment of Bertha
Pappenheim, although this deconstruction is not the main thrust of her essay.
In the preface she sets up major issues that are particularly pertinent to my
concerns here.

> For feminist readers, the accusation is not so much that Freud and
> Breuer themselves were capable of hysterical blindness in relation to
> hysteria (or femininity, for that matter), but that hysteria itself is seen by
> them as the specifically, almost normatively, feminine neurosis; Freud's
> theory of bisexuality ensures that this is so, since the confused sexual
> identifications which for him produce hysteria are themselves constitu-
> tive of femininity. (Jacobus, 199-200)

Furthermore, 'Freud treats hysteria as the special case which establishes the
general category of the unconscious, along with the role of sexuality, in the
psychic life of all desiring subjects,' and 'woman is treated by Freud as a
special case of man, her lopsided bisexual constitution at once illustrating and
reproducing the structure of his, while apparently predisposing her alone to
neurosis' (ibid). The general theory of psychoanalysis–the metanarrative–is
thus produced from an interpretation of the woman hysteric, but in pursuit of
'science' woman and the hysteric are 'special-ized,' produced as categories
labelling certain constructions and expelled into otherness:

'Femininity' and 'hysteria' name the otherness and strangeness which inhabits psychoanalytic theory (and literature) and which psychoanalysis must marginalize in order to found itself as a theoretical body of knowledge. (ibid.)

Jacobus poses a series of 'What ifs?' If these 'special cases' are not special, and femininity defines masculinity, then hysterical women's writing could define writing itself.

What if they [hysterical narratives as embodying the repressed aspects of all narratives] inscribe a hysteria that might as well be called masculine? Both the hysterics figured in, and the hysteria embodied by, women's writing ('the woman's masculine language') might then prove to be the shadow of male hysteria about women; hysterical narrative would expose the repressive assumptions of all narrative: and the so-called 'hysterical' readings generated by women's writing would expose normative readings as themselves hysterically, unavoidably, implicated in the very stories they retell. (Jacobus, 202)

One important aspect of Jacobus's approach is her attempt to avoid, or refuse, a tendency in feminist criticism to make the hysteric a heroine, an effect particularly noticeable in the extensive literature on the Dora case: 'by now a canonical feminist text, in which Dora's resistance to taking up the position assigned to her under patriarchy makes her the first feminist critic of Freud' (Jacobus, 200). The discussions of Cixous and Clément in *The Newly Born Woman* are still, perhaps, some of the most stimulating in outlining and problematizing this view. From Cixous:

Dora seems to me to be the one who resists the system, the one who cannot stand that the family and society are founded on the body of women, on bodies despised, rejected, bodies that are humiliating once they have been used. And this girl–like all hysterics, deprived of the possibility of saying directly what she perceived, of speaking face-to-face or on the telephone as father B. or father K. or Freud, et cetera do–still had the strength to make it known. It is the nuclear example of women's power to protest. It happened in 1899; it happens today wherever women have not been able to speak differently from Dora, but have spoken so effectively that it bursts the family into pieces. (Cixous and Clément, 1986, 154)

From Clément:

Yes, it introduces dissension, but it doesn't explode anything at all; it doesn't disperse the bourgeois family, which also exists only through its

> dissension, always reclosable, always reclosed. . . . For me the fact of
> being passed on to posterity through Freud's account and even Freud's
> failure is not a symbolic act. This is already more true of Freud and
> Breuer's hysteric [Bertha Pappenheim] who became the first welfare
> worker and who made something of her hysteria. The distinction be-
> tween them, between those who nicely fulfil their function of challeng-
> ing with all possible violence (but who then enclose themselves after-
> ward) and those who will arrive at symbolic inscription, no matter what
> act they use to get there, seems essential to me. (ibid., 156)

One way of reading Jacobus's argument would be that the so-called 'hysterical' readings produced by feminist criticism work to resist this reclosure.
Such readings reveal that repression, the mechanism that is operative in
hysteria itself, is also operative in hysterical narratives, those produced by
hysterical women patients and hysterical men analysts. All narratives are
revealed as hysterical by this analysis, which further reveals that hysteria is
not the special case of feminine hysteria, but that hysteria is constructed as
feminine by the disavowal of masculine hysteria. For Jacobus, this masculine
hysteria is 'male hysteria about women.' The project of feminist writing,
then, seems to be a continual critical examination of the operation of this
male hysteria about women, revealing that it is operating and attending to the
particular forms that the operation takes–investigating the specifics of each
instance of repression, rather than a reductive repetition (indeed, Jacobus
indicates this in the last chapter of the book).

   Her argument around the Anna O. case tends to suggest that the bracketing
together of femininity and hysteria is a linkage produced by masculine hysteria.
This is quite clearly a sound conclusion if femininity is understood as itself a
discursive, performative, regulatory construct. What about the linkage of woman
and hysteria? If 'hysterical' reading and writing is identified with the project of
feminism, could this mean that feminist criticism comes to specify all 'true,'
effective criticism concerned with 'hysteria about women,' no matter who performs it? Perhaps more urgent is the question that arises around the 'blind spots'
of this hysterical reading and writing. Breuer and Freud's readings of Bertha
Pappenheim are shown to be hysterical and productive of hysterical writing, yet
they were conservative, reactionary even, and damaging (initially to Pappenheim, to women) in their effects. Their product was a theory that supported the
Law of the Father, the 'othering' of woman. What is to prevent hysterical
feminist writing from doing the same–if not to 'women,' then to other others?

   Freud performed a further hysterical reading on Breuer's handling of the
Anna O. case. In a letter to Stephan Zweig in 1932, Freud wrote:

> What really happened with Breuer's patient I was able to guess later on,
> long after the break in our relations, when I suddenly remembered

something Breuer had once told me in another context before we began to collaborate and which he never repeated. On the evening of the day when all her symptoms had been disposed of, he was summoned to the patient again, found her writhing in abdominal cramps. Asked what was wrong with her, she replied: 'Now Dr. B's child is coming!' . . .

At this moment [Breuer] held in his hand the key that would have opened the 'doors to the Mothers,' but he let it drop. With all his great intellectual gifts there was nothing Faustian in his nature. Seized by conventional horror he took flight and abandoned the patient to a colleague. For months afterwards she struggled to regain her health in a sanatorium. (quoted in Jacobus, 222)

Both Jacobus and John Forrester (1990) show the importance of this (hysterical) reading by Freud of Breuer's treatment, and they also show that a major (unconscious) motivation of Freud's in revealing Breuer's blind spot (to Zweig, in 1883 to his then fiancée Martha Berneys, and to Ernest Jones) was rivalry with Breuer and the desire to devalue or master the elder analyst.

The revelation of Breuer's male hysteria and its speaking silence, its 'oversight,' clearly places Freud himself in a position of omniscience. His subtext bridges the gaping lacuna which Breuer had merely tried to conceal. Read as an unfolding sequence of revelations, Breuer's story becomes a tale-within-a-tale told by Freud, whose finger marks the hiatus in the text and turns it against Breuer himself. The all-seeing narrator proves to have a blind spot; ironized beyond his powers of prevision by an unexpected turn of events, Breuer falls through the gap and becomes a character or figure for hysteria in his own story. (Jacobus, 223)

Breuer professed knowledge about Bertha Pappenheim and her condition and claimed this knowledge had effected a cure. Freud showed where Breuer's knowledge failed and that the cure was not accomplished, displacing Breuer from the position of the knowing subject and setting himself there instead. Freud's relation to Breuer repeats Breuer's relation to Pappenheim, with the same possibility of 'oversight.' In this process, Freud not only hystericizes Breuer, he also feminizes him. In showing Breuer is lacking, Freud makes himself appear not lacking–Breuer is castrated in order to create Freud's (illusory) omnipotence, as the one who really does know, is not castrated. Freud is the image of man in the image of God. What is not perceived by Freud, his 'oversight,' is this operation of his desire to be the Father and lay down the Law. His own countertransference is overlooked.

The shifts and reverses of these relations in the case of Anna O. bear some uncomfortable similarities to much feminist criticism of Freud's texts, particularly of the Dora case. Could feminizing Freud be 'the woman's masculine language' in the sense that the aim of exposing the constructedness of femininity is itself subverted by the desire to assume a phallic position of wholeness; mastering the man as woman by becoming the woman as man? It is evident that the women analysts can be as much a prey to this as the men. Joan Rivière, for instance, wraps herself in Ernest Jones's mantle in order to assert that

> Womanliness . . . could be assumed and worn as a mask, both to hide the possession of masculinity and to avert the reprisals expected if she was found to possess it–much as a thief will turn out his pockets and ask to be searched to prove that he has not the stolen goods. The reader may now ask how I define womanliness or where I draw the line between genuine womanliness and the 'masquerade.' My suggestion is not, however, that there is any such difference; whether radical or superficial, they are the same thing. (Rivière, 1929, 306)

Perhaps Rivière does not steal Jones's penis so much as couple herself with him and it, in order to use him and it as a shield–another mask, to hide what? The fact that Rivière's position and activity in the 'man's world' of psychoanalysis is so much like that of the woman lecturer and the woman propagandist she describes. If their femininity, all femininity, is a masquerade, so is hers, and if theirs disguises masculinity 'underneath,' hers does too. Rivière's femininity as masquerade makes masculinity more 'real,' and also puts her with the men. In order to deflect attention from her own 'theft,' Riviere gives the credit, and the penis, back to Jones, and this (heterosexual) coupling with him has the further effect of distancing her from the women of her cases. Their 'masculinity' places them within Jones's categories of the homosexual woman, whereas Rivière relocates herself as heterosexual–normalizes herself. But her femininity is a mask. If Jones is 'masculine' and Rivière is 'masculine,' Rivière is, at one level, within the category of homosexual woman and, at another level, within the category of homosexual man! With Jones it's a man/man thing. More precisely, perhaps, this is a hom(m)osexual relation, as Lacan points out, heterosexuality being an impossible relation since there are not two sexes at issue but only one. Normative sexuality is all about the man, with the woman serving only as the lost piece necessary to complete him and make him whole. Rivière's analysis, as it stands, is hysterical and marked by desire for mastery. Hysterical, but normalizing in its effects.

WRETCHED, SWEATING HEADS OF HUMANS

Rivière has strong (unconscious) reasons for failing to interrogate masculinity as itself a masquerade, or what Lacanians would refer to as a 'parade,' revolving around a desire to be not lacking, not castrated, to be without desire and thus whole. This 'parade' and mastery are evidently closely allied. Interestingly, Cixous and Clément's discussion of the Dora case follows on from their exchange on the discourses of mastery and of the university, derived from Lacan. This section of the book, titled 'A Woman Mistress,' is prefaced by questions:

> If the position of mastery culturally comes back to men, what will become of (our) femininity when we find ourselves in this position? When we use a master-discourse? Mastery-knowledge, mastery-power: ideas demanding an explanation from us. Other discourses? (Cixous and Clément, 136)

Lacan's theory specifies four particular discourses–of the master, the university, the analyst, and the hysteric (Verhaeghe, 1995).[2] They all involve the same four positions, those of agent (subject, speaker, writer), other (object, addressee), product (of the relation of agent to other and of the discourse itself), and truth (the desire that drives the discourse but is repressed or hidden within it). Four terms rotate in a fixed order across these four positions and thus specify the character of each of the discourses. These terms are the master signifier (the phallic signifier), the signifying chain (knowledge), the lost object which is the cause of desire, and the split subject.

In the discourse of the master, the master as agent appears or pretends to be the master signifier–phallic, whole, complete–and addresses or attempts to impose his mastery on the other, the position occupied by knowledge. Knowledge, in this formulation, can be seen to be an effect of acceptance of mastery; knowledge is validated as knowledge by acceptance of the authority of the master who guarantees it. What is produced from the relation of master and other is increasingly the lost object, cause of desire, not satisfaction of desire (which is impossible) but proliferating dissatisfaction and repetitive and increasing will to achieve mastery. What is hidden in the discourse of the master is the fact that the master as subject is split and can never be whole. The formulation of this discourse specifies increasing alienation, masked by the 'parade' of the subject/agent as master, dependent on the collusion of the other to maintain an appearance of mastery and thus intensifying the imposition of authority.

In the discourse of the university, knowledge is the agent, addressing the lost object as other. Knowledge attempts to reach the lost object through language, to get the object (back) by achieving knowledge of it. But what is produced is only the subject as split, in effect as more and more split. All that can be achieved is the production of more and more words which themselves bear repeated testimony to the gaps or lack within them, the 'oversights' that signal continuation of desire. This discourse is also an objectifying one–the lost object is reduced to a mere object of inquiry and the inquiry itself appears objective and dispassionate. The discourse exhibits the objectivity of science, but what is hidden in it is the master signifier at the position of truth. The desire for wholeness is at the root, and knowledge is again guaranteed as knowledge (authoritative and apparently universal and objective) by the phallic signifier. Knowledge therefore has its investments (of desire) and is in the service of the master which legitimates it in the discourse of the university.

The split subject is the agent in the discourse of the hysteric, addressing or questioning the master signifier at the position of other. Here the analyst is, or is seen as the master signifier. The hysteric wants to 'get' her desire and presumes she can 'get' it from the analyst who will know what it is and thus be able to give it (back) to her. This places the analyst, in the transferential relation, as the one who knows and has everything–whole and omnipotent, the master signifier. But what is produced from their relation is knowledge, increasing words which specify more and more that the subject is split. Rather than repairing this subjective rift, the discourse underlines it, with the effect, perhaps, that the hysteric makes an accommodation to the inevitability of desire. This through knowledge, once again, derived from the master signifier. What is hidden is the truth as lost object. The cause of the hysteric's desire drives the discourse but cannot be found in it. The knowledge produced has nothing to say about the nature of her desire.

The analyst's discourse has the lost object, cause of desire at the position of the agent (the analyst) addressing the split subject (the hysteric/analysand). What is produced is the master signifier, and what is hidden in the discourse, but which fuels it, is knowledge (the signifying chain). To express the discourse of the analyst so baldly is evidently inadequate. It requires considerable interrogation, as being central to Lacan's thought and crucial to my arguments, and also because it is the hysteric's calling to call the position of the analyst into question. To examine this discourse more fully it is necessary to plot a series of twists and turns, and to relate them to the narratives or stories that have featured so far.

Freud was operating, without knowing it, within the discourse of the master in his re-reading of Breuer's treatment of Anna O. This is the trap we can all fall into. Breuer was probably operating within the discourse of the university, on one level, in his relation to Bertha Pappenheim, with the effect of producing hysteria, or himself as hysteric (split subject). Freud too, in writing about the Anna O. case, produced hysterical reading/writing. These two discourses are deeply implicated one with the other. In believing in their own objectivity, and in the possibility of objectivity uninflected by unconscious desire, both Breuer and Freud adopted the discourse of the university, but in doing so they were 'turned' that short quarter-turn of Lacan's diagrammatic representation of the discourses, back into the discourse of the master.

They were 'turned' by their transferences, or rather by their blindness to the possibilities of their own transference. And it was the same with Rivière, up to a point. But there is something else.

What if Rivière's concern in the paper was not so much with the position of her patients as with her own position? She poses a question, about her own desire, to Ernest Jones, believing him to have the answer. Jones is placed as the master signifier, placing Rivière herself within the hysteric's discourse, the split subject as agent. The beginning of her paper certainly seems to bear this out (Rivière, 1929, 303). What she gets is not any sort of answer to her question–she does not get what she wants–but ends up merely with knowledge, couched in the master's terms, that she, the subject, is split, that he is not and she really wants what he has already. The problem is that Rivière does not get past believing in the authority of the master, and does not question it. From the point of view of the master, Rivière is a good hysteric. From the point of view of feminist criticism–when it has its eyes open–she is a bad one. The good hysteric for feminism and for Lacan is one whose question to the analyst puts the analyst's assumption of mastery into question. In fact, this is the feminist critical project as Jacobus indicates it, questioning the mastery of the Symbolic order to produce a different sort of 'knowledge' of this mastery rather than knowledge validated by the master signifier in which the operation of mastery and the illusion of the 'parade' go uninterrogated. Feminism's good hysteric could go some way towards answering Heine's question 'Tell me, what signifies Man' by at least revealing that man is an effect of signification. But she cannot get any closer to answering her own question as hysteric–'What is my desire?'–since the lost object remains the engine and the hidden truth of her inquiry. If she neglects to remember the diagrams, she forgets that she is subject to desire, that she is just as split, if differently, as he is and turns back into the discourse of master in that short quarter-turn.

Maybe this good feminist hysteric has already turned when she questions the master's mastery. She recognises him as a split subject, and recognises that as woman/other she functions for him (the man) as at least the signifier of the lost object. This turn places the analyst as split subject at the position of the object and her as the lost object at the position of agent, and she is 'turned' into the discourse of the analyst. If we put the woman hysteric as agent into the discourse of the analyst, this has the effect of reversing the positions in the discourse of the hysteric. Now the analyst is the split subject as agent, addressing his hysterical question–'What is my desire?'–to her, where she functions, for him, as phallic woman. What is produced is knowledge as before, phallic inscription; knowledge in the master's terms. The man/analyst placed as hysteric by the woman/hysteric/analyst seems as if he will always be feminism's bad hysteric and receive confirmation of his own 'parade.' Unless, of course, he becomes an analyst too! Does this mean he becomes a woman and a feminist as the greatest good?

If the consequences of the imbrication of the discourses of the master and the university are fairly clear, there is more to be said about those of the hysteric and the analyst. The hysteric's discourse in this formulation cannot be specific to women, since it is the only discourse in which the split subject is in the position of agent, driven by desire and its cause, and all subjects are split in the Symbolic Order. Since no-one is whole or One, everybody is a split subject and therefore all are in the hysteric's place, unless they dissemble.

According to the preferred Lacanian readings of the discourse of the hysteric (Verhaeghe, 1995, op. cit.; Fink, 1995, 129-37), Rivière would probably not be seen to operate within it at all. Lacan identifies this discourse with true science, inquiry that really gets somewhere because it does not cover over the bits that do not fit–it does not rule out the unconscious. Science in the discourse of the university is more 'apparent' science, always with power as its aim (Fink, 132-5). The hysteric's is true science because she always keeps going until she can see that the master is flawed. She is therefore always, eventually, good by the end of analysis–provided, of course, the analysis goes to full term and the analyst is able to work it through.

I maintain, however, that this process of the tranferential relations of analysis runs the discourses of the hysteric and the analyst together. In one sense they run concurrently, and in another they consecutively represent transformations affected in/by/for the hysteric. Or they should do. For if the examination of the first two discourses embodies a warning, Lacan's formulation of the second pair could be said to embody a wish. In the discourse of the master, the agent pretends to be whole and complete, but is not. In the discourse of the analyst, the agent pretends to be the lost object, cause of desire, but cannot be it. For to be this would be to cease to be a subject, in effect to cease to really be. So he performs this for the analysand. In the discourse of the hysteric, the analyst seems to the hysteric to be the master; in the discourse of the analyst he (has to) make himself appear to be that 'whatever it is' that is missing and wanted. This 'appearing to be' the 'whatever it is' is precisely the role allocated to woman. One might ask whether there is a difference, either radical or superficial, between his masquerade and hers, and how this is articulated in relation to the phallus as master signifier.

The master signifier is the product of the discourse of the analyst. What does this mean? According to Verhaeghe, 'in Freudian terms, the oedipal determinant particular for that subject' (Verhaeghe, 96). According to Fink, 'As it appears concretely in the analytic situation, a master signifier presents itself as a dead end, a stopping point, a term . . . The task of analysis is to bring such master signifiers into relation with other signifiers, that is, to dialectize the master signifiers it produces' (Fink, 135).

> That's why the end result of the analytical discourse is radical differ-
> ence: beyond the world of make believe, . . . in which we are all
> narcissistically alike, we are fundamentally different. The analytic dis-
> course yields one subject, constructing and deconstructing itself
> throughout the process of analysis; the other party is nothing but a
> stepping-stone. (Verhaeghe, ibid.)

It is interesting how the explication of this discourse of the analyst enters a different register from the explanations of the other discourses. From theory we are shifted here into practice, specifically the practice of psychoanalysis represented–by the analysts, it has to be said–as a very special case. According to these explanations, one outcome seems to be that the discourse of analysis does not produce theory, rather the specifics of an individual subjec-tivity. Where is theory then? It is the support of this practice. And what discourse functions as this support? The discourse of mastery. What is the hidden truth of the discourse of the analyst? It is the signifying chain, knowl-edge. According to Verhaeghe:

> The knowledge functions at the position of truth, but–as the place of the
> agent is taken by *object a* [the lost object, cause of desire]–this knowl-
> edge cannot be brought into the analysis. The analyst knows, oh yes, he
> does know, but he can't do much with it, as long as he takes the
> analytical stance . . . ; he has wisely learned not to know, and this opens
> the way for the other to gain access to that which determined his or her
> subjectivity. (97)

According to Fink, this knowledge is 'obviously not the kind of knowledge that occupies the dominant position in the university discourse. The knowl-edge in question here is unconscious knowledge, the knowledge that is caught up in the signifying chain and has yet to be subjectified' (136). This knowledge then is either conscious and must be deliberately forgotten by the analyst, or is unconscious and therefore of its nature forgotten (repressed). If this knowledge is what must be consciously suppressed by the analyst it is only hidden in so far as the analyst deliberately prevents the analysand from seeing it. It is part of the analyst's masquerade, in that he pretends to be the lost object and not a subject. But this cannot be the engine of the discourse, it cannot be the truth of what impels/compels the analyst to be an analyst. The hidden truth has to be intimately connected to the analyst's desire. If this knowledge is unconscious–what the analyst really does not know, then how is it so 'obviously' not like the knowledge in the discourse of the university?

If what the analyst does not know is his desire to be whole, then it is not so distinct from the factors that impelled Breuer and Freud's 'oversights.' The only viable distinction that can be made between the agent of this discourse and that of mastery, the university or, indeed, hysteria, is that the analyst knows enough to keep his mouth shut. The analyst cannot speak, for if he does, he must fall out of the discourse of the analyst and into one of the others. However, there is something of this not speaking that characterises hysteria–an impediment that makes its presence, though not its 'nature,' felt in the symptom. This commonality of silence suggests that the discourses of the analyst and of the hysteric, and the positions of analyst and hysteric are very close together.

How interesting then that the face he presents to the analysand, what he pretends to be within the discourse, is the lost object of desire, exactly that masquerade that the woman performs for the man. He acts as if he were not a subject. He is silenced. But he knows/believes he is a subject really and decides not to speak. He knows/he believes he is the master really, but he decides to empty himself. He enables the other to become. To become what? What he has already decided she is, so that he can keep trying to be what he wants?

The moment he speaks, teaches, writes, what does the analyst become? If he writes theory he may turn to enter the discourse of the university, since his knowledge is guaranteed by the master; or the discourse of the master itself, imposing on the other. The best he can do is to question his own position and enter the discourse of the hysteric. But this discourse, despite interpretations to the contrary, has the potential to be 'good' or 'bad.'

O SOLVE ME THE RIDDLE OF LIFE

Why did the Dora case fail? Freud, eventually, puts it down to two factors, that he 'did not succeed in mastering the transference in good time' (Freud, op. cit.: 160) and that he 'failed to discover in time and to inform the patient that her homosexual (gynaecophilic) love for Frau K. was the strongest unconscious current in her mental life' (ibid., 162). Subsequent readings have very much concentrated on the countertransference and the fact that Freud resisted being placed in a feminine position.

A striking aspect of his justifications of his technique in the 'Prefatory Remarks' and 'The Clinical Picture' is that they read more like a self-justification than a methodological one. Freud is concerned to establish himself among the men of science of the medical community, while at the same time showing himself to be better than they are, but he is also trying to prove that he was himself objective and scientific in the case and that it held no erotic entanglements for him.

I am aware that–in this city at least–there are many physicians who (revolting though it may seem) choose to read a case history of this kind not as a contribution to the psychopathology of the neuroses, but as a *roman à clef* designed for their private delectation . . .

Now in this case history . . . sexual questions will be discussed with all possible frankness, the organs and functions of sexual life will be called by their proper names, and the pure-minded reader can convince himself from my description that I have not hesitated to converse upon such subjects in such language even with a young woman. Am I, then, to defend myself upon this score as well? I will simply claim for myself the rights of the gynaecologist–or rather, much more modest ones–and add that it would be the mark of a singular and perverse prurience to suppose that conversations of this kind are a good means of exciting or of gratifying sexual desires. (Freud, ibid., 37)

One of the most interesting interpretations of the case comes from Forrester:

As a number of writers have pointed out, Freud found it exceedingly difficult to accept the position of woman in the transference. He found it impossible to conceive, or was reluctant to allow, that such a transference would be possible with him. But in Dora's case it was not just a question of Freud appearing in feminine garb; the psychoanalytic situation would have to receive a new meaning once Frau K.'s significance had become the centre of attention. For the relation that Dora had with Frau K., and with the governess who had also sacrificed her to her desire to seduce a man (her father), was one of intimate talk about sexual secrets between two women. The most hidden of all Dora's secrets that Freud's technique failed to uncover was that the psychoanalytic conversation itself, in which Freud thought he held all the keys, had become the scene in which two 'women' talked about sex, Dora's scene of 'gynaecophilic' satisfaction. The opposition between logos (Freud's technique, explicitly analogous to gynaecology) and philia (Dora's secret), which Hertz draws out, is what Freud wishes to maintain, so that psychoanalysis retains its scientificity, and is prevented from degenerating into natter, into old wives' tales. (Forrester, 53)

So for Dora the conversations were a 'good means' of 'exciting or gratifying sexual desires,' which might make her a special case of 'singular and perverse prurience.' But if they were for one, could they just as well be for the other in the analytic situation? The link to Frau K. is a transferential turn, and also a homosexual turn in the case. Dora's homosexual love turns Freud into a woman homosexual. But hysterical readers, when they follow Freud, tend to turn the homosexual woman into a man. Forrester again:

> But what this overlooked, as Freud was the first to argue, was Dora's orientation towards the mysterious and beautiful feminine, the body feminine in particular. Yet the array of identifications by which Dora came to have such a homosexual desire already implies that she has marked herself as a man; her desire for Frau K. is 'hers' in so far as she identifies with her father and with Herr K. What is important for Dora's 'case' is not so much whether her desire is for a man or a woman, as discovering how the masculine and feminine components were articulated together. (Forrester, 52)

Whether Dora desired a man or a woman might not be so important for the case, but it could be quite important for lesbian theory. What do we have here? Dora turns Freud into a woman, and Freud is bent on positioning Dora as a woman, that is, as a heterosexual woman. He insists on her love for Herr K., and Herr K.'s *love* for her. But it is evident that Freud identifies with Herr K. and presumes Dora also identifies him with Herr K. This places Freud in a heterosexual pairing with Dora, and she with him, thereby resisting Dora's homosexual placement and his own feminization. However, if femininity is a masquerade, as another follower of Freud, Rivière, argues, then Rivière's patients, and Rivière herself, are masculine 'underneath.' And what makes them homosexual is the articulation of this 'masculine component.' If Dora's femininity is masquerade, and Freud is placed under that same sign by Dora, and if Dora's desire is homosexual and therefore she is masculine too, we now have two men in the case. It has turned from a man/woman, to a woman/woman, to a man/man thing. What does it mean that Freud tries so hard to instate the heterosexual pairing? Perhaps that it guarantees his own heterosexuality?

If we are concerned with countertransference, it might be useful to ask what was on Freud's mind at the time, so to speak. One thing was the break-up of his long friendship with Wilhelm Fliess, the man of science, the medical man, who Freud himself said was the first audience or first reader of Freud's scientific papers. This break-up was also linked to Breuer, whose handling of the Anna O. case Freud seems to have forgotten and which should have sounded a warning about erotic entanglements and transferential involvements. In a letter to Fliess on August 7, 1901, Freud wrote:

> What is your wife doing other than working out in a dark compulsion the notion that Breuer once planted in her mind when he told her how lucky she was that I did not live in Berlin and could not interfere with her marriage? (Masson, 1985, 447)

And in the very same letter:

And now, the main thing! As far as I can see, my next work will be called 'Human Bisexuality.' It will go to the root of the problem and say the last word it may be granted me to say–the last and the most profound. For the time being I have only one thing for it: the chief insight which for a long time now has built itself upon the idea that repression, my core problem, is possible only through reaction between two sexual currents . . . The idea is yours. You remember my telling you years ago, when you were still a nose specialist and surgeon, that the solution lay in sexuality. Several years later you corrected me, saying it lay in bisexuality–and I see that you are right. (Masson, 448)

His core problem, theoretically, was repression, and in practice too in the Dora case, where his repression is the problem. Perhaps here he was on to the cause. Earlier, on January 30, 1901, Freud wrote to Fliess specifically about the Dora case which he had then written up, and which was titled 'Dreams and Hysteria':

'Dreams and Hysteria,' if possible, should not disappoint you. The main thing in it is again psychology, the utilization of dreams, and a few peculiarities of unconscious thought processes. There are only glimpses of the organic, that is, the erotogenic zones and bisexuality. But bisexuality is mentioned and specifically recognised once and for all, and the ground is prepared for detailed treatment of it on another occasion. It is a hysteria with tussus nervosa and aphonia, which can be traced back to the character of the child's sucking, and the principal issue in the conflicting thought processes is the contrast between an inclination toward men and an inclination toward women. (Masson, 434)

Oddly, very little of this is explicit in the case history as we have it. Most of the mentions of homosexuality occur in the footnotes, some added considerably later in the 1920s. Something strange seems to be going on, and this can be picked up from a letter Freud wrote to Ferenczi in 1910, when Ferenczi wanted a closer relationship with Freud, like the one he had had with Fliess:

Not only have you noticed that I no longer have any need for that full opening of my personality, but you have also understood it and correctly returned to its traumatic cause. Why did you thus make a point of it? This need has been extinguished in me since Fliess's case, with the overcoming of which you saw me occupied. A piece of homosexual investment has been withdrawn and utilized for the enlargement of my own ego. (quoted in Mahony, 1996, 22)

The break-up of Freud's relations with Fliess was finally caused by an argument over bisexuality, with Fliess believing that the importance of it was his idea and that Freud had conveniently forgotten this and stolen it as his own. This was on Freud's mind during the treatment of Ida Bauer and the writing of the Dora case: bisexuality, homosexuality, hysteria. What is this bisexuality which is repressed from the Dora case history? Perhaps for Freud it becomes a matter of 'the articulation of masculine and feminine components.' The paper referred to in his letter to Fliess is 'Hysterical phantasies and their relation to bisexuality' of 1908. According to Forrester, this paper corrects one error in the Dora case by 'showing that all (or nearly all) hysterical fantasies (and hence symptoms) represent a fusion of masculine and feminine components' (Forrester, 52). For Freud and so many of those who have followed him–whether good or bad hysterics–bisexuality seems to come down to this, and hysteria too, since the question that the hysteric poses to the analyst is most often expressed as two questions: 'What is my desire?' and 'Am I a man or a woman?' which are taken to be synonymous. For feminist hysterics, perhaps, they might as well be, but for lesbian hysterics the answer to the second does not answer and cannot be allowed to erase the first.

O TELL ME, WHAT SIGNIFIES BI?

What has all this to do with the problem of how to 'do' lesbian theory, teaching and writing that is the concern of this paper? Anybody can produce hysterical writing, operating within the discourse of the hysteric, and I have argued that this is the best anybody can do if they are to avoid laying down the Law or being pressed into its service. Unless, of course, they become the analyst. I have indicated how, I think, the discourses of the hysteric and the analyst are linked. So the lesbian theorist has to start by being hysterical, but needs to be a good hysteric. Yet even the good hysterics of feminism have not provided that much that is directly of pertinence to the lesbian theorist. To be our own good hysterics we have to find the oversight, what it might be that these good hysterics have overlooked–the dead stop or limit where, having made the passage to the place of the analyst, they produce the master signifier out of the hat.

You could say that the Dora case history is an example of the discourse of the analyst in operation, in fact, since Freud held on to the phallus and brought the case history to a dead stop–the case history, that is, read as a case about Freud rather than Dora. Subsequent hysterical readings have been prompted by that dead stop, that oversight, so that the case functions as a point within the wider trajectory of interpretation and is part of a continuing discourse of analysis. Perhaps that could sustain and comfort us in our errors and forgetfulness–except that we are impatient and cannot afford complacency.

So what is the oversight that we might identify as such and move forward? I suggest it is an attachment that appears necessary to both feminism and lesbian theory (and even lesbian sexuality itself), the attachment to masculinity and femininity. Current theory has demonstrated that these are constructions, regulatory norms, effects of language in the Symbolic, but even while knowing this, the attachment is still there. Perhaps it is not so much to masculine and feminine as to man and woman. Fundamentally, feminism is still attached to woman, even though any *body* can be a good hysteric, and can still define its project, with Jacobus, as being attention to 'male hysteria about women.' Lesbians are certainly attached to women–isn't that what specifies lesbian? But what if one productive oversight is precisely in the framing of the hysteric's question, or in the way the hysteric frames the question? It is not really a matter of 'Am I a man or a woman?' at all. Similarly, Freud may have retreated when he framed bisexuality as a matter of an originary state from which man and woman, masculine and feminine, get fixed according to the articulation of these two components. Even for Lacan, and even at his most hysterical when, as analyst, he puts himself in the woman's place, that articulation still revolves around the master signifier, the phallus as dead stop.

Maybe lesbians can examine their attachments to women theoretically through the idea that bisexuality is the key, but may not be a man or woman thing. Cixous ends the chapter that began by asking, 'what will become of our femininity when we find ourselves in this position [of the master]?':

> I keep coming back to this: we are all bisexual. The problem is, what have we done with our bisexuality? What is becoming of it? (Cixous and Clément, 146)

To say that we are all bisexual tends to make it easy to disregard bisexuality, to settle for Freud's evasion, or to fall back into the man/woman thing and make bisexuality a special case. But after all, this could be a starting point and not a dead stop. Cixous and Clément begin their chapter by evoking the dream of a new discourse in their attempt to interrogate mastery:

> Mastery-knowledge, mastery-power: ideas demanding an explanation from us. Other discourses? (Cixous and Clément, 136)

Why not move through the hysterical and the analytic turn into perversion, or the discourse of the pervert not formulated by Lacan? He spoke of perversion in his quest for a reality 'beyond the phallus' in answer to Freud's old question 'What does the woman want?' (Mitchell and Rose, 1982, 138 passim). In his attachment to woman, Lacan still kept the phallus under his hat. Bisexual and lesbian theory should have a strong investment in not just tilting but twisting, turning, raising that hat and revealing the conjuring trick as an illusion–the illusion of the man/woman, woman/woman, man/man thing. If we continue to collude in this illusion, we end up with the same old rabbit and the same old hat.

NOTES

1. The poem by Heine reads, in translation, 'His heart full of sorrow, his head full of doubt.' The sub-headings used here, apart from the last one, come from the translations in the Pelican Freud Library translation of Freud's 1933 lecture 'Femininity' (Freud, 1973, 146), or Mary Ann Doane's article on masquerade (Doane, 1982, 75).

2. I take the general interpretation of Lacan's formulations of the four discourses largely from Verhaeghe (1995) and Fink (1995), so far as I understand them. There is scope for misreading here, and I also freely intersperse my own interpretations.

WORKS CITED

Bernheimer, C. and Kahane, C., eds. 1985. *In Dora's case*. London: Virago.

Cixous, H. and Clément, C. 1986. *The newly born woman*. Manchester: Manchester University Press.

Doane, M.A. 1982. Film and the masquerade: Theorising the female spectator. *Screen* 23: 3-4.

Fink, B. 1995. *The Lacanian subject*. Princeton: Princeton University Press.

Forrester, J. 1990. *The seductions of psychoanalysis*. Cambridge: Cambridge University Press.

Freud, S. 1973. Femininity. *Pelican Freud Library vol. 2*. Harmondsworth: Penguin.

———— 1977. Fragment of an analysis of a case of hysteria. *Pelican Freud Library vol. 8*. Harmondsworth: Penguin.

Freud, S. and Breuer, J. 1974. *Studies on hysteria*. Pelican Freud Library vol. 3. Harmondsworth: Penguin.

Jacobus, M. 1986. *Reading woman*. London: Methuen.

Mahony, P.J. 1996. *Freud's Dora*. New Haven and London: Yale University Press.

Masson, J.M., ed. 1985. *The complete letters of Sigmund Freud to Wilhelm Fliess 1887-1904*. Cambridge, Mass: Harvard University Press.

Mitchell, J. and Rose, J., eds. 1982. *Feminine sexuality*. London: Macmillan.

Rivière, J. 1929. Womanliness as a masquerade. *International Journal of Psychoanalysis* X: 303-13.

Verhaeghe, P. 1995. From impossibility to inability: Lacan's theory of the four discourses. *The Letter*. Spring: 76-99.

Hard Times and Heartaches:
Radclyffe Hall's *The Well of Loneliness*

Heather Love

SUMMARY. This paper considers recent critical responses to Radclyffe Hall's 1928 novel *The Well of Loneliness*. While Hall's portrayal
of mannish invert Stephen Gordon has had a troubled reception in this
century, recent work celebrating butch-femme identity and practice has
gained the novel wider acceptance among lesbian critics. While these
recuperations are significant in working against homophobic readings
of *The Well*, they often overlook the real difficulties Hall described.
This paper argues for the historical significance of Hall's work as a re-
flection of the lived experience of lesbians in a homophobic society.
*[Article copies available for a fee from The Haworth Document Delivery Service:
1-800-342-9678. E-mail address: getinfo@haworthpressinc.com <Website: http://
www.haworthpressinc.com>]*

KEYWORDS. Mannish lesbian, butch-femme, inversion

*What to do, then, with the figure referred to, in various times and
circumstances, as the "mannish lesbian," the "true invert," the "bull
dagger," or the "butch"? You see her in old photographs or paintings
with legs solidly planted, wearing a top hat and a man's jacket, staring
defiantly out of the frame, her hair slicked back or clipped over her
ears; or you meet her on the street in T-shirt and boots, squiring a*

Heather Love is a PhD candidate in English at the University of Virginia working
on the relation between literary modernism and the formation of lesbian identity.
    Address correspondence to: Heather Love, English Department, Bryan Hall,
University of Virginia, Charlottesville, VA 22903.

[Haworth co-indexing entry note]: "Hard Times and Heartaches: Radclyffe Hall's *The Well of Loneli-
ness.*" Love, Heather. Co-published simultaneously in *Journal of Lesbian Studies* (Harrington Park Press,
an imprint of The Haworth Press, Inc.) Vol. 4, No. 2, 2000, pp. 115-128; and: *'Romancing the Margins'?
Lesbian Writing in the 1990s* (ed: Gabriele Griffin) Harrington Park Press, an imprint of The Haworth Press,
Inc., 2000, pp. 115-128. Single or multiple copies of this article are available for a fee from The Haworth
Document Delivery Service [1-800-342-9678, 9:00 a.m. - 5:00 p.m. (EST). E-mail address: getinfo@
haworthpressinc.com].

brassily elegant woman on one tattooed arm. She is an embarrassment
indeed to a political movement that swears it is the enemy of traditional
gender categories and yet validates lesbianism as the ultimate form of
femaleness.

–Esther Newton, "The Mythic Mannish Lesbian"

In her groundbreaking 1984 article "The Mythic Mannish Lesbian: Radclyffe Hall and the New Woman," Esther Newton offered a radical new
reading of *The Well of Loneliness*, and of its heroine, Stephen Gordon, whom
Newton introduced as "[w]ithout question, the most infamous mannish lesbian of all time" (559). For fifteen years Hall's 1928 novel had been the
subject of intense criticism in the lesbian community. With its "third sex"
heroine, butch-femme romance, and tragic ending, *The Well* found few cham-
pions among the lesbian feminists of the 1970s, whose model of lesbianism
"as the ultimate form of femaleness" did not account for the likes of Stephen
Gordon. Challenging the "anti-*Well* approach" of earlier critics, Newton
placed Stephen's mannishness in context, refusing to condemn Hall's representation and instead pointing to its historical significance. Newton credited
Hall with disrupting "the asexual model of romantic friendship" (560) of the
nineteenth century and with giving us the first self-defining and fully sexual
lesbian character in literature.

If Stephen is no longer quite so infamous as she once was, it is in large part
due to the influence of critics such as Newton, who during the 1980s and
early 1990s worked to revalue butch-femme identity as a space of political
resistance, erotic self-definition, and aesthetic free play. Critics like Joan
Nestle, Amber Hollibaugh, Cherríe Moraga, Sue-Ellen Case, Theresa de
Lauretis, Elizabeth Lapovsky Kennedy, and Madeline D. Davis sought to
recuperate the abjected figure of the stone butch, and their work in turn
helped to shift responses to Radclyffe Hall's female invert in this decade. As
a result of what Bonnie Zimmerman has called "the decline in the hegemony
of feminism over lesbian theory" (2), the most virulent attacks on
Hall–which labeled her as both homophobic and misogynist[1]–have come to
an end. Critics have accepted and, at times, revelled in Stephen's butchness,
remembering her courage and celebrating her role in the formation of modern
lesbian identity. Such an upsurge in critical interest in Hall is reflected in the
recent increase in Ph.D. dissertations and Master's theses devoted to her
work, as well as in sympathetic treatments of Hall in the last fifteen years by
critics like Jonathan Dollimore, Gillian Whitlock, Teresa de Lauretis, Terry
Castle, Adam Parkes, Julie Abraham, and Joanne Glasgow. In addition, the
publication of Glasgow's edition of Hall's love letters to Evguenia Souline in
NYU's Cutting Edge series has made an important biographical resource
available to students of Hall's work.

However, despite this revaluation of butch-femme identity and increased interest in Hall, critics remain resistant to several aspects of her work. In particular, readers continue to criticize *The Well of Loneliness* for its extremely abject tone, overblown expressions of self-hatred, and tragic ending. While some recent lesbian critics have made their peace with Stephen's much-vaunted masculinity–with her neckties, riding breeches, and even her "narrow-hipped, wide-shouldered" body–few have been able to find any value in her sacrifice, her suffering, or her loneliness. Though Stephen's butch pleasures are no longer anathema, her butch pains remain extremely problematic for many readers. Few would argue with Hall's intention to champion the female invert's right to exist but many are still troubled by the means she employed to this end, and have rejected *The Well* as excessively dark. In the 1990s, critics continue to argue that her portrait of Stephen as a "freak" and a "mistake of nature" offers lesbians a poor role model and that it reinforces the homophobic beliefs of the general reader.

For most critics *The Well* remains a bitter pill, one that, as Jaime Hovey points out in her 1995 dissertation, is still difficult to swallow. Hovey writes,

> [Hall's] championing of masculine valor, the voluntary sacrifice of Stephen's lesbian desires made sublime through the imagery of Catholic martyrdom, the evocation of homosexual culture through the language of racism and degeneration, the denigration of male effeminacy, and the final humiliating appeal to 'normal' society for the inclusion of congenital inverts, all are strategies which have made this a hard novel for many lesbian readers to stomach. Although recent celebration of butch identity has somewhat rehabilitated *The Well of Loneliness* from its characterization in the lesbian canon as the representative of, in Blanche Weisen Clark's famous phrase, 'the "butch," the tears, the despair of it all'; lesbian critics still distance themselves from its embarrassingly needy, earnest plea to God and country for tolerance, preferring to retool its disquieting sentimental 'pathos' into a happier, campier 'strain of kitsch.' (113)

Critics who have taken these recalcitrant issues head-on have continued to lament *The Well*'s status as *the* lesbian novel, and to challenge its centrality in the tradition. Only critics who have attempted to "retool" the pathos of Hall's novel–to coat its bitterness with a campier, kitschier, and more ironic sensibility–have more fully embraced *The Well* as an essential and valuable text in lesbian history.

Hovey astutely identifies the two competing strains of Hall criticism at the present moment: the continuing dismissal of Hall's work as "too sad" and the more recent "happier, campier" strain of Hall criticism. In the following pages, I would like to argue in particular against the second strain of criticism, which seeks to recuperate Hall's work by de-emphasizing its tragic aspects. While I see the value of that gesture, especially given the many homophobic readings to which Hall has been subjected, in my view it is precisely the tragedy of Hall's text that makes it so compelling. I would suggest a reading of Hall's work which neither rejects nor retools its most challenging and melancholic moments, but rather takes them as a starting point in exploring the difficulties of lesbian public identification. The pain of Hall's text is instructive and, I would argue, ultimately irrecuperable for any happier narrative of the formation of lesbian identity.

*   *   *

Love me, only love me the way I love you. Angela, for God's sake, try to love me a little–don't throw me away because if you do I am utterly finished. You know how I love you, with my soul and my body; if it's wrong, grotesque, unholy–have pity. I'll be humble. Oh, my darling, I am humble now; I'm just a poor, heart-broken freak of a creature who loves you and needs you more than its life . . . I'm some awful mistake– God's mistake–I don't know if there are any more like me, I pray not for their sakes, because it's pure hell.

–The Well of Loneliness

Unhappy lovers write unhappy letters–painful to write, painful to receive, painful to read weeks, months, even years after the fact. But Stephen Gordon's lovemaking reaches depths of self-abasement few have ventured, as she throws herself entirely on the mercy of the beloved; while her naming of herself as "heart-broken" and "humble" is fairly typical of this genre, her appeal for pity as a "freak" and as "God's mistake" takes us into another territory entirely. It is in these desperate tones that Stephen addresses herself to Angela Crossby, the married neighborhood woman who conducts an ambiguous affair with the young and inexperienced Stephen and then "throws her away." Angela, who is occupied with an affair with a neighborhood man, rejects Stephen's continued advances and finally betrays her by exposing this same letter to her husband, who then turns it over to Stephen's mother. Her mother continues the pitiless scourging of Stephen's frail subjectivity as she expels her from Morton, their ancestral home, saying, "I shall never be able to look at you now without thinking of the deadly insult of your face and body to the memory of the father who bred you" (200). Immediately after the confrontation with her mother, Stephen is drawn by a "strong natal instinct" to her father's study. There she is overcome by a horrible loneliness; Sir Philip, who passed away during Stephen's childhood, had been one of the only characters in the novel to treat her with understanding. It is at this moment that Stephen reaches a low point in her self-hatred and self-pity, bottoming out deep in the well of loneliness. Hall writes,

> All the loneliness that had gone before was as nothing to this new loneliness of spirit. An immense desolation swept down upon her, an immense need to cry out and claim understanding for herself, an immense need to find an answer to the riddle of her unwanted being. All round her were grey and crumbling ruins, and under those ruins her love lay bleeding; shamefully wounded by Angela Crossby, shamefully soiled and defiled by her mother–a piteous, suffering, defenceless thing, it lay bleeding under the ruins. (203)

Critics have argued that this dark portrait simply reinforces normative cultural values, and demonstrates Hall's internalized homophobia, her inability to conceive of homosexuality on her own terms. However, what seems most interesting in *The Well* is precisely Hall's engagement with the condition society imposes on her. Rather than imagining a society on other terms, Hall is attentive to the destructive power of society as she currently experiences it. Stephen's self-hatred and self-pity are effects of this power, reflections of the continual rejection she is subjected to as a result of her "aberrant" sexuality and gender-identification. Through this portrait, Hall describes the experience of bearing an abjected identity within the dominant society. Hall exposes the extent to which society's "shameful wounding" is not incidental to but rather constitutive of Stephen's innermost self. Unwonted or illicit desires determine Stephen's very being as "unwanted," permanently marked by refusal and by the tragedy of her unassimilable existence. Hall does not offer a humanist vision of Stephen's "true self," separate from society and the traumas it inflicts. Nothing is held in reserve; no corner of the self is untouched. Hall's portrait of the tragic lesbian comes into distinct conflict with later utopian visions of lesbian identity as outside or beyond the terms of patriarchy (Stephen's love most emphatically does not "surpass the love of men" . . .). In place of such arguments, Hall offers simply a plea for social acceptance, which, in her radically historicist view, is necessary for any shift in identity or consciousness.

Following this difficult scene, we witness Stephen's pivotal acquisition of a determinate identity, as, searching for "an answer to the riddle of her unwanted being," she finds her father's copy of the sexological work of Richard von Krafft-Ebing. There Stephen discovers that she has a place in existence, as she finds in the "battered old book" the necessary clues to identify herself as a female invert. Stephen's embrace of the medical discourse of inversion offers a textbook example of Michel Foucault's concept of "reverse discourse," which he describes as the process by which a marginalized group begins to speak on its own behalf in the same terms by which it has been rendered marginal.[2] Hall herself made just such a move in *The Well of Loneliness*, as she embraced Havelock Ellis' portrait of the female invert, even including an introduction by the famous sexologist. Hall's appropriation of this discourse allowed her to represent in Stephen a sexual, self-identifying lesbian character arguing for her right to existence. Even so, the costs of adopting such a strategy are evident throughout the novel, for Stephen is haunted by the associations of the abjected identity she claims. Though she attempts to resist its stigmatizing effects, she is marked by the refusal and scorn to which such a public identification exposes her. The tragedy of Stephen's "unwanted being" culminates at the end of the novel in her sacrifice of her lover Mary to a happy heterosexual union with Martin Hallam. In *The Well*'s final scene, Stephen martyrs herself to the discourse of inversion, giving up the happiness she has known with Mary to open herself to the horrible army of inverts who physically possess her, demanding that she speak on their behalf and "tearing her to pieces" (436-7).

Several critics, also torn to pieces by the end of *The Well*, have taken solace in the differences they have been able to locate between Hall's novel and her life story. Arguing against the homophobic confusions of fiction and life which have plagued even recent accounts of Hall's work (such as Lovat Dickson's 1975 biography, *Radclyffe Hall at the Well of Loneliness: A Sapphic Chronicle*), many lesbian critics have insisted that Hall's life was not so maudlin, pointing out that she lived with Una Troubridge through to the end of her life, and that she "maintained a steadfast interest in her own sexual integrity and satisfaction" (Glasgow, 204). I would not argue that Stephen's story is Hall's story; however, I find little to be gained from detailing their biographical differences. The fact that Hall stayed with Una, lived comfortably for much of her life in England, or experienced sexual satisfaction with her lovers does not change Hall's deep identification and concern with "the melancholy of the invert."

Joanne Glasgow takes up several of these points in her introduction to *Your John*, Radclyffe Hall's late letters to Evguenia Souline. These late letters do describe many of the pleasures and passions of their affair, but what is more striking in them is the extent to which these pleasures are interwoven with the birth-pangs of Hall's lesbian identity. Hall's words significantly echo many of the most troubling passages of *The Well of Loneliness*, as she confronts in a variety of more or less explicit ways the difficulty of bearing a visibly deviant sexual identity in 1920s British society. Like her invention Stephen Gordon, Hall was intimately familiar with this difficulty, what Carroll Smith-Rosenberg has called "the price paid by those who literally used their bodies and their emotions to invert received order" (279).

Hall discusses this difficulty at length in the following passage from a 1934 letter:

Last night I had one of my fits of the glooms. When the weight of my life lay heavey [sic] upon me, when everything seemed dust and ashes in my mouth, when I felt that I had not made good at all, that I would never make good being what I am–that the scales were too heavily weighted against me–I get like that sometimes & have done for years–it is the melancholy of the inverted. I tell you this because it is God's truth that you can lift me right out of such moods, that when I am lying in your arms & you in mine such moods cannot touch me . . . I feel battle-weary, and you are my rest, my joy and my ultimate justification. (80)

Throughout *The Well of Loneliness*, Hall describes Stephen as having "the nerves of the abnormal" (407), a description which she echoes in this letter to Souline. Hall's characterization of herself as "battle-weary" may sound like a hackneyed convention of the love letter, and yet, in reading a passage such as this, it is significant to recall that Hall and others like her were fighting an almost daily battle with powerful forces of homophobia. Hall's invocation of Souline, with whom she had fallen in love earlier that year, as her "ultimate justification," may give some indication of just how tenuous were the foundations of Hall's claim to identity.

Like Stephen, Hall conceives of herself as a congenital invert, explaining herself and her desire to Souline in those terms. In response to Souline's calling their love "emotionally wrong," Hall responds that this love is the only right one for her, given her inverted nature. She writes,

I have never felt an impulse toward a man in all my life, this because I am a congenital invert. For me to sleep with a man would be an outrage against nature. Can't you try to understand, to believe that we exsist [sic]–we people who are not of the so[-]called normal? Where's your medical knowledge? (50)

Apparently, Hall found Ellis's account of the invert not only politically useful in an appeal to the reading public, but also personally useful as a meaningful self-description in this much more intimate context. Such a warm embrace of the discourse of inversion begs the question, difficult to modern readers, of the attractiveness of this medical category to Hall. In Glasgow's introduction to the letters, she ignores this troubling evidence, arguing that Hall did not see herself as masculine, and that she "certainly did not confuse gender perfor-mance with inversion" (10). Such an account would mark a great difference between Hall's theory of inversion and Ellis's, but Hall, for one, had not lost track of her medical knowledge. In several passages in the letters, Hall draws heavily on Ellis's account of inversion in explaining identity, alluding fre-quently to the masculinity as well as the melancholy of the female invert. Though current feminist critics may not now "confuse gender performance with inversion," for Hall the link between her love of women and her "natural" gender identity was close indeed.

Despite the oversights of such apologist readings, Glasgow is right in pointing out that Hall's discussions of gender and sexuality in the letters are more varied and expansive than in her infamous novel of inversion. Though Hall names herself repeatedly as an invert, and accepts what she sees as the inevitable difficulties of that identification, her understanding of sexual identity is somewhat more flexible in these letters that in *The Well of Loneliness*. For instance, in one letter, Hall ventures that Souline is "probably bisexual." She writes, "Nature, my darling, is not limited by the views . . . of a hospital matron" (52). Nonetheless, much of Hall's courtship is taken up with an effort to educate this young (and resistant) Russian nurse in Paris into an acceptance of the naturalness of inversion. As such, her seduction is played out in the discursive field of female same-sex desire, where she constantly struggles to respond to dominant images of lesbian existence. Often, Hall battles with invisible enemies, as when she expresses her concern about what Souline may already "know" about lesbian existence. She writes,

> Oh, you who know so much in "in theory" as you once told me very proudly–you know less than nothing, but nothing at all! And God only knows what you have learnt "in theory." I tremble to think what you have learnt, surely something about very freakish things indeed, otherwise why this fear? (48-9)

In her attempts to win Souline, Hall draws on her personal experience and her study of sexology to argue for a medical understanding of same-sex desire as an inevitable but largely innocuous variation in Nature's plan.

In forwarding these arguments, Hall betrays a serious anxiety about her lover's perception of her body and her desire. On occasion, Hall confronts these fears directly, as when she writes, "I am not such a freak that the thought of the love of my body need scare you" (49). Hall finds it necessary to reassure Souline again and again, vouching for the benignity of her love. She writes, "you are not a morbid unnatural creature who has fallen deeply in love with a devil" (52). Another strategy Hall employs is to give Souline a kind of mantra to repeat to herself: "Look the thing straight in the face and say: 'I have fallen very much in love with an invert, and thank God, she has fallen in love with me. There is nothing to make me feel lonely & bitter'" (52). Or again: "Just say to yourself 'I'm a normal woman and when my John loves me my response is normal'" (69).

Throughout the letters, Hall is at great pains to distance herself from dominant images of female same-sex desire. In these arguments, Hall argues against both accounts of medical inversion more pathologizing than Ellis's (e.g., Krafft-Ebing's *Psychopathia Sexualis*) as well as decadent images of lesbians circulated in the works of such authors as Baudelaire, Pierre Louys, or Emile Zola. On the one hand, she betrays an anxiety lest Souline perceive her love for her as a morbid indulgence, the vice of the schoolmistress or the courtesan. For instance, when Hall reminisces to Souline about their time together in Paris, she writes, "You'r[e] so shy that it[']s like making love to a school girl–not that I have ever done such a thing!" (60). At other times, Hall seems to be offering an implicit response to pathologizing medical images of the invert as diseased or degenerate. For instance, Hall sends a note to Souline along with a photo of herself in which she writes, "This snapshot was taken in Mickie's garden. The spots on my arm are not a fell disease, they are frightful mosquito bites . . . " (49).

The logic of Hall's protest may not make sense until we consider it in the light of another photograph of Hall, the one published on the front page of the *Daily Express* on Sunday, August 19th, 1928, under the banner headline "A Book That Must Be Suppressed." The article that followed–James Douglas' violent homophobic attack on Hall and her novel–began the legal process that would result in the banning in England of *The Well of Loneliness* in November of that year. Douglas, using every weapon at hand, attacked Hall's lesbianism both as a corrupt vice and as a medical disease. Douglas describes the public menace caused by the publication of the novel. He writes,

> I am well aware that sexual inversion and perversion are horrors which exist among us today. They flaunt themselves in public places with increasing effrontery and more insolently provocative bravado. The decadent apostles of the most hideous and most loathsome vices no longer conceal their degeneracy and their degradation. (Quoted in Brittain, 54)

Douglas furthers his argument, explicitly invoking the concept of inversion as sickness in a section of the article entitled, "The Plague," in which he calls on British society to "clean itself from the leprosy of these lepers" (54-5).

What is striking in this collection of letters is the repeated intrusion of history onto the scene of a private seduction. In order to win Souline's love, Hall must convince her not only of her true love for her (which proves difficult as Hall is living with Troubridge as she writes) or of her worth as a lover (Hall is confident on this score), but also of the morality of their sexual union. Hall understands the success of her seduction to depend upon her ability to recontextualize female inversion as normal and natural rather than freakish, perverse, or sinful. In her anxiety, Hall demonstrates the inescapably political nature of "the love of the invert," as even the most private domains of desire and sexuality are marked by the traumas of public identification. Hall establishes this connection in *The Well of Loneliness*, as the utopian and romantic spaces she describes are repeatedly shut down by the realities of a homophobic society. The first major difficulty for Stephen and

Mary occurs when their friend Lady Massey withdraws her Christmas invitation to them after she discovers the nature of their relationship. Hall describes the night that follows:

> That night Stephen took the girl roughly in her arms.
> 'I love you–I love you so much . . . ' she stammered; and she kissed Mary many times on the mouth, but cruelly so that her kisses were pain–the pain in her heart leapt out through her lips: 'God! It's too terrible to love like this–it's hell–there are times when I can't endure it!'
> She was in the grip of a strong nervous excitation; nothing seemed able any more to appease her. She seemed to be striving to obliterate, not only herself, but the whole hostile world through some strange and agonized merging with Mary. It was terrible indeed, very like unto death, and it left them both completely exhausted.
> The world had achieved its first real victory. (371)

In Hall's personal letters as in *The Well of Loneliness*, it is remarkable how frequently "the whole hostile world" ends up in these lovers' beds. This scene is reminiscent of the "strange and agonized" tone of many of Hall's letters to Souline during periods when Souline had ceased to respond to Hall sexually. Though despair and fanaticism are the stock-in-trade of the unrequited lover, the extremely painful insistence of these letters is remarkable in its excess and, I would argue, in its overdetermination. Defeated by both Souline's indifference and the world's cruelty, Hall bears a deeper wound, and she lashes back with extreme cruelty. Abandoning her coaxing tone, Hall imagines a sexual encounter between them, threatening, "I could kiss you till you bled–I could tear you to pieces Evguenia" (141). In a moment of erotic teasing, Hall jokes, "So you need calling down, being quite out of hand. Very well I'll beat you when I get to Paris–trouble is that I really believe you'd like it" (97). Reminding Souline of her financial support of her, Hall stakes her claim on her:

> You belong to me, and don't you forget it. You are mine, and no one else[']s in the world. If I left you for 20 years you'd have to starve. No one but me has the right to touch you. I took your virginity, do you hear? I taught you all you know about love. You belong to me body & soul, and I claim you. And this is not passing mood on my part–it[']s the stark, grim truth that I'm writing. (140)

Hall's desire to control Souline, to punish her, and to take utter possession of her grows in the letters as she becomes more and more frustrated by her inability to enter into a legitimate and public bond with her. While we might read such passages simply as expressions of Hall's personal desires, I would argue that they only become fully legible in the historical context of Hall's public identification and the stigma attached to it. These moments represent the incursions of "the whole hostile world" into the most private of spaces.

Hall's letters to Souline reveal again and again the inseparability for her of the public discourse of inversion from her private experience of desire and sexuality. A similar slippage between the public and the private appears in an interesting passage in *Boots of Leather, Slippers of Gold*, Elizabeth Lapovsky Kennedy and Madeline D. Davis's oral history of a working-class lesbian community in the 40s and 50s. Reporting on the feedback they received from their narrators, they quote the criticism of one narrator in particular, a woman named Vic:

> 'It sounds like it was pretty much the good side of the whole thing. It didn't sound like there was much on hard times or heartaches, or what-ever you want to call it that really happened. I don't know how you took your interviews, if you just took certain things out. It sounded like it was a really nice life, and it wasn't . . . ' When we asked her what she meant–had we left out how bad people felt over breakups or how badly people treated one another–she replied, 'Mostly how society treated you when you were out and things like that, not so much the people you were with.' (14)

Perhaps one reason why Radclyffe Hall's work has remained so contro-versial in the lesbian community is that she rarely, if ever, "left out how bad people felt." This melancholic and even pathetic quality is the most salient feature of her novel, what remains with most readers in spite of protests, denials, and dismissals. While many readers have suggested that we move on from this exceedingly grim portrait, I would argue that it is precisely this abject remainder–the stubborn traces of Hall's suffer-ing–that most warrants our critical attention. In this regard, I find the confusion between heartbreak and homophobia–the slippage between "how bad people feel" and "how bad people treat you"–an immensely compelling aspect of Hall's life and writing. While critics have for the most part dismissed such a confusion as Hall's internalized homopho-bia–and left it at that–I would argue that it is in further exploring this confusion that we can begin to understand the formation of modern lesbian identity in its properly historical context.

In *The Well of Loneliness* and in her letters, Hall described the pleasures and pains she experienced in claiming a deviant identity as the starting place for a movement for political and civil rights. It is no wonder that such an account should make lesbian readers uncomfortable, for it calls attention to the ambivalent legacy of our own still-marginal identity. While modern les-bian existence may seem a long way from Stephen Gordon's anxiety and self-abasement, Hall's novel nonetheless serves as a troubling reminder of the difficulties of our own position, the fear, prejudice, and self-hatred against and through which we continue to struggle. Hall's ambivalent representation captured the awkward mixture of pride and shame, resistance and complicity, which remains our peculiar inheritance. *The Well* is not the reason for our suffering, but rather a record of it. Rather than rebuke, reprimand, or condescend to Hall, we ought to lay claim in her novel to our own complex and difficult history. Despite the bitterness, we ought to swallow hard, and thank Hall for the butch, the tears, and the despair of it all.

ENDNOTES

1. See in particular Lillian Faderman and Ann Williams, "Radclyffe Hall and the Lesbian Image" *Conditions* 1.1 (1977); Blanche Weisen Cook, "'Women Alone Stir My Imagination': Lesbianism and the Cultural Tradition" *Signs* 4.4 (Summer 1979): 718-739; Lillian Faderman, *Surpassing the Love of Men* (New York: William Morrow and Company, Inc., 1981); Vivian Gornick, "The Whole Radclyffe Hall: A Pioneer Left Behind" *Village Voice* June 10-16, 1981: 45+; Catherine R. Stimpson, "Zero Degree Deviancy: The Lesbian Novel in English" *Critical Inquiry* 8.1 (Winter 1981): 363-79. For later examples of the "anti-*Well* approach," see Lillian Faderman, "Love Between Women in 1928: Why Progressivism Is Not Always Progress" *Journal of Homosexuality* 12.3/4 (May 1986): 23-42 and Sheri Benstock, *Women of the Left Bank: Paris, 1900-1940* (Austin: University of Texas Press, 1986).

2. Foucault's most famous discussion of the concept is in the following passage from *The History of Sexuality*: "There is no question that the appearance in nineteenth-century psychiatry, jurisprudence, and literature of a whole series of discourses on the species and sub-species of homosexuality, inversion, pederasty, and 'psychic hermaphroditism' made possible a strong advance of social controls into this area of 'perversity'; but it also made possible the formation of a reverse discourse: homosexuality began to speak on its own behalf, to demand that its legitimacy or 'naturality' be acknowledged, often in the same vocabulary, using the same categories by which it was medically disqualified." Michel Foucault, *The History of Sexuality, Vol I: An Introduction* (New York: Vintage Books, 1978), p. 101.

WORKS CITED

Abelove, Henry, Michéle Aina Barale, and David M. Halperin, eds. *The Lesbian and Gay Studies Reader.* New York: Routledge, 1993.

Abraham, Julie. *Are Girls Necessary? Lesbian Writing and Modern History.* New York: Routledge, 1996.

Benstock, Sheri. *Women of the Left Bank: Paris, 1900-1940.* Austin: University of Texas Press, 1986.

Brittain, Vera. *Radclyffe Hall: A Case of Obscenity.* New York: A.S. Barnes and Company, 1968.

Case, Sue-Ellen. "Toward a Butch-Femme Aesthetic." Abelove, Barale, and Halperin 294-306.

Castle, Terry. *The Apparitional Lesbian: Female Homosexuality and Modern Culture.* New York: Columbia University Press, 1993.

_____. *Noel Coward & Radclyffe Hall:* Kindred Spirits. New York: Columbia University Press, 1996.

Cook, Blanche Weisen. "'Women Alone Stir My Imagination': Lesbianism and the Cultural Tradition." *Signs* 4.4 (Summer 1979): 718-39.

De Lauretis, Teresa. *The Practice of Love: Lesbian Sexuality and Perverse Desire.* Bloomington: Indiana University Press, 1994.

_____. "Sexual Indifference and Lesbian Representation." Abelove, Barale, and Halperin 141-58.

Dollimore, Jonathan. "The Dominant and the Deviant: A Violent Dialectic." *Critical Quarterly* 28 (1986): 179-92.

Faderman, Lillian. "Love Between Women in 1928: Why Progressivism Is Not Always Progress." *Journal of Homosexuality* 12.3/4 (May 1986): 23-42.

_____. and Ann Williams, "Radclyffe Hall and the Lesbian Image" *Conditions* 1.1 (1977).

_____. *Surpassing the Love of Men.* New York: William Morrow and Company, Inc., 1981.

Foucault, Michel. *The History of Sexuality, Vol. I: An Introduction.* Trans. Robert Hurley. New York: Vintage Books, 1978.

Glasgow, Joanne. "Rethinking the Mythic Mannish Radclyffe Hall." *Queer Representations: Reading Lives, Reading Cultures.* Ed. Martin Duberman. New York: New York University Press, 1997.

Gornick, Vivian. "The Whole Radclyffe Hall: A Pioneer Left Behind." *Village Voice* June 10-16, 1981: 45+.

Hall, Radclyffe. *The Well of Loneliness.* New York: Anchor Books, 1990.

_____. *Your John: The Love Letters of Radclyffe Hall.* Ed. Joanne Glasgow. New York: New York University Press, 1997.

Hollibaugh, Amber, and Cherríe Moraga. "What We're Rollin' Around in Bed With: Sexual Silences in Feminism." *Powers of Desire: The Politics of Sexuality.* Ed. Anne Snitow, Christine Stansell, and Sharon Thompson. New York: Monthly Review Press, 1983.

Hovey, Jaime. "Imagining Lesbos: Identity and National Desire in Sapphic Modernism, 1900-1930." Diss. Rutgers, State University of New Jersey, 1995.

Kennedy, Elizabeth Lapovsky and Madeline D. Davis. *Boots of Leather, Slippers of Gold: The History of a Lesbian Community.* New York: Routledge, 1993.

Newton, Esther. "The Mythic Mannish Lesbian: Radclyffe Hall and the New Woman." *Signs* 9.4 (Summer 1984): 557-75.

Nestle, Joan, ed. *The Persistent Desire: A Femme-Butch Reader.* Boston: Alyson Publications, Inc., 1992.

_____. *A Restricted Country.* Ithaca: Firebrand Books, 1987.

Parkes, Adam. *Modernism and the Theater of Censorship.* New York: Oxford University Press, 1996.

Ruehl, Sonja. "Inverts and Experts: Radclyffe Hall and the Lesbian Identity." *Feminism, Culture, and Politics.* Eds. Rosalind Brunt and Caroline Rowan. London: Lawrence and Wishart, 1982.

Smith-Rosenberg, Carroll. "Discourses of Sexuality and Subjectivity: The New

Woman, 1870-1936." *Hidden from History: Reclaiming the Gay and Lesbian Past*. Eds. Martin Duberman, Martha Vicinus, and George Chauncey, Jr. New York: NAL Books, 1989.

Stimpson, Catherine R. "Zero Degree Deviancy: The Lesbian Novel in English." *Critical Inquiry* 8.1 (Winter 1981): 363-79.

Whitlock, Gillian. " 'Everything is Out of Place': Radclyffe Hall and the Lesbian Literary Tradition." *Feminist Studies* 13.3 (Fall 1987): 555-82.

Zimmerman, Bonnie. "Lesbians Like This and That: Some Notes on Lesbian Criticism for the Nineties." *New Lesbian Criticism: Literary and Cultural Readings*. Ed. Sally Munt. New York: Columbia University Press, 1992.

Index

Abraham, Julie, 116
Academy Awards
    for Best Director, 61n
    for Best Foreign Language Film,
       40,60n,61n
Afrikete, 33-34,37n
Allen, Jeffner, 3,77-78
Allen, Paula Gunn, 2
    "A Lot Changed After She Fell,"
       28-30
    Sacred Hoop: Recovering the
       Feminine in American Indian
       Traditions, 37n
    "Who Is Your Mother? Red Roots
       of White Feminism," 37n
    "The Woman Who Fell From the
       Sky," 27-28
    The Woman Who Owned the
       Shadows, 27-30
Allen, Paula Gunn, 35-36,36-37n
Al tikrei, 50
Amazons, 77-78
Andermahr, Sonya, 1-2
Anna O. *See* Pappenheim, Bertha
Antisemitism, 43,44-45,56-57,63n
Antonia's Line (film), 61n
Anzaldúa, Gloria, 2
    Borderlands/La Frontera: The New
       Mestiza, 23-25
    "Bridge, Drawbridge, Sandbar or
       Island: Lesbians-of-Color
       Hacienda Alianzas," 35,36
    mestiza concept of, 23-25,35-36,
       84
Aphanisis, 53
At First Sight (film), 40,43-44,61n,63n
Athene, 75,77
Auschwitz concentration camp, 41

Bacril, Jean-Pierre, 46
Barnes, Djuna, 71
Bauchau, Patrick, 47
Baudelaire, Charles Pierre, 122-123
Bauer, Ida, 11-12,112
Beauvoir, Simone de, 78n
Berneys, Martha, 101
Bisexual body, 91
Bisexual inflections, literary, 83-89,
    91-92
Bisexuality, Freud's theory of, 4,98,
    111-112,113
Black feminism, diversity within, 10
Black lesbian writers. *See also* names
    of specific writers
    gender identity construction by,
       32-35
Blanchard, Saga, 46
Bodies That Matter (Butler), 36n
Boots of Leather, Slippers of Gold
    (Kennedy and Davis), 125
Borderlands/La Frontera: The New
    Mestiza (Anzaldúa), 23-25
Brant, Beth, 2
    "Coyote Learns a New Trick,"
       31-32
    Giveaway: Native American
       Writers, 30
    Mohawk Trail, 30-32
    "A Simple Act," 30-31
Breuer, Josef, 11,97,100-101,104-105,
    110
"Bridge, Drawbridge, Sandbar or
    Island: Lesbians-of-Color
    Hacienda Alianzas"
    (Anzúalda), 35,36
British lesbian writing, 65-80, *See also*
    names of specific British
    writers
    Gender Trouble: Feminism and the

*Your John: The Love Letters of
   Radclyffe Hall (Hall)*, 120

Zami: A New Spelling of My Name
   (Lorde), 32-33

Zeus, 75,77
Zimmerman, Bonnie, 116
Zola, Emile, 122-123
Zweig, Stephen, 100-101